THE INTRUDER

The man jumped over the king-sized bed and landed in front of Chris, lifting him again, hauling him into the air. "Where the hell is the Western Key?"

Chris reached out with hooked fingers and dragged them across his opponent's face. His fingers clawed into skin, dragging over the flesh and causing his enemy to let go of him in order to cover his face.

Chris hit the ground swinging, using his fist to hammer the side of the man's head. He felt something crack and didn't know if it was his hand or the man's skull, either way he rather liked the sound and he absolutely loved the way the bastard staggered back.

He stopped cold when the man's hands went up to ward off the blow and showed his face again. Or at least where his face had been. What looked his way now was mostly mouth, a gaping angry wound filled with wicked-looking fangs that would have shamed a shark. Chris's mind reeled; there was no way what was in front of him was a mask. The change in the bones and muscles had warped the shape of the face but not far enough for him not to recognize the general structure and hairline. The thing lunged forward, snapping its jaws angrily. . . .

Other *Leisure* books by James A. Moore:

FIREWORKS
UNDER THE OVERTREE

JAMES A. MOORE

POSSESSIONS

LEISURE BOOKS NEW YORK CITY

A LEISURE BOOK®

June 2004

Published by

Dorchester Publishing Co., Inc.
200 Madison Avenue
New York, NY 10016

ISBN 0-8439-5171-0

The name "Leisure Books" and the stylized "L" with design are trademarks of Dorchester Publishing Co., Inc.

Printed in the United States of America.

Visit us on the web at www.dorchesterpub.com.

The start of this book is, in some ways, semi-biographical. The idea came to me while I was in a hospice where my mother was passing. This book is dedicated to the memory of Ingeborg Keller Moore, my mother and one of the finest people I have ever had the privilege to know. You are missed more than words can say.

POSSESSIONS

Chapter One

1

The restaurant was fairly crowded, but Chris Corin wasn't bothered by the noise. Most of it was coming from his friends and family. They were celebrating his birthday and the day was turning out to be a fine one indeed. Now and then life was kind.

DeLucci's was hardly a five-star dining establishment, but that had more to do with the waitstaff and the casual attire than with the food. As far as Chris was concerned, no one made a better pizza and few could come close to the nearly orgasmic quality of their linguini and clam sauce. "Classical Gas" was playing on the speakers in each corner of the place, and even that was good, despite the slightly tinny sound of the battered old speakers. He'd always loved the Mason Williams song.

His mom was over to the right, a smile on her

1

pretty face. Her skin was showing her years, a scattering of crow's feet around her eyes and lines around her mouth when she smiled, which she did often, but in style of clothes and attitude, Eileen Corin could have been a peer instead of his mother. Her auburn hair was longer than most people considered "proper" for a woman in her forties, but neither she nor her children could have given a damn. She worked hard six or seven days a week, and if she wanted to relax properly, that was her business.

Eileen was laughing at something inane and probably risqué that had come out of Jerry Murphy's mouth. Almost everything that poured past Jerry's lips qualified as inane and risqué. It was part of his charm. To Jerry's right, Katie Gallagher was chastising him for whatever he'd just said. The admonishment was in good humor instead of in anger, though Chris had seen and heard both in his time. Katie and Jerry had been dating since they were fifteen and he knew all of their moods. That was to be expected; Jerry was his best friend. Katie was a close second. He'd had to play referee between the two of them on several occasions, which was a task he never enjoyed. If she hadn't been with Jerry, Chris could have fallen for her in a bad way when they first met. With long dark hair and hazel eyes, creamy skin and an infectious smile, she had close to everything he considered worth noticing in a member of the opposite sex. She was also extremely intelligent and quick-witted. These days it wasn't even a consideration, despite the fact that she had a body that could stop a man's heart and a face that was just as fine. She was officially off-limits, and Chris was smart enough to know it. She caught his eyes on her and smiled. He winked a casual all-is-well-with-the-world wink, and looked over to her right, where Courtney was sitting.

Courtney was cute, with short-cropped dark hair that made her look like a pixie. It worked for her. She was Katie's best friend, and while she too was attractive, Chris had put paid to any chance of a relationship with her a long time ago. High-maintenance was the best term to describe Courtney. Even Katie admitted that the girl had a crisis a week on the average. Chris preferred a relationship to be less like work and more like fun. They'd dated for about a month before she dumped him for someone who could treat her in the manner to which she was accustomed. There were no hard feelings; it just wasn't meant to be. For Chris that had been a long month. Enough time had passed for Courtney to move through around seven more boyfriends. Her latest victim, a slightly dazed-looking jock named Stu, was shaking his sun-bleached blond head, trying, it seemed, to figure out exactly what everyone at the table was laughing about. Chris figured Stu might last as much as two months before Courtney nuked him.

Next to Stu was Brittany, Chris's personal thorn. What little sister isn't? Brittany was fourteen, with light freckles that actually complemented her sweet features and hair like their mother's but only if you took all the brown out. There had been several peo-

ple over the years who accused her of dyeing her
tresses to get them that rich shade of red, but she
didn't. It was just natural. Brittany had officially become a pain in his ass the day she turned thirteen
a little over a year before. It was like magic, the way
puberty and sudden mood swings came over her
on that day. Sometimes, like now, she could be a
sweetheart, as fun to be around as she ever had
been. But mostly she was a brat. If you looked at
her funny—and to Brittany any expression at all
could be interpreted as funny—she was likely to go
ballistic or, just to keep things interesting, break
into tears. Her body was stuck in that awkward
stage writers sometimes called "coltish," and it was
only when he looked at his little sister that Chris
really understood the term. She looked almost
starved, she was so skinny, but in truth she ate like
a horse. Her legs took up about two-thirds of her
body and the rest of her was slow to catch up on
the last growth spurt. She was wearing a bra these
days, though it could hardly be called necessary.
For the present time he decided he loved her. Later
on, he'd probably hate her again. The conflicted
feelings were definitely mutual.

By and large there wasn't a group of people he'd
rather be with, and that included both his sister and
his ex-girlfriend. They were the focal points of his
day-to-day experiences and most of them, excluding Stu, whom he barely even knew as yet, seemed
to think he was a bit of all right as well.

And if anyone had told him that one of them
would be dead before the night was over, he would

have scoffed at the notion. Bad things didn't happen on birthdays. It was an unwritten rule.

The party dragged fairly late for a school night, but that wasn't very surprising. School was out of session, and in Chris's case would be for at least a few months. He'd saved his money and worked his ass off and now, in just a few weeks, he had plans to go to Europe and do a little backpacking through the places he knew he'd never get to if he delayed for too long. One last summer before college started and he was forced to swing into the grind of the real world. He intended to make it last.

His mom stood up and stretched, and Chris was both annoyed and amused by the eyes of both Jerry and Stu watching her body. Annoyed because she was his mom and amused because he saw that reaction all the time. She knew how to keep herself fit. She moved over to him and gave him a quick peck on the cheek. "Happy birthday, hon. I'll see you tomorrow."

He hugged her back and frowned. "Still sucks, you having to work tonight."

"Hey." She shrugged and grimaced. "Bills gotta be paid. They aren't gonna take care of themselves." There was a brief flash of guilt over the trip to Europe, but he quelled it. They'd discussed all of that before and she'd insisted that she could handle the bills just fine. He decided not to doubt her on that. She'd managed his entire life and while they weren't exactly living on easy street, they weren't crawling through back alleys and calling cardboard boxes home, either.

She turned away from Chris and looked at Brittany. "Remember what I said." Her voice was pleasant, but Chris knew well enough that she'd just given his sister the warning to behave herself.

As if someone had flipped a switch, Brit's face went from happy to stormy. "I will, *Mother....*" Her use of the word "mother" was a perfect example of how his little sister's mind worked. She was using the proper word for referring to the woman who was, in fact, her mother, but the way she said it dripped cold, lethal venom.

Eileen flashed a smile at her daughter, which put an immediate stop to the attitude. His mom had a lot of different smiles, depending on what she was trying to say, like the *knock-it-off-or-I'll-clock-your-ass-for-you* one that put Brittany back into a proper mode of behavior. "Okay, see you tomorrow." And off she went, walking through a hail of good-byes from his friends. Chris stood up too, while Jerry collected money from everyone and laid it out with the check and a decent tip. Maybe not a great tip, but fair enough for the service they got.

Five minutes later they were making plans to meet back at Chris's place for a little more rest and relaxation. As eighteenth birthdays go it might have been mild, but it was enough. He just wanted to relax. School had been hectic and now he was in the unwinding stage of the summer. Partying would come later, in Europe. Besides, there was Brittany to consider. Even if she wasn't at an age where she could make his life miserable by telling on him for any bad thing he did, she might use him as a role model. His own rule of the day when it came to her was not to lead by bad example. It had less to do with worrying about what sort of trouble she'd get into than it did about the hell he'd catch for whatever she did that he'd done first.

II

Eileen Corin shifted gears and slid effortlessly into the left-hand lane. One of the rare advantages of working the graveyard shift was dealing with less traffic, and while she hated the hours, she loved the traffic flow. Still, Chris was right; it stank that she had to work on his birthday. But the bills, as she often told her kids, didn't believe in paying themselves, and just of late they'd been piling up. She should have learned her lesson a long time ago about using credit cards. Some lessons just refused to be learned.

The night was cooler than she'd expected, and she rolled down the window a crack as she sped down the interstate. The only music she could find on the radio was more along the lines of the bubble gum Brittany listened to, and she hit on a talk station where a man with a deep, resonant voice was talking about terrorism. It was a subject she could have done without, but his voice was pleasant. In her mind she drew the picture of a handsome man who matched the voice, tall and lean and attractive, but in a nice, slightly rough way. A man whose face had character and strength. If he had a nice ass too, that would just be a plus.

She needed something pleasant to hear, something pleasant to think about. Just of late the only subject that wanted to stay in her head was the one she wanted to avoid the most: Her mother had been calling her at work, and that was something she didn't want to deal with. Any and every thing about her mother was something she didn't want to deal with. Her hand slid up to finger the necklace she always wore, only to find a void where it should have been. She cursed herself under her breath and remembered setting it down on the bathroom counter just before she had taken her shower earlier in the afternoon.

Not good, she decided, *but not really a reason to panic. Just stay calm and everything will be fine. It'll still be there when I get home, and that's only a few hours from now. Hardly enough time for anything to happen.*

The wind outside the car was pleasant, a soft cool breeze that just plain felt good. It hardly ever seemed to be the right temperature out in the real world these days, without at least the benefit of the air conditioner. Maybe she'd break down and open the window in her little office when she got to work. She felt her mind drifting, imagining what it would be like to hit the beach in a few weeks when the weather finally permitted; the soft warm breeze, the scent of the ocean and the sweet feeling of the sun on her skin, warming her and relaxing her muscles. . . .

She was still enjoying the weather when the winds suddenly shifted. The force of the gale was strong enough to shake the car and almost force her into the next lane. She snapped out of her light daze and looked around, shocked to see that she was no longer the only one on the road. There were two SUVs and a tractor-trailer near her now. She'd barely been aware that she was so tired and now she'd damn near gone to sleep behind the wheel. What the hell was wrong with her?

She was almost willing to put it off to depression at the thought that her baby boy was eighteen today. How had the years gone by so damned fast? But there was that nagging voice in the back of her head, the one that had kept her free from her mother's influences for all of these years. That voice told her the sleepiness she felt might not be completely natural.

She shook her head and sucked in a deep breath, trying to make herself come more fully awake. Damn, but she hated those thoughts. Almost twenty years away from her mother and still the woman could pull her into a dark pit of fear. But that very fear had kept Eileen alive and free for a long time, and she intended to stay that way.

Something out there in the darkness had different ideas. She heard it, first as a faint flapping noise and then soon enough as the sound of thundering wings, cutting through the air with hellish intensity. Eileen's eyes scanned everywhere, seeing nothing but almost desperate to find the source of the noise.

"Jesus, please, not now . . . Please just let me be jumpy. . . ."

The voice on the radio laughed good-naturedly

at someone's joke, the handsome voice that she wanted to hear again and again softly chuckling at some witticism or another. All she could think was how badly she wanted to be back at home with Brittany and Chris and away from the noises that were growing louder but not showing her anything that could let her know where they were coming from. The fantasy voice she'd been halfway to falling in love with was now just another source of distraction when she desperately needed to have her eyes on the road and her hands firmly on the wheel.

On her right the eighteen-wheeler suddenly shifted roughly in her direction, tilting awkwardly and surely ready to jackknife. She yanked the wheel hard to the left and looked at the mountainous bulk as it teetered, plainly able to see that the wheels on her side were taking too much weight, bulging and threatening to explode under the pressure. Her eyes looked upward toward the top of the Trans-State Delivery Services trailer and saw that the metal roof of the thing was actually visible. And beyond that, a hulking blackness that shifted and pushed and rammed itself against the side of the truck, its wings pounding the air, its thick legs flexing in an effort to keep its balance as it sailed along next to the truck, traveling at over sixty miles per hour.

And she knew that she was right to be afraid, right to worry over the loss of the necklace. Her mother had found her again.

Fear can save and fear can kill. Under the right circumstances the raw emotion will kick in with a heady dose of adrenaline and allow for the fight-or-flight instincts to do their thing. It's seldom possible to use it to your advantage when a truck is falling toward you on the interstate. True, Eileen's car swerved away from the truck and that could have saved her, but she was already in the far left lane and instead of getting clear of the massive truck and its terrified driver—she could see his grizzled, wide face, his mouth open in a scream that showed too well the color of his teeth—she slammed into the solid concrete barrier and felt the world tip her toward the very vehicle she tried to get away from.

Her seat belt held her firmly in place as the road was suddenly over her head. Her hair, caught by the breeze she'd been admiring, was pulled out against the hood of the car, her shoulders yanked violently as the hair was torn from its roots in her scalp, and she let out a small, inconsequential yelp as she saw the truck rolling toward her through the pain she felt in her last seconds of life.

Eileen was killed by the impact of the fully-loaded tractor falling onto her car and collapsing the structure around her. She never even felt the airbags that deployed in a vain effort to save her from impact. She never felt the asphalt that shredded the hood and windshield along with those safety bladders as both vehicles continued their slide down the road and through the concrete barrier that separated them from oncoming traffic. She never saw the oncoming Exxon tanker that never had a chance to stop before it rammed into the entire twisted sliding mass. She never felt the explosion as the gasoline spilled and ignited and bloomed into a fireball large enough to rattle windows for several blocks around the road, waking people and sending dogs into a frenzy of barking. She didn't hear the trucker who hit her screaming as he slowly roasted alive, trapped in the cab of his company truck.

She died quickly. It was a small blessing, but a blessing nonetheless.

III

Christina Aguilera was bleating out another song on the radio and Chris didn't care. Anything to lighten Brittany's mood. She'd been in a funk ever since Mom had reminded her that she was still just a kid. Sometimes he enjoyed watching her get into one of her moods, but just then he didn't want to deal with it and the music seemed to help her get back into party mode. By the time "Genie in a Bottle" was done playing, she was almost cheerful again.

"I love that song, she is sooo talented." Brittany smiled, her eyes crinkling up as she bopped along to the music that had already stopped.

"Well, she's fun to look at, at least." He grinned back, turning onto Longfellow Avenue. "At least when she isn't poodling her hair."

"Shut *up*, her hair looks *awesome* that way."

"If you ever do that to your hair, I'll give you a buzz cut." He winked, and she got an indignant look that seemed possible only on little sisters: one part irate and two parts happy with a dash of shock that he would *dare* even consider such an act.

"I'd kick your butt!" She mock-glared at him, ready for a good fight. She was a scrapper at heart, and that was one of the things he liked about his younger sibling.

"Maybe, but you'd still have hair as short as mine." He ran his fingers through his short, stiff hair, grinning back at her.

"Oh, hush! Here come the numbers!"

On their way over to DeLucci's, Brittany had begged him to stop for a soda, and he'd given in rather than hear her pout. While she grabbed up the Diet Pepsi for herself—he assumed in case she ever had a weight problem, because she sure as hell didn't need to lose weight and she wasn't diabetic—and a regular for him, he'd counted out his money and on a whim filled out a form for the Big Game. He used the day and month from his birthday, from Brittany's and from their mom's, figuring if he won they'd all be rich. The take was somewhere around sixty-nine million dollars to a single winner. He decided if he won he could share.

Really, the only reason he'd bothered to buy one was because he could. It was like a rite of passage in a way, finally being legally old enough to blow his money on a pipe dream. Brittany, on the other hand, swore she had a good feeling about it, so he shut up and listened with her as the overly-cheerful voice on the radio started calling out the winning numbers.

"Six . . . seventeen . . . four . . . eleven . . . thirty-one, and the power ball number is seven." Chris forgot to breathe, forgot about the road in front of him, forgot even that he was behind the wheel of the family station wagon as he contemplated those numbers and compared them to the ones he'd chosen at the 7-Eleven. He listened carefully as the announcer repeated the string of digits, his heart beating almost hard enough to crack his ribs. Beside him, Brittany was defying physics by actually bouncing in her seat despite the safety belt.

"OHMIGOD! CHRIS! OHMIGODOHMIGOD! Those are YOUR numbers!!!" Her voice was a high shriek, the sort of noise that usually made him tell her to pipe down, but right then he couldn't have cared less. She could have called over Yoko Ono and joined her in a duet performed to a band performing with badly rusted saxophones and tubas and he wouldn't have cared in the least. She still would have had the most beautiful voice in the world.

He started jumping in his own seat, trying his best to pull free of the restraining belt, his eyes wide and his smile even wider, knowing full well that he had to be dreaming, had to somehow be imagining everything.

He barely managed to pull the car to a stop in front of his house in a screech of brakes. Jerry's Mustang made a screech behind him and Stu's Corvette did the same. They'd been following closely, but not so closely that there was a worry about a collision. Still, he'd stopped abruptly and caused a

chain reaction. And he couldn't have cared less.
Chris leaned over and pulled Brittany close, kissing
her on the mouth before he fought free of the seat
belt. She moved faster, fairly leaping from the car,
screeching happily about the winning numbers, her
feet lifting off the ground and coming back down
in a dozen excited little jumps. He could hear Jerry
talking, hear the excitement growing in his voice,
but couldn't make out the words. Chris was too
busy grinning like a chimpanzee and trying to
imagine the look on his mom's face when she found
out. Then Jerry was hugging him hard, pounding
on his back with both hands and Katie was hugging
Brittany and Stu was looking confused and Courtney was squealing and doing her best to imitate
Brittany a few seconds earlier, looking at Chris with
a strange gleam in her eyes. He blinked and it was
Katie hugging him, kissing his cheek warmly and
smiling. He blinked again and Stu was pumping his
hand up and down hard enough to shake his whole
body and he blinked and Courtney was kissing him
on the mouth, leaving him feeling decidedly breath-
less. Damn, but she knew how to make him flustered. And he blinked again and everyone was
inside and it was slowly really starting to sink in
that he had won and how much he had won. Even
if ten other tickets had the same numbers, it was
more money than he'd ever thought he'd really
have.

They celebrated well into the wee hours of the
morning, drinking a bit too much and even letting
Brittany have a beer before it was all over. He

should have been exhausted when he woke up at seven-thirty but he wasn't. Every time he thought about being tired, he remembered the winnings coming his way and the adrenaline kicked in again.

The end of the night—or the early part of the morning if you need a little accuracy—was very, very blurry. His head throbbed when he woke up, and his body was sore in a few places. Mostly it was sore in ways that left him a little puzzled. He wasn't the most experienced man on the planet, but he'd had sex a few times. Whatever he'd been doing, the soreness focused on the same muscle groups that were sore after his first real marathon bout with a partner. That had to be nonsense, of course. Drunk or not, he was pretty sure he'd remember a serious bout of hardcore carnal knowledge.

He let Brittany sleep in, and dragged Jerry along with him to the main office of the lottery. It was buried in the bowels of an office building and a nightmare to find, but once they got there it was easy enough to confirm that he had indeed won. There were no other tickets with the same numbers. Within a few months, he would receive his first check. Until then, there were papers to confirm that he had won and there were other papers that had to be filled out and filed.

By the time they were done it was almost noon, and Chris decided that he and Jerry could risk a dent in his first credit card. He took Jerry out to lunch, both of them pleasantly tired and enjoying the hell out of the feeling.

"I can't fucking believe you won the lotto, man. That's too weird."

"You think it's weird? I can't really grasp it in my head, Jerry. It's like, okay I won, cool. And then I want to start screaming, 'cause, you know, I'm about to be fucking rich."

Jerry shoved his hand through his mop of brown hair and positively beamed. "Yeah, well, about that fifty you owe me . . . I'm gonna have to charge interest now. Nothing personal."

"I don't owe you fifty. . . ." Chris looked at his friend with a dubious smile growing on his face. He knew he was being set up, but couldn't quite figure out how.

"Yeah, back in fifth grade, man. I loaned you fifty cents for a second milk, and you never paid me back. I was willing to let it slide before, but now that you got all this money coming in, I figure a hundred and fifty thousand dollars ought to just about cover it."

"Yeah, and your sister's a nun, man."

Jerry's older sister had managed to gain quite a reputation for herself when she was still in high school. It had nothing whatsoever to do with religious piety. Jerry, who'd just taken a swig of his sweetened iced tea, almost snorted the drink out his nose when he started laughing. Most people might have thought he'd take offense to the comment, but most people didn't know that Jerry and Chris had no hesitation to bash each other's families. It was all harmless and neither of them took offense. Of course, with Jerry and his rather large collection of

17

siblings, Chris could almost always find a member of the group to pick on. Chris only had Brittany, but Jerry was more than glad to smear her reputation. All insults, by unspoken agreement, were strictly kept to when the two of them were alone. Under no circumstances did either of them actually make any accusations—real or imagined—in public.

The group of businessmen at the next table over looked at Jerry's face—which was turning almost frighteningly red as he laughed harder still—and looked away with expressions of annoyance and disgust. That just got them both laughing harder. When they finally left the restaurant and headed back to Chris's place, they were ready to call it a day and get some actual sleep. All the money in the world could only keep you giggling and high for so long.

His mom's car wasn't in the driveway on Longfellow Avenue, but he expected her sometime soon, so he parked in his usual spot in front of the lawn, hugging the curb. He looked at the house where he'd been all his life and wondered if his mom would want to stay there or move into a place that actually had space. The house on Longfellow was hardly a palace, but it was most decidedly home. The windows were dirty—his fault, he was supposed to clean them a few weeks ago—and the sky-blue paint was buckling in a few spots, threatening to actually peel away before the summer was over. The short driveway was just exactly long enough for one car, which meant he normally parked at the curb. The grass was shorter than his own hair, which was only because he'd mowed it two days earlier, and the flowers around the base of the windows were coming along nicely, even if they had to dodge a few curious bees every day.

His own bedroom had been big enough when he was younger, but these days it seemed crowded. His face split into a smile again when he realized that just a few months from now, he'd never again have to worry about having a big enough place. It was weird, the idea that he could buy damned near anything he wanted without having to worry about the cost.

Jerry climbed out of the passenger's side, looking around with eyes half closed and smiling contentedly. Jerry should have been a cat; he had that sort of face. No matter what he was doing, he always looked at the world with eyes that looked half narrowed in contemplation and he always walked with a loose-boned, easy grace that was positively unsettling. Chris had never once in his life seen Jerry fall down or even stumble. It just wasn't in his nature. His best friend looked over his way and stretched in a leisurely fashion, his long arms extended over his head and joined together in a casual fist.

"Your couch is sounding like a damned fine place to crash, bro."

"My couch is your couch, but you'll have to fight Brittany for it."

"I can take her."

"You wish. She'll kick your ass."

"Naw, all I have to do is pick on 'N Sync and she's out of there."

Chris chuckled and yawned himself, tired now that he was home again and the first wave of excitement had petered out. "She's over them. I think she's graduating to the Backstreet Boys."

"No, man, she already got over them."

"One of the boy bands . . . they all sound alike." They walked toward the house. "You can always ask her when we get inside."

Jerry mock-grimaced. "No thanks, dude. Last thing I need is an intellectual discussion on the merits of geek boys in ready-made bands."

"Jealousy's showing, my man." Chris pushed on Jerry's shoulder, and true to form, he didn't even stumble. "You know you can't carry a note or they'd have snapped you up a long time ago."

"I don't want to be on stage; I just want the women."

"You already have one; don't be greedy."

Jerry opened the door and stepped inside, with Chris right behind him, trying to will his eyes to adjust faster to the complete darkness inside the house. All the blinds were drawn and the TV was off. He didn't even hear Brittany on the phone with one of her friends. It was a little unsettling, especially during the summer. His first thought was that she'd gone out and his mom was going to be pissed, because he was supposed to be watching his little sister and she'd flown the coop. His jaw clenched automatically as the idea of tracking her down and getting her home before Mom found out crept into his head. Sleep was a nice dream, but not likely for a while.

He opened his mouth to start the official piss-and-moan-at-Brittany's-latest-stunt speech, but stopped when he ran into Jerry's back. "Dude, forward motion! I want to get inside the damned house."

Jerry didn't make a retort. Jerry just vanished, moving faster than Chris would have ever imagined possible, bolting through the clutter of the short entryway and over to the couch in a leap that would have shamed most predatory cats. Chris barely managed to track Jerry's speed, but he could see where Jerry stopped.

Jerry was on his knees in front of the couch, his hands on Brittany's slender shoulders, his face inches from hers, looking into her blue eyes, his own brown ones showing no humor, no hint of amusement, but only deep concern. "Brittany? Honey? What's wrong?"

Brittany looked at Jerry dazedly for a second, her eyes barely focusing at all, the skin of her eyelids red and puffy, her cheeks still wet from tears. Then her arms wrapped around Jerry's neck and she pulled herself to him like a constrictor, half choking him as she shoved her face into the crook of his neck and started crying anew. Her words were mumbled and came from a throat made ragged by crying. All he could see of his sister's head was the back of her skull and the ponytail she'd pulled her red hair into. What Chris focused on was Jerry's long, worried face crumbling a bit as he listened to the words Brittany spoke.

Brittany's voice—croaking and sounding jagged in comparison to the one he knew her to use—came to him as if through a long tunnel, and he felt his world slow down to a crawl as the words registered in his mind. "Mommy's dead . . . my mommy's dead." And the bright shining morning grew dark as the impossible came to pass. His mother couldn't be dead. His mother couldn't possibly have been taken from him.

But she had been, and not all the money in the world was going to bring her back.

Chapter Two

I

There were things that had to be done, and Chris did them, though not by himself. On his own, or even with Brittany's help, nothing would have been accomplished in the proper ways. Katie was the one who called the newspapers to announce Eileen Corin's passing from the world. She was the one who asked Chris questions and got the information she needed so she could then call a funeral home and arrange for someone to come by and discuss arrangements for his mother's burial. She was the one who haggled and dealt with the details, merely coming to Chris and Brittany to let them answer questions regarding style of coffin and what sort of service they wanted. The service would be closed casket, out of necessity. What was left of their mother's body wouldn't fill a bucket and most definitely wasn't to be viewed by any but the most disgustingly morbid.

Jerry was the one who comforted Brittany, taking turns with Katie. Chris, for his part, stared at the walls a lot and tried to remember what thinking or feeling felt like. He was managing to breathe pretty well, and walking was okay, but for the most part he felt like a robot going through preprogrammed motions.

There were phone calls, endless waves of phone calls, with people he felt he should be able to actually recognize, speaking to him on the subject he least wanted to contemplate, and expressing their condolences for both his loss and his sister's. He made conversation, spoke when he was supposed to, but none of it really connected on a conscious level. They were just buzzing voices and words and in the long run they meant nothing at all to him. They were just there; just sounds to fill his head and stop him from screaming at the world. He wanted to scream though, almost desperately. If he could have screamed, maybe the pain would have lessened, but he didn't seem capable of anything stronger than a soft voice.

There were vague recollections of several of Brittany's friends coming into the house and staying with her, holding her hands or hugging her, and if he really thought hard about it, he could remember Courtney coming over and crying all over the front of his shirt, but the only ones who mattered at that precise time were Jerry, Katie and Brittany. Them, and the cold aching wound that roared through his soul whenever he thought of his mother.

And after a few days of non-reality, he came to in the lawn of a cemetery he'd seen a thousand times before. The grass was green, except where the coffin that held his mother's remains crouched mournfully like a specter. Father Fullford was speaking in kind terms about his mother's soul and her memories and how, as long as she was recalled fondly, she would never really be dead, and how God in His Heaven had called her to His side. Chris blinked his eyes, almost as if he were finally waking from a deep sleep, and looked at the small ocean of mourners, many of whom he couldn't recognize to save his life. They were the people who worked with his mom at the IGA grocery store where she was one of several managers. Where she would no longer head off for longer spans than he cared to think about and from where she would never again come home tired and worn and smiling just the same because she had good people to work with. Or come home groaning because someone at work had proven to be a complete moron. Or smile when she saw that they'd waited up for her or that Chris had made her dinner or that Brittany had cleaned the living room without being asked or when one of them gave her a hug and asked her how her day was or laugh when Jerry made one of his slightly off-color remarks or leered at her only half in jest or beam when Katie came over and told her what she'd missed on the soaps that day or . . .

Chris stifled a sob and reached down to the soil set neatly to the side and grabbed a double handful to scatter over the top of her lowering coffin. His body trembled and he felt the sting of tears that he refused to let fall. Mom wouldn't want him making a spectacle of himself in public. Besides, someone had to be strong for Brittany's sake and he couldn't expect Katie and Jerry to do that too, on top of everything else they'd done lately. He watched the coffin descend with a gentle mechanical rumble and dusted off his hand while Brittany repeated his gesture. And maybe it wasn't considered proper or right in the real world, but Jerry followed suit after Brittany was done and so did Katie and Courtney and he loved them for that simple gesture.

People came toward him in small clusters, all of them dressed in black and a good number of them crying, and they spoke their words of mourning and condolences again and he thanked them for their kindness and hugged those that hugged him first though there were many he could barely recall. And he hugged Brittany fiercely as she cried into his chest, her shoulders shaking almost violently with her grief. And he loved her then, loved her with all of his heart and cried himself, letting his grief out in small increments, afraid that if he really started screaming he'd never be able to stop, afraid that he would shatter like fragile glass and nothing would ever be able to put him back together again. This way he felt like someone had only cored out his insides instead of shattering him.

Katie hugged him just as fiercely as his sister had, and he hugged back, grateful beyond words for all that she had done. He kissed her forehead softly and whispered his thanks, and did the same again when Jerry came to him and held him. Jerry, who'd cried more than a few tears himself for the loss of Eileen Corin from the world. She'd practically been a second mother to him over the years, and if his grief was not connected by blood it was no less real and no less powerful.

There was a wake as well, once again planned properly by Katie. Chris went along with everyone else and in the quiet of the station wagon that Jerry drove for them, he held Brittany in his arms and promised that they would get through it all somehow. She nodded and listened and cried, and he thought about his mother and cried with her, slowly accepting the fact that she was dead and gone, never to come through the door of the house again.

He barely remembered the wake, save a few fond recollections from people over things his mother had done over the course of her life. People milled around and brought food with them and offered it to him and Brittany, and Katie thanked them and played the perfect hostess when his mouth refused to work, though he could see that she was tired. And the day became the night and slowly, oh so very slowly, the strangers left the house and Chris found something to do with himself. He cleaned and wiped away the messes that the strangers he should have known had left behind. Brittany blinked tired eyes and drifted to sleep on the couch and he covered her with a blanket and looked down on his little sister, amazed that she could possibly be tired when he felt like he was finally really waking up for the first time in several days.

Jerry and Katie left last, offering to stay the night if he needed them to. He shook it off and smiled for them, a genuine smile of gratitude for all they had done and all that their being a part of his world meant to him. He hugged the two of them to him, and felt the comfort of their presence and then shooed them off to have some time alone together for a change of pace, because he could remember the last few days well enough to know that they'd never left his side for more than a few minutes at a time.

And it was over, except for the echoes. The sound of his mother's voice ringing in the back of his head and the falling feeling in his stomach that he was almost certain would never go away.

Sleep wasn't even a possibility. Despite the silence in the house, Chris's mind was working at high speed and he knew there was no chance of him closing his eyes and getting comfortable. Even his favorite shows on TV would be wasted on him, and staying in his room was completely out of the question. He stared at Brittany, asleep on the couch, for several minutes. She was his world now, and he was hers, and he promised his mother's memory that he'd take care of her and protect her. Brittany rolled over on the couch, turning her back to him and nuzzling her pretty face against the sofa's pillow. He crept up the stairs as quietly as he could and changed into a pair of shorts and a T-shirt with a few holes in all the most comfortable places.

Then he took a deep breath and steeled himself to go into his mother's room. He needed a little time with her possessions, with her life's collected things, and he knew that sooner or later a lot of it would have to be packed away or given to charity. There was no time like the present for handling the tasks. He was alone at last and maybe the work would help him recover a little more of his internal balance.

The walk to the other side of the hallway was one of the longest he'd ever made. Ten feet from one door to the other and it seemed to take a few thousand years. But finally he managed to reach the door to her private sanctuary and push it open and step through the threshold of memories he knew would cut him like a blade.

And into the chaos of her violated bedroom.

Chris looked around without really seeing anything but the desecration of the room. There were items he'd seen all his life—his mother's jewelry box; her chest of drawers that he'd helped her refinish when he was ten, if helped was the actual word that was appropriate; her clothes, normally in good shape if a few years out of high fashion; her bed, that massive antique four-poster bed that he'd bounced on a thousand times, much to his mother's chagrin—all of them hurt in one way or another, torn or cut or emptied and left to rot for all the thief cared. Seeing them broken and battered set off a switch in his head. Gone for the moment was the deep loneliness of his mother's death. And in its place was a blossoming fire of rage fueled by the thought that the perpetrator might still be in the house.

Chris walked into his mother's bedroom, stepping over broken memories that he'd hoped to hold and savor for a time. Her collection of crossword-puzzle books was scattered like a newsprint avalanche, the pages torn out and discarded. He slipped on a pile of clean but scattered underwear as he neared the foot of the bed and almost fell, but caught himself. His chest felt constricted, like someone had tightened a dozen belts over his ribcage when he wasn't looking, and his knees were shaking with the onslaught of unspent adrenaline.

He sat on the bed, pushing aside still more of his mother's undergarments. The phone was still where it had always been, on the nightstand next to her bed, though the drawers had all been pulled out and emptied. He'd dialed the nine and the first one when he saw the closet door. Had he heard movement in there? It was hard to say past the thudding of his heart in his temples. He set the phone back down and stood up. If there was someone in the house other than him and Brittany, he didn't want it to be someone waiting for his guard to go down.

The closet door was open. The closet door that his mother always neatly closed as part of her morning ritual was open, its contents partially disgorged, spilling across the thin sea-green shag carpet. Chris reached for the cut-glass doorknob and pulled the closet door open more, his eyes trying to see into the darkness of the small room.

He managed to duck the fist that came right at

his face, more by instinct than because he'd really expected to see anyone lurking inside. It was just too damned Hollywood to ever happen in real life.

He didn't dodge the foot that lifted up and kicked him in the stomach. That one hit nice and clean and sent him staggering back to hit the bed and land on his back. He blinked and looked up at the darkness beyond the entrance to the closet, seeing the shabby-looking man that came out of the space the door normally held in darkness.

He wasn't a big man, but he looked it from Chris's prone angle. His face was covered in sores, and his skin looked like it might have last known the use of soap and water at least a few months earlier. His clothes looked like they belonged in a garbage dump, covered as they were in bits of a dozen or more meals and decorated with a flurry of rents and holes worn through them. The man's hair was long and stringy, gray with a peppering of brown. His beard was the same, and so were the bushy brows over his eyes.

His eyes, though, stood out. They were wrong, watery and unfocused despite the fact that Chris knew the man was looking straight at him. Chris braced himself against the bed with his left leg and kicked high with his right, striking the man solidly in his bearded jaw. The man grunted and fell back, hitting the wall near the doorway with a resounding thump. The framed picture of the family and Jerry that hung near the closet fell down, the glass breaking on impact. And that, more than anything else, sent Chris into a rage.

He was off the bed and swinging before he could think clearly. His fist slammed into the man's head, which in turn hit the wall again. Chris's body fell forward and his knees rammed into the man's ribcage. For his part, the stranger grunted and gasped, then lifted his hands to defend himself. Waves of a stale beer odor wafted from the derelict with every move, and Chris had to fight to not gag on the scent alone.

"Motherfucking come into MY house and you do THIS?!" Chris hit him again, liking the way the man's skin seemed to slide under his fist. He realized there might actually be something wrong with that sensation when the features of the burglar's face suddenly shifted to the left under his fist and the wet-looking eyes stayed where they were.

By the time Chris realized the man was wearing a rubber mask, and that he had not, in fact, knocked the intruder's face off, it was too late to recover lost ground. The "bum" under him caught him in the chin and made his teeth snap together with an audible clack. Chris fell back a second time, hitting the heavy wooden frame of the bed hard enough to make his vision blur. Then the shabby stranger was pulling off a bearded mask with a low growl of frustration. Chris saw his attacker's real face for the first time, but it was no more familiar than the mask had been. He was younger than Chris expected, maybe in his early twenties, but he looked at Chris with eyes that seemed far too old for his average face. His dark hair was plastered down from being inside the cheap mask, and his face was pale, like he hadn't bothered to actually be in the sun at all in the last few months. There was something about him that was almost familiar, but Chris didn't really have a chance to consider where he might have seen him before.

The man didn't hesitate; he grabbed Chris by the front of his T-shirt and heaved him into the air with enough strength to make him cry out in shock. He was no larger than Chris, but he hefted him with no obvious effort. The baggy clothes wrinkled even more as the pseudo-bum—complete with all-too-authentic stench, thanks just the same—pulled him up to look him directly in the eyes, holding Chris off the ground and looking up at his face with a snarl of nearly insane rage.

"Where is the key?"

"What? What the fuck are you talking about?" The question was as good as a splash of cold water, and Chris snapped to his senses despite the lump rising on the back of his skull. The man shook him like a rag doll and Chris lashed out with every limb, swinging wildly. His left foot connected with the his attacker's crotch, sinking through the billowing overcoat he wore and connecting with solid flesh. If anything, the man holding him seemed more annoyed than hurt by the size twelve in his testicles. He threw Chris across the room, sending him spinning through the air to land with a very loud cracking noise against the opposite wall. Chris groaned as he fell toward the ground, all of the fight taken out of him along with the wind.

The man jumped over the king-sized bed and

landed in front of Chris, lifting him again, hauling him into the air. "Where the hell is the Western Key, you moron?" The voice was impatient, like a man who was expecting his lunch in a hurry and found out there would be a waiting period. Chris wanted to make a snappy comment, but just then he was actually trying very hard to take in a lungful of air.

Chris reached out with hooked fingers and dragged them across his opponent's face. Boxing lessons be damned, the man was on something and Chris would take any edge he could get. His fingers clawed into skin this time, dragging over the flesh and causing his enemy to let go of him in order to cover his face.

Chris hit the ground swinging, using his fist to hammer the side of the man's head. He felt something crack and didn't know if it was his hand or the man's skull; either way he rather liked the sound and he absolutely loved the way the bastard staggered back. This time when his enemy hit the floor, Chris used the bottom of his foot to do his best to grind the man's solar plexus through the ground. Hands still over his face, the man whoofed out all of his air and Chris cocked back his leg to try the same trick on any other appropriate target.

He stopped cold when the man's hands went up to ward off the blow and showed his face again. Or at least where his face had been. What looked Chris's way now was mostly mouth, a gaping angry wound filled with wicked-looking fangs that would have shamed a shark. Chris's mind reeled; the bum face might have been a mask, but there was no way that what was in front of him was cheap latex. The change in the bones and muscles had warped the shape of the face but not enough to not recognize the general structure and hairline. The thing lunged forward, snapping its jaws angrily and letting fly with thick ropes of saliva, screeching in a voice that sent shivers running down Chris's spine. The angry maw slammed shut and opened again inches from Chris's foot. Chris jumped back, too shocked to make any sound louder than a squeak.

When it stood back up, the creature hissed in his direction—he couldn't really say it looked, because for the life of him he couldn't find eyes anywhere on that face anymore. "This isn't over, boy. I'll have the Western Key." The voice wasn't even remotely human, but he could hear the words clearly enough. Panic set in when it came a step toward him, and Chris pushed himself against the wall, a scream building in the back of his throat.

Then that warped, vile head turned away from him, looking toward the window where it must surely have gained entry, and the figure ran leaping through the narrow opening, fitting where it should not have been able to go and doing so with frightening ease. Chris watched it scramble out the window and didn't dare move, didn't dare breathe, afraid it might come back again.

He waited five more minutes, and then grabbed the phone, finishing what he'd started earlier by calling the police. It took three tries to actually dial the simple number. His hands were shaking too badly.

II

Chris had just barely managed to get a tired and fussy Brittany up to her own room and back into a proper slumber before Detective Walter Crawford showed up. Crawford was not overly tall, but he was big, with hands that looked like ham hocks and a wide body that was leaning toward flab more than muscle. His suit fit well enough for an over-the-counter special, and his thinning brown hair matched the caterpillar he had growing on his upper lip. Despite his appearance, he gave off an air of confidence. Despite the air of confidence, he still reeked of cheap aftershave that was used a little too liberally. The stuff didn't actually make Chris's eyes water, but he suspected it could if he stood too near the man.

Chris led him into the living room, and the two sat down to discuss what had happened.

"Let's get right to it, Mr. Corin. Can you give me a description of the man you caught in the house?"

"He was in good shape, around five feet ten inches in height. Short brown hair and dark eyes, pale complexion and clean shaven."

The detective blinked and gave a small smile of approval. "You think you could come up with a good likeness if I sent over an artist? That you could recognize him if you saw him again?"

"Oh yes, definitely." *No doubt about it, Detective. You don't see a monster every day of the week.*

"Good. Let's go take a look at your mother's room, if that's all right. I want to see what shape he left it in."

Chris led the way, and the man followed behind him, every step sagging under his weight. The door to Brittany's room was closed, which was just fine. He didn't want the man leering at his little sister. Something about him just made Chris think he was the sort that would do it. The room looked exactly the same as when he'd left it: like a small hurricane had exploded all over the place.

Crawford looked over the area, making several "tsk" noises as he did, and looked over at Chris. "Any idea what was taken?"

"Nothing that I can figure out." Chris shook his head and felt his jaw clench with anger as he viewed the devastation. "He said he was after some sort of key, but the only keys my mom kept were with her when"—he took a deep breath and made himself finish the sentence—"when she died last week. I don't know of any keys she had except the ones on her key chain."

"My condolences about your mother." There wasn't exactly a lot of sympathy in the comment, but Chris made a small noise of appreciation. "So you think whatever key he was looking for was with her?"

"Like I said, she didn't carry a lot of extras around."

The interview continued, and Chris retraced

every step he could remember from the encounter. Working quickly and efficiently, the detective took several fingerprints, lifting them carefully from the doorknob and one very clean one from the outside windowsill.

Almost as an afterthought, Chris brought up the change in the intruder's face. It wasn't really something he hadn't thought of from the beginning, but he played it like it was. "Listen, I know it sounds weird, but I think his face changed at the end."

"Changed? How?" The detective looked his way, his bulldog face pinched in concentration.

"Well, for a second or two there, I'd have sworn his mouth grew a lot bigger." No way in hell was he going to mention the loss of eyes or nose, or how the face shape itself was altered.

The detective shrugged. "I've seen some people manage to look a lot different when they were stressed." He broke a small smile. "One cop I know swore up and down the man who attacked him had three arms. He didn't, of course. He just had two. But the creep was hopped up on amphetamines and he was swinging so fast with what he had that it felt like more than two arms and the cop just substituted what his mind felt with what he really perceived."

"Seriously?"

"Happens all the time. Listen, you were in a high-stress situation, and it can't have been any better for you having buried your mother earlier today." The eyes under the thick brows showed sympathy. "If he'd had two heads and a tail, I wouldn't have been surprised. What does surprise me is how good your description of the perpetrator is. Just leave out oversized mouths when you talk to the artist, okay?"

Chris let out a breath he hadn't even realized he'd been holding. It was nice to know he wasn't going completely off the wall. "That's a deal. Do you need me to go down to the station? For the artist, I mean?"

"No, I'll have someone out here soon. You might actually want to write down a description while it's fresh, and I can take a copy and give it to our artist. Be as thorough as you can, face shape and skin color, everything you can think of." And that was a relief, too. Chris didn't want to have to rouse Brittany from her sleep and he was so damned tired he could barely think. The adrenaline had worn off a long while back and at the present time, curling up on his bed sounded like a wonderful idea.

"That sounds like a deal to me."

"It isn't exactly procedure, but I figure we can make it work. If you want, I can come by tomorrow with the sketches and any mug shots I can find that come even close."

"That'd be perfect."

"You're sure your mother didn't have any extra sets of keys anywhere?"

"Almost positive. I'll double check with my sister when she wakes up and let you know when you come back by."

"Your sister was here when everything happened?"

"Yeah, but she was asleep. I didn't want to wake her if I could avoid it. She's been through enough."

The detective nodded and moved carefully out of the room, walking with more grace than Chris would have thought him capable of under any circumstances. Chris led Crawford down the stairs and escorted him through the front door. "This is my personal card, hooks you straight up to my cellular phone, which is always with me, even if I don't always answer. You have any questions, you call me, okay?"

"Thanks, Detective, I appreciate your help."

The man shrugged again and got an almost embarrassed smile on his face, which took ten years away from his haggard face. "Just doing my job, Mr. Corin. Again, my condolences on your loss. We'll see what we can do to bag this creep fast, okay?"

Chris set the card down on the dining-room table and staggered up the stairs. He closed the window in his mother's room and went back into the messy environs of his own. He was asleep only a few minutes later.

III

The following morning Chris and Brittany set about cleaning up their mother's room. Brittany was in a mood, actually ticked off because he hadn't awakened her to talk to the police. The fact that she knew absolutely nothing about the fight or where their mother might keep a second set of keys meant nothing at all.

"Look, I just think I have a right to know if the damned house gets broken into, that's all."

"Okay, point made, Brit. The next time I catch someone breaking in, I'll stop everything and call you right away, okay?" His voice was a bit harsher than he meant it to be, but he was also in pain. Every bruise and tender spot he'd been able to ignore the night before was now busily making certain that he didn't manage it a second time. And his sleep had been for crap; every time he drifted off, he heard a noise—nothing bigger than a settling of the house or a neighbor's dog barking—and every time he came wide awake, half expecting to find a mouthful of nasty fangs dripping over his face.

Brittany smacked his arm half in jest at the snide comment, and winced with him when he let out a gasp. She'd naturally selected the spot with the biggest bruise from hitting the wall, with the sort of surgical skill only permitted to younger siblings. Part of him wanted to backhand her right then and there but he forced himself to be calm, and decided all was forgiven when she smiled apologetically. She had the sort of eyes that would bring him nothing but grief in his life and he knew it. "Puppy dog eyes" was what Jerry always called it. He felt briefly uncomfortable with the fact that his little sister could use sad puppy eyes on him. She was a member of the opposite sex, but she was his sister. He was supposed to be immune to that sort of thing from her.

Brittany picked up their mother's jewelry box and started sorting through the pieces, while Chris gathered the clothes scattered all over the floor. "What should we do with Mom's clothes?"

Brittany blinked her eyes rapidly, on the verge of tears again, and looked at the assortment of earrings and necklaces in her hands. "I guess she'd want them to go to Goodwill."

He nodded. "Anything in this stuff that you want . . . you know, to help remember her?"

"I'm gonna keep her jewelry if that's cool."

"Of course it's cool. She wouldn't very well want me to wear it."

"Smart ass." She smiled a bit and that made him feel better.

"Better than being a dumb ass like you." The words were automatically said without venom. They'd been throwing small insults at each other for as long as either of them could recall.

"I keep expecting her to come through the door and yell at us for being in her stuff." Brittany's voice was small, filled with a desperate desire for their mother to come home, which he could understand all too well.

"I know. I do too."

"You think she's in Heaven?"

"Of course. Where else would she be?"

Brittany shrugged. "Dunno."

"If there is a Heaven, and I'm pretty sure there is, that's where Mom is now."

She nodded, as if his judgment alone made it true. He wished he could believe so easily. It had been a long time since he'd given much thought to God and Heaven. They weren't really a big part of his life.

"Will you let them take me away?"

"Huh?" *What the hell?*

Brittany shivered despite the heat of the morning. "Social Services. Will you let them take me away?"

"No! Don't even think like that."

"They will, you know. They always take kids away who aren't old enough to be on their own. They'll put me in some goddamned foster home." Her voiced hitched as she spoke and he could see from the way she was holding herself that she was ready for another crying jag.

Chris set the clothes down gently on the bed and slid to the other side, sitting on the ground next to her. She looked at him with the puppy eyes again and he knew it wasn't an act, that she was terrified. As he watched her, the tears started in her eyes. He put an arm around her skinny shoulders and pulled her close until her face rested at the crook of his shoulder and chest. "No one's going to take you away, Brittany. I won't let them."

"You promise?" Damn, she was going to break hearts when she was older.

"Yeah, I promise. You're my sister, not a house-plant. I'm not letting anyone take you away." He kissed her forehead and she nuzzled against him, seeking comfort from one who was normally a source of grief for her. He held her that way for a few minutes and then patted her side. "Come on, let's get this finished."

The rest of the work went quickly, with Brittany's mood better than it had been.

Within an hour or so, you could barely tell that there had been a break-in—just as long as you didn't look too closely at the tears in the mattress. Brittany went off to take her morning shower and Chris went down to make breakfast for them both. Brittany got to clean the dishes while he took care of his own shower. She'd left about four minutes worth of warm water before the icy cold spray took its place, which was typical, but he let it slide.

By the time he was done cleaning up and dressing himself, she'd gone out, leaving a note that said she was over at Renee's house. The note promised she'd be back by dinnertime.

Chris was getting ready to call Jerry when he knocked on the door. "What's up, bro?"

"Yo, Jerry. I was just gonna call you."

"Yeah. Well, I figured you might want to get out of the house for a while, maybe catch a movie or something."

"I can't leave."

"Why not?" Jerry's face didn't show anger, just mild surprise. Except when he was arguing with Katie, Jerry very seldom showed anger. Everything about him was more pronounced around his girlfriend, be it happiness or anger. Katie had that effect on him and that was probably half the reason they made a good couple. She made Jerry more alive than he was on his own, like she finished the Jerry Equation in some obscure way.

Chris sighed and told him about the night before and the break-in. Jerry's face looked as pissed as Chris imagined his own had been, but he calmed down quickly enough. "So when's this detective supposed to be by?"

"He said sometime this morning."

"You holding up okay?"

"Yeah, I guess. Just still trying to figure everything out." Jerry nodded, leaning back in the recliner that he'd long since adopted as his own. "Do you know what Brittany asked me earlier?"

"Tell me."

"She asked if I was going to let Social Services take her out of the house."

"Seriously?"

"Yeah, she was actually worried about that."

"You set her straight?"

"Yeah. But I mean, what if they decide I'm not fit to be her legal guardian?"

"Then you tell them to fuck off. You can do that. You're rich." Jerry shrugged his shoulders and walked into the kitchen, grabbing each of them a Pepsi from the refrigerator.

"You know, I'd almost forgotten about that. The rich thing, I mean."

"Well, you've had a little on your mind, man."

"No shit . . . You think that'll make a difference to the courts if it comes up?"

They both popped their sodas and Jerry took a deep swig before answering. "Yeah, I think it'll make a difference. It means you can hire an attorney to take care of all the forms that have to be filed." He belched loud and long and grinned at Chris. "I'm not saying it'll make everything peaches and cream, but it sure as hell makes your chances better than they would be otherwise. Besides, you're her family and most courts would rather see family stay together. Less paperwork that way."

"Know any good lawyers?"

"I'll ask my dad. Anyone he doesn't know, he can find out about."

Chris nodded his thanks. "You know what bothers me the most?"

"What?"

"I have absolutely no idea how to handle being in charge of her."

"And that surprises you?"

"Well, no, not really, but I mean, what am I supposed to do if she does something stupid?"

"Same thing your mom would do, man."

"Mom would talk to her. You know that."

"Yeah? So you talk."

"Have you ever known Brittany to listen to me?"

"Now and then. Maybe not all the time, but when it counts."

"Yeah, right."

"Give her a chance to fuck up before you convict her, all right?" Jerry's voice took on that edge it got when he was in scolding mode. Normally he reserved it strictly for Katie—a point that Chris refused to bring up, because he rather liked his head where it was, as in attached to his neck—but now and then he used it on Chris as well.

"What do you mean?"

"I mean you're not the only one who just lost a mother. I know that's harsh, but you have to give Brittany a chance to adjust too. She's scared for a reason, man. What does she have now except for you?"

"Okay, point made."

"Seriously, Chris. Think about it, okay?"

"I got it!" he snapped and almost immediately apologized with his eyes. Jerry responded in the same way: no harm no foul.

"So other than your sister and the break-in, you okay?"

"Nothing I won't survive."

"Want me to hang around and wait for this detective to show?"

"Sure, but only if you don't have plans with Katie."

"Yeah, well, we sort of planned on coming over here and hanging out. She'll be over when she's done at the restaurant. She couldn't blow off another day."

"Shit . . . I wish she hadn't done that. I don't want her getting herself in trouble with her boss."

"What? You don't think you guys are a little more important than that?"

"You know what I mean. She shouldn't risk losing her job."

"Chris, it's a fucking nowhere job to give her spending money."

"That's not the point, Jerry. She's got to make money too."

"And money isn't the point. You and Brittany are our friends, Chris. And we both loved your mom a lot. There's no way in hell we were gonna sit on the sidelines and forget about you for a week. The decision was hers and the decision was mine and get the fuck over it."

That pretty much ended the discussion. They went on to other subjects and waited for the detective. Later in the afternoon, when Katie showed up, Chris left a message on the answering machine at the number Crawford had given him and they left as a group to get out of the house and actually do something for a change of pace.

They took in a movie—Katie's choice, and while it was okay, there weren't nearly enough explosions—and then went out for munchies and to grab a couple of videos. This time Chris and Jerry chose. There were explosions aplenty on the tapes. They got back to the house a little after six, loaded down with Kentucky Fried Chicken and their cinematic selections. There was no sign of Brittany in the house.

Chris decided to worry a little after nine in the evening, when he called her friend Renee's house and found out that she hadn't been over there all day.

IV

Brittany came home just after five in the morning, barely coherent and probably bordering on a serious case of alcohol poisoning. By that point, Chris and Jerry had been searching for several hours every place they could think of, and Chris was ready to commit murder. They were still out on the street when Katie called to let them know she was okay.

Katie was there when they got back, and Brittany was in bed with a stainless-steel pot next to her bed in case she suddenly decided to void her stomach again. She'd already done that several times according to Jerry's girlfriend.

It took both Jerry and Katie to prevent Chris from waking his sister. He wanted blood after all the worrying he'd been doing. Jerry physically restrained him for a full two minutes, while Katie went over the litany of times she knew of when he'd pulled similar stunts.

"I have never stayed out until five in the fucking morning without a call or advance notice to my mother."

"No, Chris, you just came home so drunk that you couldn't see the wall." Her words were said without heat, with a slow and gentle patience that made it damned hard for him to get upset with her or to argue the point. "You aren't a saint, either, and I know this is a bad time for her to pull a stunt, but she needs to unwind and maybe she thought this was the best idea."

"Lying to me is the best idea?" He laughed bitterly as he spoke, knowing full well that Katie was right and not caring in the least. "Jesus, Katie, like I don't have enough worries right now?"

"And you were always worried about your mom's thoughts and feelings when you and Jerry used to go out partying?" Her eyebrows knitted together over her brown eyes, and the look on her face said she was perfectly willing to go 'round and 'round with him until he saw reason. There was no part of him that wanted to give in on the argument, but he also had a strong enough sense of self-preservation to know he wasn't going to win this one.

"Fine. I'll let her sleep and blister her ass when she wakes up."

"Oh, no." Her voice grew serious, and there was a slight hint of danger in it, a warning that he had best be kidding. "None of that. You can talk to her in the morning, and I'll be here to see that's exactly what you do."

Chris reared back as surely as if she'd slapped his face. "What?"

"Chris, I'm not letting you take it out on Brittany. You can talk it out, but I know you with your fists."

"You can't really think I was serious? I'd never hit Brittany. Besides, that was one fight, a long time ago."

"Never is a long time. Now, go on up to bed. Jerry and I will lock up and we'll be back later in the day. Don't you even think of talking to Brittany before then."

Chris looked to Jerry for support, and Jerry looked back, shrugging his shoulders. "Hey, is it my fault my girl is a mother hen?"

She poked him playfully—if a little too harshly—

in the ribs in response. "Ten A.M. We'll be back then. Until then, get some sleep. That's an order."

"You're not the boss of me. . . ." The words had no heat to them. Katie was very good at calming down situations. It probably had to do with the fact that she could give the cold-shoulder treatment better than any woman he'd ever known aside from his own mother. She could be positively Antarctic when she wanted to, and Chris had seen Jerry suffer under that curse more times than he cared to think about. He wasn't willing to risk it.

Jerry and Katie left, and Chris moved up the stairs, looking in on Brittany, who was curled into a slightly green lump on her bed. She moaned softly in her sleep and he moved closer to her, looking down. Had he ever been this stupid? Yes, yes he had. He pulled her blanket up over her body and moved quietly back to his own room.

Sleep didn't come easily. In his dreams he kept seeing Brittany being captured—or worse—by the thing with the giant mouth. The smell of alcohol on her breath brought back the reek from the damned freakish nightmare he'd painted after the man escaped.

V

The confrontation came all too early in the morning for Chris and for Brittany, who was still looking green around the gills. Katie was looking wide awake, and Jerry was looking mostly asleep, but mentally able. That was more than Chris could say for himself. He was barely conscious and desperately wanted to go back to bed for a few weeks. Crawford was supposed to come over at some point, and that meant Chris had to stay awake.

What should have been a simple and easily-contained argument about when Brittany should be home blew up in Chris's face. She listened to exactly five words—where the hell were you?—before she exploded, screaming that he was not her father and she had rights.

From there it went downhill fast. Chris was about as willing to let her scream as he was to let her take a machete to his nose. The whole thing was over in roughly two minutes, when she stormed out of the house in a full-scale tantrum.

Katie looked truly stunned, and Jerry wasn't far behind, but Chris knew better. He'd pretty much been expecting something along those lines.

Katie looked directly at him and smiled apologetically. "I never guessed she could be so . . ."

"Completely psychotic?" Chris smiled sweetly.

"I was going to say high-strung."

"You are far too kind."

"Well, maybe we can talk to her later. . . ."

"Maybe I can get a tranquilizer gun." Jerry's voice was a remarkable imitation of Katie's just then, and she shot him a warning look. He backed away with a big grin and held his hands in the air in mock surrender.

"Look, I appreciate the effort, Katie, but this is one that's going to take more than one sit-down discussion. In the meantime, I have that detective coming by and I need Jerry to get hold of that lawyer his dad knows."

"Well, we can arrange that." Jerry stepped in fast, wanting to smooth over the comment that still had Katie sending him a murderous glance. "I'll make a call right now and we'll set it up, okay?"

"Fine." Chris nodded and then looked at Jerry and Katie, his eyes serious. "And thanks. Seriously, for everything."

Chris wound up making breakfast for them, using his tried and true methods for making pancakes, which meant they were palatable, but not very pretty. After that, the two lovebirds flew the coop to find out more about the lawyer, and Chris waited by the phone as best he could. He gave up his nervous pacing and fidgeting and eventually fell into a light sleep on the sofa.

He'd likely have slept the entire day away if Jerry hadn't called a little after three in the afternoon. "Hullo . . ."

"Chris, man, you sleeping?"

"Nyeaahh. But that's cool. What's up?"

"Found you a lawyer. He can meet with you tomorrow morning, right around nine."

"Cool."

"Brittany come home yet?"

"I don't think so."

"The cop come by?"

"Nope. I figured he'd at least call. . . ." He frowned, wondering what was taking the man so damned long. Then he shrugged. Likely as not, he had a lot of cases. By his reckoning, it wasn't exactly the calmest job in the world, and a breaking and entering where no one was seriously hurt and nothing got stolen probably wasn't the top priority. Still, he reached over to the dining-room table, dragging the phone half off the end table in the process, and grabbed the detective's card. He'd give him a ring when he was done with Jerry.

"You want us to come over?"

"No, man. You guys have been great, but I'll take care of things on this end. Want to meet in the morning, though? Maybe hit the lawyer with me?"

Jerry's voice was slightly breathy, and Chris could just about envision Katie doing something hideously distracting while he was on the phone. He'd seen her do it a few times. Once, while Jerry was trying to call home and sound like he was both calm and sober—and he'd been neither at the time—Katie had slipped up next to him and traced the inner curves of his ear with her tongue. Jerry'd gone stiff as a board, his whole body positively rigid and his eyes closed as he tried to concentrate well enough to speak lucidly to his mother. It had taken all of Chris's self-restraint to not break into laughter right then and there. He'd also had a few impure thoughts about Katie later in the evening when he was drifting off to sleep. "Umm. Yeah . . . I can do that, my man."

"Cool. Tell Katie to be nice."

"She always is. . . ." There was a smile on Jerry's face that even made it through the phone lines. Chris hung up and left his best friend with his lady. Part of him, as always, was a little jealous.

He tried Detective Crawford's number and left a message, hoping the man would get back to him quickly. He let himself worry briefly about Brittany and then decided she could handle herself for a few hours. By eight that evening, he couldn't stand being stuck in the house anymore and went out to get himself something to eat.

He wanted pizza, but there was no way he could go over to DeLucci's for it. The memories of his final night there with his mother were still a bit too fresh. He settled for a local shop he'd never tried before and found the meal disappointing at best. Maybe it was just his mood, but everything tasted flat.

After that he went back home, prepared to settle down and watch television for a while and hope that the detective would call him back. He opened the door and stepped inside, barely bothering to look where he was going. Three steps later he was in the living room and heard surprised gasps. He looked up quickly, his entire body going tense after the recent break-in. Thoughts of finding his little sister held by the freak from the night before, still looking for his key and maybe playing the interrogation game with Brittany sent him into high alert.

Brittany was on the couch, half prone, her eyes wide with fear and something else . . . what . . . guilt maybe? He could just see her face over the shoulder of the man on top of her. For an instant Chris thought she was being attacked, but then his eyes took in the details of exactly what was happening.

The man who was leaning over her looked his way. Chris guessed his age at somewhere between eighteen and twenty-two. Brittany scrambled back, her bare chest breaking contact with the hand that had been fondling her developing breast. Her hand pulled away from the crotch of the man's jeans, which were still on, but the fly was open.

"Motherfucker!" It was the only word that came to Chris's mind, and he let it fly from his lips like a battle cry as he leaped the distance to the couch. Brittany screamed out something in response, but he didn't really hear her through the red haze that was sweeping over his vision. His hands reached out and grabbed the creep groping his sister, hooking his fingers into the black button-up shirt and feeling the fabric tear and stretch as he yanked with all his might.

He and the pervert went backward, the backs of Chris's knees catching the edge of the coffee table he'd cleared with ease and both of them went over the top. The guy let out a sound that was one part growl and three parts shriek, his arms windmilling madly, even as he landed on top of Chris.

He didn't stay on top for long. Chris rolled over and took him along for the ride. Chris's fist was cocked and ready to drop before he stopped himself from pounding the man into hamburger. For his part, the Romeo now pinned under him bravely held out his arms, his eyes begging for mercy.

"Chris! Stop it! Leave him alone!" His sister's voice was loud and scared, not at all as ferocious as it had been that morning.

"You shut your mouth, Brittany! You're already in deep enough shit!" He looked her way, and whatever she saw in his gaze made her take a step back.

"Don't hit him. Please don't hit him."

Chris glowered down at the man under him and lowered his face until they were only a few inches apart. "How old are you?"

"Nineteen?" Wide brown eyes looked at him, and the long, curly brown hair around the pinched face shook slightly.

"My sister is fourteen. I catch you anywhere around her again, and I'll break your balls. Then I'll have you arrested for statutory rape. Do I make myself clear?" Oh, how he wished the little prick would give him attitude. He wanted desperately to cave his head in.

Instead, the creep nodded very, very carefully, as if afraid that any other action might get him beaten to death. That was the wisest thing he could have done. Chris crawled backward and stood up, dragging the man's dead weight with him. He didn't bother to let the bastard gather anything he might have left behind. He hauled him over to the door and physically threw him outside. Chris figured it was better than going to prison for manslaughter.

The guy took off like a deer in hunting season.

Chris slammed and locked the door and then turned to face Brittany. He could see it on her face, the desire to confront him. He could also see the fear she felt when she looked him in the eyes.

He looked at her without speaking for several

seconds, looked at her arms covering her chest, looked at the fear winning out over the anger on her face, and looked at her even longer, until she finally averted her eyes.

She very quietly and meekly went up the stairs. He didn't dare speak. Whatever words might come out of his mouth weren't the type that would easily be forgiven later.

VI

He waited until he'd calmed down, sitting in the silent living room and merely listening, letting his mind drift. He wasn't really capable of thought, not clear, concise, rational thought at any rate. He didn't call Jerry or Katie, though he knew he could have and they would have been there in a matter of minutes. He didn't call because they needed a break from the pressures of his life and because he was afraid that if he tried to explain what had happened he'd go ballistic right then and there. So he just waited.

And while he waited he heard his sister go through several different emotional reactions. She went through a silent stage as strong as his, and she went into a crying jag that almost broke his heart. Ten minutes later she was screaming into her pillow—a habit she'd had since the age of nine whenever she wanted to vent steam—and from there into another crying jag. Through it all he stayed where he was, breathing slowly and not thinking until he was fairly certain he could approach her room without exploding.

He knocked and then opened her door without bothering to wait for an answer. She looked his way, her face sullen and stormy, her hair scattered on her pillowcase. She was wearing pajamas, which was good. He'd had a brief flash of finding her naked or fully clothed, and didn't know which one would have been worse. Naked meant embarrassment. Dressed maybe meant her trying to sneak out of the house. The latter of the two would probably have ended badly, despite his efforts to remain calm.

"Listen to me very carefully." She nodded, her eyes in full puppy-dog mode and having no effect whatsoever. "I'm going to a lawyer tomorrow morning. I'm going to talk to him about getting legal custody of you, so we don't have to worry about you winding up in a foster home or any of that shit."

She sat up, looking all of ten years old, her eyes were so wide.

"I meant what I said about us being family and you not going to a foster home. But if I catch you pulling anything like that again, there will be hell to pay."

Brittany nodded again, her body relaxing a little. Whatever she was fearing, his words had eased that dread a little. He closed her door and went to his own room.

He slept very little. Brittany slept almost the same. From time to time he heard her crying. He understood the desire, but wouldn't allow himself the luxury.

Chapter Three

I

Although Chris did not see the detective, a package was left leaning against the door on the front porch, the following morning. Chris thumbed through several photocopied pages of mug shots and found that none of them looked much like the freak who'd broken into his house. The sketch done by someone with more talent than he'd actually expected was closer, but not quite right.

Chris made himself a cup of instant coffee—not because he really liked the taste, but he felt a dose of caffeine might do him some good—and drank it with a breakfast of toasted frozen waffles. If someone could have removed the sandpaper from the insides of his eyelids, he felt pretty certain there would have been a new best friend in his life.

Still, Chris was plenty satisfied with the old best

friend when he showed up just after eight in the morning. They took off for the lawyer's office and made it through the early-morning traffic with around four minutes to spare.

Sterling Armstrong looked just like his name. He had been bred for success and power and it showed in everything about him and about the offices he employed. If his secretary wasn't a model, she should have been, with her long hair pulled into a ponytail and her suit that probably cost more than Chris's mother had ever made in a single month. She smiled sweetly when they came in and completely glossed over the fact that both were dressed in jeans and T-shirts.

Upon hearing their names, she immediately called her employer and a moment later escorted them into the sort of office that very likely made most people tremble in fear. *His rates have got to be astronomical*, Chris thought as he looked around. Solid oak desk, matching book cases, a wet bar and leather seats all around.

Sterling Armstrong rose from his seat behind the desk and walked over, offering a manicured hand and a smile that would have shamed most politicians. If his secretary was dressed for success, Armstrong looked dressed for world conquest. His suit was gray silk and very likely hand tailored. He looked like a model who was past his prime, but just barely, and positively reeked of confidence.

He greeted Jerry like an old friend, and Chris like the friend of an old friend. Not for the first time, Chris found himself idly wondering how it was that

Jerry's father knew so many influential people.

They had coffee around a small glass table in the corner of the office that overlooked most of downtown, and Chris brought the man up to date on the situation with his mother's passing, the lottery winnings and his little sister.

"Are you sure you're ready to take on your sister as your legal responsibility?" The man's voice was as smooth and cultured as the rest of him.

"Absolutely. She's my family and I don't want her stuck in some foster home somewhere for the next four years."

"There are other options. . . . Have you considered a live-in nanny or a private-school education for her?"

"The nanny wouldn't work out. She wouldn't listen." Chris shrugged his shoulders, watching the light-brown eyes of the man across the table. Armstrong's perfectly coifed hair was shot with silvery strands that were almost strategically placed, and Chris had to wonder if the gray was natural or had been added to make him look a little older. "Private school isn't happening, at least not yet. She has friends at her school now, and I don't want to yank her away from where she's comfortable. I think she's had enough changes in her life already."

"Fair enough. You understand that there might be a good deal of paperwork involved in handling this . . ."

"Well, that's sort of where I figured you come into the picture."

Armstrong laughed lightly, and nodded. "True

enough, but what I mean is that it gets expensive."

"If it isn't breaking twenty thousand dollars, I don't figure I'll have to sweat too much."

"I can get it done for considerably less than that, I imagine."

"Good. Now, I don't really know what all is going on, and from what Jerry's been telling me, you're one of the best." The man nodded his thanks to Jerry for the compliment. "Is it possible to keep you on with a retainer fee?"

"Oh, yes. That can be done."

"Good." He looked at Jerry and Jerry nodded. "I guess that's all for now, Mr. Armstrong."

"Sterling."

"Sterling it is. I'm Chris."

They were on their way a few minutes later, escorted out with another dazzling smile from the secretary that Chris was pretty sure would haunt his midnight fantasies for a while.

After they'd reached the parking garage, Chris climbed into the passenger's side door. "So, where does your dad know this guy from?"

"They went to college together." Jerry sat down and closed his door, starting the Mustang's engine.

"And what does your dad do again?" Both of them buckled up and Jerry smoothly backed out of his space.

Jerry smirked. "Makes money hand over fist."

"Is Sterling your dad's lawyer?"

"Yep."

"Okay. If he's good enough for your dad, he's good enough for me."

64

"Goddamned better be good enough for you, rich boy."

"Jealous?"

"Well, yeah, I mean, I'll have to go to college now. You? You can just go on all the spring breaks and fake it."

Chris snorted. "Screw that. I'm going to college."

"Why?"

" 'Cause spring break is only a few weeks. I intend to spend as much time as possible around the college chicks."

"Yeah? What are you gonna do with Brittany?"

"I'll take daytime classes."

"You and she ever get everything worked out yesterday?"

Chris sighed and took a deep breath before telling Jerry what he'd walked into the night before and how he'd handled it. Jerry made several comments throughout, but none of them were dealt with his usual sarcasm.

"This is Brittany we're talking about, right?" Jerry shook his head as he drove, his face looking almost as stunned as Chris had felt the night before. "Your little sister? The cute one who hasn't grown out of her Keds?"

"That's the one." He looked out the window at the houses and cars passing by, trying not to let himself get angry all over again. "I think if I ever see that fucker again I'll go through with the threats, too."

"Jesus, Chris, I'll help."

The car slowed down for a red light and finally

stopped, idling with a faint, rather pleasant rumble from the powerful engine. Chris rolled his shoulders, trying to ease the tension that he felt sinking teeth into his muscles. Several soft, muted pops sounded faintly in his ears and vibrated through his neck at the same time.

Any sense of relaxation that had started creeping into his system was destroyed a few seconds later, when he saw the face of the man who'd broken into his house drive by. The man was sitting behind the wheel of an old sedan that had last seen a good car washing some time in the previous century. The grungy brown sedan went speeding past in the opposite direction. "Jerry! Sonuvabitch! That was the guy who broke into my house!"

Jerry didn't even bat an eye. He just looked once in each direction and then gunned the engine. The car's tires screamed as if shocked as he cut smoothly in a semicircle and floored it in pursuit of the car.

Chris batted an eye several times and damned near let out a girly scream. He hadn't quite been prepared for the action. "Shit, Jerry!"

"Hey, you said he's the guy, so let's check it out." Jerry steered with one hand, going through the gears on the transmission at record speeds with the other. When he was done—all of seven seconds later—they were gaining fast on the sedan and he grabbed for the cell phone on his hip. "Here's the phone. Call Katie and ask her to go watch Brittany. Then call your detective. We're gonna find out where this fucker's headed."

"Good plan, just for the love of God, give a guy a little warning." He punched in the speed-dial number for Katie and held on as Jerry spun the wheel to the right and followed the land yacht in front of them. The man in the car they followed apparently caught wind to the fact that he was, in fact, being tailed, because he accelerated hard, the old Buick almost jumping as the engine roared. For a piece of shit, it had heavy horsepower. Jerry kept pace, but didn't try to gain on him.

Katie answered the phone on the fourth ring. "Hi Katie, it's Chris. Listen, don't really have a lot of time to talk just now, but can you head over and watch Brittany for a while? Sweet. Thanks. What am I doing? Jerry and I are playing detective. The guy who broke into the house is right in front of us and we're following him." He pulled his head back a bit as she screamed into the phone. Jerry got that damned grin of his going again and shook his head. Chris suspected his friend knew exactly what she was saying, word for word. "No . . . no . . . nothing like that. We're just going to see where he's going, and if it looks like he's gonna stop somewhere, we'll call in Detective Crawford and let him know. No. Not a chance in hell. No. I won't do anything too stupid and I won't let Jerry do anything either."

"Make sure you don't, Chris. I mean it."

"Look, Katie, even if I wanted to get macho right now, and I don't, Jerry is driving his Mustang. Do you really think he'd let anything happen to his second-favorite girl?"

She sighed into the phone. There'd been a month

or so last summer when she and Jerry had fought almost constantly. That had been around the same time he'd purchased the beat-up old car and started rebuilding the engine. When Jerry set his mind to something, he was rather like a juggernaut. He'd set his mind hard on the idea of fixing up the classic car, and before it was all said and done, it had almost cost him Katie. During that month he spent almost every waking hour retooling the interior, painting the exterior and building the engine virtually from scratch. That meant he'd had little time for Katie. For her part, she had little patience for being second fiddle to a car. Chris had had to physically pull his best friend from his garage and give him a serious ass-chewing before Jerry saw the light of reason. Though it had been almost a year, there were times when Katie still got edgy about the cherry red Mustang. Jerry had done his best to make it up, but she still tended to look at the car as a rival for his affection. Girls could be strange, Chris mused, but then, that was what made them interesting.

"Get him and his car back in one piece, Chris. I mean it. I don't like you guys going off and being macho."

"I will. I promise. Besides, this isn't macho, it's just trying to get one asshole off the road and make sure he stays away from the house."

He smiled at her response and handed the phone over to Jerry, who scowled and grabbed it before putting on his mollify-the-missus voice. "Hi, gorgeous. What? No. You know better than that. No, I won't. No. I said no, didn't I?" He paused, the phone between his chin and his shoulder as he took another hard right turn, the wheels of the Ford whining slightly in protest. "We'll be back at Chris's place in an hour or less. If it's more than that, I'll call. I love you too. Yes. I will. Bye." Jerry straightened out the car and threw the phone at Chris. "Call your detective."

The area around them was degrading fast into the heavy poverty district. The houses were trashed, the people walking around had apparently given up on dressing for success a long time ago, and the streets themselves were full of potholes. The Mustang bucked over the torn-up asphalt, but Jerry managed to stay on course.

In front of them, the Buick wasn't faring quite as well. A hubcap spun off from the right side and darted crazily over to the sidewalk where it jumped hard and then ran into the brick wall of a liquor store. At the same time, the muffler on the old sedan gave up in a shower of sparks and fell to the road. The creep behind the wheel wrenched it hard to the right and the whole battered wreck slid sideways, almost going up on two wheels before it stopped.

Jerry managed to not ram the car, but it was a close thing. He pumped the brakes furiously and the Mustang's tires let out a squeal of protest that was rivaled only by the screams that Jerry and Chris both let rip. There were roughly four inches between the nose of the Ford and the side of the Buick when they stopped.

The driver's side door of the other car slammed open, and the figure behind the wheel, visible only as a silhouette, vanished from sight. "Oh, hell no!" Chris fought against his seatbelt for a moment and then pushed open his own door. He was moving for the Buick even as Jerry was screaming for him to get back over to the Mustang.

Chris bounced off the front bumper on his way over to the open door on the older car, cursing under his breath and wincing at the sharp pain that scraped over his upper shin. It took some rather dynamic arm waving to keep him on course, but he managed it. When he stopped, he was looking through the open door into the car proper, his hands balled into fists and his stomach fluttering madly. There was the need to find and punish the man who'd dared to violate his mother's memories via her room and then there was the clear image in his head of that mouthful of teeth that had taken the place of an actual face; the fury and terror were not mixing well at all in his mind or in his body.

The thought of the thing in his house, near his own room and that of his sister was enough to make him think about what was waiting for him. He focused on the car's interior and saw nothing but seat covers, a steering wheel and a dashboard. The man—or thing—that had been driving the car was gone. Chris spun on his heel and looked around, trying to see anything out of the norm. Aside from the car and Jerry, who was looking rather pissed, thanks just the same, there was nothing.

"Have you lost your fucking mind?" Jerry was stomping his way, his face reddening even as he came closer. "I told you we'd follow him! I didn't say you could go out and try to get yourself killed!"

"He's not here, Jerry. He's gone." Chris's voice sounded funny to his own ears. Weaker than he wanted it to, and stressed.

"Bullshit!" Jerry came around from the back of the car, his eyes never once leaving Chris's face. His eyes were damned near murderous, but there was an underlying hint of fear in that expression. Chris knew him well enough to read that.

"Then you find him, dammit! I sure as hell can't!"

Jerry ducked his head down, and the rest of him followed as he dropped to the ground, looking like nothing so much as a man caught halfway through a push-up. He looked under the car, his whole body still twitching from the near miss with the vehicle. When he popped back up the anger was gone, replaced by a puzzled look. "Where the hell did he go?"

Chris walked around the car himself, frowning, and checked under the hulking thing before shaking his head. "I don't know." His mind flashed to the way the face of the man had changed, the fluid shifting of bone and muscle that had allowed the sharklike mouthful of fangs to appear and had taken away the angry features that had been there before. *If he could do that with his whole body . . .*

He didn't let himself finish the thought.

"I have no fucking idea."

The two of them stared at the car for a few more

moments before the distant sound of police sirens dragged them back to the present moment. Chris jotted down the license plate and then they were off, heading back toward his house.

He made the call from Jerry's cellular phone, leaving yet another message for Detective Crawford. He would have been far more annoyed about the lack of response if his mind wasn't so damned busy trying to figure out what had happened to the burglar. He hadn't just vanished, he had to have gone somewhere, but Chris couldn't imagine where. There hadn't been a manhole cover on the street, and there hadn't been anything besides the two cars that was large enough for him to hide behind. There was absolutely no way in hell the man could have gotten away without being seen by one of them. The only possibility that came to mind was one he didn't like to think about. There'd been a drain at the edge of the road, not five feet away and facing the same direction as the driver's side door on the Buick. The opening was all of four inches tall, maybe five. Nothing remotely the size of an adult male could have slipped through that opening, unless it was pureed first.

But Chris kept seeing that face, so warped and altered, torn away from its previous dimensions and distorted into something from a nightmare.

Nothing human could have fit through that drain.

Unless it could change shape enough to make itself fit.

If Jerry noticed the nervous twitch that mani-

fested at the left corner of Chris's mouth, he didn't
bother to mention it.

II

They got back to the house on Longfellow only a
few minutes after Katie managed to get there. Brittany was in fine spirits until she saw Chris, and
then she clammed up. It was like watching a switch
flip, the way her face went from bright and cheerful
to sullen.

Chris looked at his sister for all of three seconds
and then went into the kitchen. He came back with
a Pepsi from the refrigerator and sat down in the
recliner where he always sat. Brittany watched the
television, or at least aimed herself in that general
direction. That suited him just fine. He still wasn't
over the heavy-duty pissed off he'd managed to
catch when he found her with her hand in a guy's
pants and her shirt off. He knew it was irrational,
but she was his little sister and she was supposed
to *stay* little. That meant not copping feels at the
first opportunity. Katie and Jerry both sensed the
extreme tension without any difficulty. The difference was that Jerry knew why it was there. Chris
watched the two of them exchange questions and
answers without words, using only their facial expressions. Katie asked what was happening and
Jerry told her they would discuss it later. Brittany
just stared at the TV.

Finally Chris broke the tension by telling his sister that he'd been to the lawyer and set everything in motion. She looked his way and for just the briefest moment showed her gratitude before remembering that the two of them weren't on speaking terms at the time.

For a while they all watched television, and Jerry spoke softly, filling Katie in on what had happened to them on their little adventure. There really wasn't much to say, but he said it all.

Eventually Chris's bladder made him get out of his seat and take care of nature. He walked down the hall, did his business and flushed. When he came out of the bathroom, Katie was waiting for him.

"Just how bad is it between you and Brittany?" Her voice was low, but not quite a whisper.

"What do you mean?"

"I mean you two won't even look at each other." She pointed down the hallway and shook her head. "I could cut the tension between you two with a knife, Chris."

"I came home to her with a guy who was older than me. They weren't actually screwing, but it was close." Even thinking about it made his lips press together and his eyebrows pull closer.

"Okay . . . well, she was stupid, but it's sort of to be expected."

"Excuse me?"

"I mean, not expected, more like inevitable."

"Are we talking about the same thing here? I'm talking about my sister being molested by a grown man." His voice wanted to rage, but he wouldn't let it. "I'm not talking about her getting drunk for the first time or playing hooky."

"How old were you when you first did it?"

"That's not the point."

"Why not?"

"Because I'm not a fourteen-year-old girl." He knew the second the words came out of his mouth that they'd been a mistake. He was right.

Katie stared at him for a few heartbeats, her face getting angry and then slowly calming down. "No, you're just an asshole."

"Katie, you know I didn't mean it that way."

"Which is why you still have balls." Katie wasn't exactly a screaming feminist on the warpath and hungry for the blood of all male chauvinists, but she did not take well to the double standard that still divided the sexes. She made her opinions known and she had never taken well to the notion that it was okay for men to start early but not for women.

"Katie, she's my little sister." He spoke in a desperate whisper, needing her to understand why he was angry, and knowing even then that she did. Katie came from a family of seven kids; she knew all too well what he was talking about. "I'm supposed to protect her and I want to, but unless I get her a bodyguard, I'm screwed here."

"Or she is." Katie winked lewdly and it took him completely off guard. Her finger poked into his ribs and he had to cover his mouth to stop from breaking out in laughter.

"God, Katie, that's rough. . . ."

"Yeah. I know." She looked away from him for a second and sighed. "You want me to talk to her?" He couldn't have nodded his head faster without giving himself whiplash. "I will, but not while you and Jerry are here."

"You're a god, Katie!"

"Don't forget that, either."

They walked back out to the living room where Brittany immediately went back into stone-sentinel mode and turned away from Jerry, focusing on the *Buffy the Vampire Slayer* rerun that was airing. Jerry stood up and moved toward the door without a word being exchanged. Chris had been set up, but it was all right. They were just looking out for him again and he knew that sometimes he needed that.

"So, me and Chris are gonna go get Chinese food." He looked at Brittany and tilted his head like a bird that thought it heard a strange noise sneaking closer. "Sweet and sour pork or shrimp with lobster sauce, Peewee?"

Brittany's face lit up. "Shrimp with lobster sauce, egg rolls and lots of wonton soup."

"Pig. Where do you put it all?"

"I am not, and don't call me 'Peewee' either."

"When you grow up to be big and strong and can kick my ass, you can tell me what to call you."

Brittany looked over Jerry's solid frame, wavy brown hair and shoulders that were twice as broad as hers and stuck out her tongue.

"No thanks, I use toilet paper."

"That's disgusting!"

"So's your breath." He leaned over and kissed

Katie on the cheek and then he and Chris were out of there.

When they got out to the car Jerry waited for Chris to sit down and looked at him with a curious, almost mischievous smirk. "Wanna go find your buddy?"

"How do you figure we do that?"

"Guess we could go look at his car again, see if it's still there."

"How long you figure we should be gone from here?"

"Maybe a couple of hours."

"Okay. I don't think we'll find him, but okay." He swallowed the fear that wanted to deny the very idea of the expedition. Screw what he thought he'd seen. Crawford was right about that, it had to have been the stress of the situation. And, frankly, he was leaning toward following his mother's philosophy about the whole thing anyway: Face your fears head on and get over them.

"Rockin'. Let's get the hell out of here." Jerry was not known for liking arguments, and the idea of being around Katie and Brittany when they got into it apparently scared him as much as it did Chris. Too many possibilities for things to go wrong.

Finding the spot where they'd last seen the car of the man who'd broken into Chris's house was easy enough. The battered old Buick was still there, in fact, though someone, somewhere, had managed to push the vehicle off the main stretch of road enough to let other cars pass. Jerry drove right on past, and then pulled the Mustang onto the next road over.

When Chris looked over at him quizzically, he shrugged and looked back. "I can see the car from here. Anyone comes up to it, we'll know and we'll see."

"You think he'll come back?"

"Probably. He might have shit in the car that he needs."

"Yeah, well, whatever he has in there probably is shit. I didn't see anything worth coming back for."

"Chris, you ever think what he has might be small or hidden?" Jerry looked at him as if he were looking at a very small and not terribly bright toddler. "Like, oh, just for starters, drugs or a weapon or even a phone book?"

"Okay. I get it. We'll wait. So what do we do if we find him?"

"We can either follow him again or try your cop friend one last time. But I gotta tell you, I'm not real impressed with this detective so far. He hasn't called you back about what happened earlier, and that was almost two hours ago. He needs to either solve a few cases or get a secretary."

"I haven't been dazzled myself." Chris looked out the window, staring at the obscene graffiti someone had scrawled on the worn brick wall of what claimed to be a diner but managed not to offer anything remotely like a pleasant odor. He guessed if he was actually starving or had a gun pointed at his head he might be convinced to try eating there, but otherwise, not a chance in hell.

Fifteen minutes idled away in the car before Jerry slapped him lightly on the arm. "Lock your door when you get out. Your buddy is back."

The two of them slid out of the car as quietly as possible, and gently closed and locked the doors. Chris could see the man rummaging in the trunk of his car and finally grabbing a small bundle that he held tightly enough to make Chris think it must be something extremely significant to his life.

When the man moved, they followed, the sun behind them making long shadows. It was still a few hours until the sun would actually set, but that didn't mean Chris wanted to be in the area any longer. The houses dipped into a shallow bowl of a valley, and spilled outward toward more level ground in the more reputable area. From where they were Chris could look across the bowl of the valley to see the houses on the other side. The interior of the depression was already getting dark as the sun lowered toward the west. It got dark early around here and the people around them were not exactly reputed to be model citizens. In fact the neighborhood was one he normally avoided looking at, mostly because it was ugly but also because it was rather notorious in the local news. If there was a murder in town, it normally came from somewhere in the area.

There had been a time when the area was considered posh, but it had been decades before Chris was born. Before the turn of the last century there had been a great number of palatial homes buried amid a large run of farmland. The farms eked out a survivable living and the homes stood in their spots like grand old dames among the peasants. The

Great Depression had brought an end to all of that. The farms couldn't survive in most cases and the estates were sold off a little at a time to keep the families in them afloat. Before it was all said and done, the area was practically abandoned.

Back in the mid-fifties, the place had been rebuilt as low-income housing for families just starting out. Most of the houses were small and comfortable. Sometime in the seventies, he figured, things had started going wrong. The tiny houses were meant to be starter properties for new families and instead became the homes of lower-income groups who felt it was pretty neat sleeping a few dozen to a room. His mom had told him stories about the sorts of people who lived in the area. They were mostly from other countries and often perfectly decent people, but the bad apples in the bushel soon started to change that. By the time Chris was born there were crack houses and other, far less savory sorts moving in and claiming the area by whatever means they felt necessary. His mom had pretty much been of the opinion that most of the places needed to be burned to the ground to make way for a proper garbage dump.

If most of the people in the area were as pleasant as the one they were currently following, he felt he could agree with her rather radical assessment.

He looked over the man he'd seen before, surprised only because the clothes he wore spoke, if not of money, then at least of a comfort zone substantially higher than his own. Despite that fact, the man was walking away from his car. Leaving it for the local criminals to do with it what they would.

Jerry cast a few nervous looks behind him and Chris knew he was worrying about what would be left of the Mustang. Chris made a mental promise to himself to pay for any repairs, or to buy his friend a new one if it came to that, just as soon as he got the first installment from his lottery winnings.

They followed the man for several blocks— through neighborhood houses that actually managed to continue looking worse and worse. What started as low income soon degraded into full-blown derelict or only slightly better than condemned—and while the man looked around from time to time, he never bothered to look behind himself. It made tailing him a lot easier than it could have been.

When he finally stopped, they were glad. It was getting darker in the neighborhood. The night people would be coming out soon and neither of them much wanted to be around when that happened. The buildings had descended from crappy to abysmal somewhere along their path. Most of the houses and shops were closed and likely to stay that way indefinitely. Some of the buildings still had windows, but not nearly all of them. They skirted a run-down house with a rickety fence where three dogs that were at least half German shepherd were barking frantically at the figure they followed, and the voice of a man who sounded like he gargled with granite chunks was screaming for them to shut their "goddamned pie holes" before he had to get out of his chair and shut them himself. Chris guessed he wasn't exactly the nicest man to be around and decided not to drop by for a social visit any time soon.

Their target made an obscene gesture in the direction of the dogs and then crossed the broken asphalt of the sun-bleached street before he climbed the warped and broken stairs leading to a house that had once been elegant and worth calling a home. The wooden slats of the walls had probably been painted at one time, but the paint had long since faded to nothing and flaked away. What little remained looked more like severe acne scars than actual protection for the lumber. There were a few rosebushes that had long since gone wild close to the property, and they had full heavy blooms on them, which seemed almost like a sad joke when one considered the nearly-bald lawn and shriveled shrubs.

He didn't knock, but simply stepped through the door and closed it behind him. Jerry looked at Chris and handed him the phone. "Call your buddy."

Chris dialed and waited, pleasantly surprised when the detective answered on the third ring. "This is Crawford."

"Detective Crawford, this is Chris Corin."

"Yes Mr. Corin. I got your earlier message. I should be down there in about fifteen minutes. I'm actually heading there now."

"Well, you can skip that. We came back out here and found the guy and I can tell you exactly where he is."

"That wasn't very smart of you. What if he has a gun?"

"We were careful. I'm looking at the house he just entered. It's at either eleven thirty-eight Tillinghast Lane or seventeen thirty-eight. I can't see if the second number is a one or a broken seven."

"Not living in the fast lane, is he?"

"Hardly. Listen, we'll wait here for you. I can identify him on the spot if you want."

"Make sure you stay out of sight. It won't do anyone any good if he sees you and runs or decides to do something about you being there."

"Not a problem. Most of the windows are boarded up. But we'll be careful."

"Where are you, exactly? I want to see you before I knock on that door."

"Side of the house facing his. You won't be able to miss us."

"I'll be there as soon as I can. Stay where you are." Half a second later Chris heard a dial tone. He shoved the phone into his pocket and told Jerry what was going down.

"So what are we supposed to do?"

"Wait here."

"Sweet. I love waiting in the darkness in a neighborhood like this."

"On the bright side, maybe he can give us a lift back to your car when it's all over."

"Okay. Good point."

The sky darkened a bit more, and Chris kept looking at the dilapidated house where the man had gone. Jerry kept himself occupied by flicking small stones through the dead lawn of the house where they were sitting.

"So, did Crawford say how long he'd be?"

"Soon as he can get here." Chris scowled and looked at the house across the street. It was a dump, but then, all of them in the area were less than savory. "I'm going over there to take a look." Chris rose and crouched, his head and torso almost perpendicular to the ground.

"Didn't he just say to sit your ass still and wait?"

"Yeah, and?"

Jerry gave him the look that said he was being stupid. "Don't you think maybe you should listen to the nice cop?"

Chris gave him the look that said *go screw yourself*. "No. Not really. I want to know what's going on over there. You coming?"

"Well, duh . . ." Jerry rose from his sitting position and dusted off his ass. "Let's get this over with." They looked around carefully and darted across the street, hunched over to make spotting them harder—well, it always worked in the movies at least—and in a few seconds they were at the window, trying to peer between the slats of wood.

The inside of the house was in better shape than Chris might have imagined, with actual wallpaper— a tacky yellow floral print that had been ugly in its glory days and was now just plain ludicrous—on the wall as opposed to say, a few dozen gang-related slogans. There didn't seem to be any furniture and the hardwood floors had warped quite a bit, but that was all he could see of the interior.

There were several people inside, but they didn't seem to be doing much of anything except sitting in a circle and talking in voices too low to hear. Chris spotted his friendly neighborhood burglar almost immediately. He was off to the left, fondling the small package he'd brought with him from the car. Chris desperately hoped it was something hideously illegal for when Crawford showed up. The sort of narcotic that would ensure a nice long stay in prison.

Jerry bumped up against him with the regularity of a metronome, trying to see inside the place. Jerry was normally a little too full of energy for his own good and at the present time it was even worse. It took an effort not to smack him on the head and tell him to back off. When the phone rang inside the house, it was moot anyway. The shrill cry of the telephone had them both jumping back away from the window in a hurry. Less than a minute later they were back across the street.

"How many people did you see, Chris?"

"Maybe ten. It was hard to tell."

"I couldn't get a count. Your big fat head was in the way."

"Yeah, well, I wanted to see if he was in there."

"Did you see him?"

"Yeah. The guy in the blue shirt. It's him but he took off his jacket."

"Not really a big guy, there, bucko. I'm surprised you didn't kick his ass."

Chris swallowed, that damned freaky face trick still messing with his head. "I got him to leave, dude. It's enough." He knew he sounded testy about it, and maybe that was just because he was. Still, he didn't want to get Jerry pissed at him too. He was annoying enough people lately.

"Chill out. You know I'm just giving you shit." Jerry put a placating hand on his shoulder and squeezed for a second.

"Yeah? Well, I've had enough shit dealt in the last few days if that's okay."

"Not a problem." Jerry let out a rattling breath. "Sorry, amigo. I'm just a little nervous."

"That's both of us." Chris looked over at the road between the houses, wondering if any of the street-lights in the area were actually in working order. The sun had almost set and there was no sign of the two lights he could see even thinking about lighting up.

Jerry started to say something else. He got as far as "So when is this—" before the wall next to him exploded in a hail of wooden shrapnel.

Chris never thought Jerry capable of jumping anywhere near as far as he did. He never thought himself able to make a scream so loud, either, but he barely even heard the gun's report. They'd been watching the road and the front of the house. They never thought to look anywhere else.

They looked now, and weren't at all pleased by the sight coming their way, heading toward them from the back of the house where they were wait-ing. The sonuvabitch had crept up on them without them ever noticing. Police Detective Walter Craw-ford was moving toward them at a light jog, and holding a gun that looked exactly the right size to kill them both.

He pointed the pistol at the air between the two of them and spoke calmly as he slowed to a stop one house away from them and two houses away from where the thief and his friends were waiting.

"Hello, boys." The man tried to smile, but it looked all wrong. His face was strained and his skin looked pasty in the faint dusk light. "I really wish you hadn't come here. I don't want to hurt either of you, so let's just make this easy. Tell me where the Western Key is and you can go on your way. No one gets hurt and no one ever has to think about this little mess again."

"Crawford? What the hell are you doing?"

"I just told you, Chris. I want the Western Key. That's all anyone here wants. So let's make this easy. Hand it over and we'll call this business done."

"You're a police officer! I called you, remember?"

"Yes you did." The man nodded. "And I thank you for that. But now I need the Western Key." From the yard next to him, the barking sounds they'd heard earlier got louder, almost drowning out the detective. The three mutts ran from the side of the house nearest Crawford and doubtless would have delighted in attacking him, but the chains hooked into their collars stopped it from happening. He shifted his stance and studied the dogs, his pistol still sighted directly between Chris and Jerry.

A figure started out of the house to scream at the dogs again and managed half a word or so before he noticed Crawford. The man very meekly backed into his house, calling the dogs by name. They reluctantly stopped barking and slunk toward the safety their owner offered. Crawford shuffled his feet a bit and looked back at his prey.

"Where's the key, Chris?"

"What the hell are you talking about?"

"The Western Key." He spoke with slow, deliberate patience, his pistol never moving. His eyes looked black in the dying light. Chris wondered if the man in the house was calling the police. He had his doubts.

"I don't know what a 'Western Key' is, mister."

"That was your one chance."

He aimed right at Chris and fired again, his face looking almost demonic in the fading light of the day. The bullet missed, but only by a few inches at best. Chris could feel the force of the wind from it as it passed.

Neither Jerry nor Chris bothered with anything like words after that. They just ran like hell. Chris looked to his left and Jerry to the right, old reflexes from their four years on the football team coming into play. They cut straight across the street and bolted toward the house where the man Crawford was supposed to be coming after was waiting.

The door to the place opened quietly, the only giveaway being the light that spilled from the inside of the dump. The light didn't last long. The bodies spilling out from the entrance to the house eclipsed it very nicely. Ten figures came spilling out onto the battered front porch and not a one of them looked friendly. The first of them—none other than Chris's special breaking-and-entering friend—hurdled the short railing and dropped to the ground not two feet from him. Chris stiff-armed him across the neck while he was still trying to get his balance, pumping his legs, barely taking the time to look back. He was glad he did. The bastard was choking and coughing behind him, struggling weakly to get to his hands and knees. Sadly, the other people from the house didn't seem to care much how he was doing. They wanted blood and it looked like Chris and Jerry were supposed to be the main donors around these parts.

A brilliant flash of pain lanced across Chris's left shoulder, just left of center, and he suddenly found himself spinning halfway around as he ran. His arm went numb and for a second he was fairly sure he'd been kicked by a mule. He caught himself on the edge of the house and tried very hard to remember what was going on aside from the pain. Then he saw Crawford and the rest moving toward him and remembered. It was just a shame he couldn't convince his body to do anything about it.

Jerry grabbed his arm and pulled hard. Chris came along with him, staggering to catch up. Jerry looked behind them and Chris looked ahead. Then they changed views, one of them almost always looking at the freak patrol bringing up the rear. Crawford had apparently given up on the pistol and was now doing an admirable job of catching up with the rest of his pack of runners. For their part, the people from the house were getting closer and closer. Chris started pumping hard with his arms, hoping for an extra inch or two in every step, ignoring the warmth running over his bicep and the pain from his shoulder above it.

Jerry had been silent until then, saving his breath for running. But he looked back at Chris now with wide eyes and an expression that said someone just had to be pulling his leg. "What the fuck did you get me into, bro?"

Chris looked back and was immediately sorry that he did. It was happening again, that strange distortion of his perspective. It had to be, because if it wasn't, then the people behind him weren't looking very human anymore. There was a man behind him, one he'd never seen before, who was in the process of stretching, his limbs growing longer as he ran toward Chris, who would have sworn on a stack of Bibles that the balding, pudgy figure had easily been five inches shorter a moment before. But that was one of the lesser changes. The man who'd broken into his house—who should by all rights have been choking on his own crushed windpipe— was low to the ground and moving like a bloodhound, his body shifting for better speed and less wind resistance as Chris watched.

The others were too far away in the fading light of the dying day, and watching them closely was impossible as he was still running for all he was worth, but he could see their shapes, and they were changing too, growing further and further away from human. A few of them were making noises, too. Noises that had nothing to do with human speech. One of them uttered a noise that sounded like a bullfrog on testosterone had been bred with a lion. The long warbling bark sent shivers through Chris.

Chris looked at Jerry. "Fuck this! RUN!"

He didn't have to tell Jerry twice. They separated, Chris bolting to the left and Jerry cutting hard to the right. It had nothing to do with deserting each other and they both knew it. They'd been in a few tight spots before that were close enough for easy comparison. There'd been a time back in the tenth grade when they'd managed to piss off Bryce Darby—who, they were both convinced, spent his spare time as an actual wrecking ball—and several of his friends. One on one they each could have taken Darby—maybe—or any of his friends—definitely—but as a group there was no chance in hell. They'd done the only sensible thing and split up, thus dividing the forces of their attackers.

It had almost worked. Darby caught up with Chris and knocked the living crap out of him. Chris got in a few good licks himself, enough that Darby left him alone for a while at least. That was the most anyone could hope for from Bryce Darby. But the tactic was sound then and it was sound now. They split up.

Most of them took off after Chris, and while he was glad to see Jerry doing a little better, he still didn't like what was following him. He didn't bother looking back as much as he had; the road ahead was broken and ragged, desperately in need of repairs, and besides that, there was the fact that he really didn't want to see the things following him. They weren't human; he was convinced of that. He didn't need to see them to know it either. The sounds they made were enough to settle the matter. The things moving behind him were grunting and barking in low, dangerous ways that brought to mind sounds he'd heard before, though he was damned if he could place where. Whatever the source of the memories, it sent his skin into a crawl and pumped enough adrenaline into his system to make running seem easy. At least for the moment. He knew it wouldn't last. He'd be winded and tired all too soon.

Despite the passionate desire to forget what he'd seen, Chris had no choice but to look again. The noises weren't all that much closer-sounding, but he didn't trust his ears. The sound of his own pulse was too loud. He looked. He would have given almost anything to take it back.

Whatever they were that chased him through the darkening night had given up any pretense of looking or being remotely human. No two of them were alike but they all seemed to be vying for the most obscene appearance. Worst of all, each and every one of the things seemed like it had been designed solely for the purpose of out-racing him. The closest of the abominations was only around ten feet away from him, and ran with a graceless stride that tore up the distance, its scaly legs tapering down to heavily clawed feet that hooked the ground and let it leap more than run. The long torso almost weaved like a snake's body and the arms cut through the air, with webbed, impossibly long hands that caught the wind and propelled it toward him. The face above that thrashing, jostling body lurched forward with every stride, its open maw writhing with what looked like a million small worms. The bulbous eyes glared at him without blinking.

The thing running close on its heels moved on all fours, with a rolling gait that carried it forward on thick legs. Chris couldn't see a head on the thing, just a stumpy torso that ended in a writhing mass of whipping feelers. Each one beyond the two in the lead managed to look more like an abstracted nightmare.

He pushed harder and damn the consequences, his body screaming in protest. The darkened houses around him—most surely abandoned—blurred past. There was nowhere around where he could hide from the things coming after him, nothing nearby that he could use as a weapon. His throat was already feeling properly sanded and his lungs were starting to burn with the need for more oxygen.

He took the corner onto the next street, heedless of what lay ahead and far more worried about what was pursuing him. Something back there roared—*roared for chrissakes!*—and he damn near wet himself.

He only looked forward when the car horn honked in front of him. The headlights hadn't even registered. He couldn't see beyond the high beams, but something big was bearing down on him, and

Chris let his reflexes do the talking for him, dodging hard to the right and losing his balance when his foot hit the broken curb. Four years of football practice under the kind tutelage of Coach Hank "Hardass" Malloy had resulted in several badly bruised body parts, one ankle that popped more often than the Three Stooges fought among themselves, and an uncanny ability to get back on his feet as fast as they were taken out from under him. Chris rolled after he lost his footing and managed to get back up and running again before the car he'd almost met head-on could come to a halt.

The first of the things behind him was not as lucky, at least if Chris could judge by the sounds. Something heavy met with the grillwork on the vehicle and Chris heard a satisfying crunching noise mixed in with the sound of breaking glass. Several of the things behind him erupted into angry growls and sounds he didn't really want to consider.

Whoever it was driving the car was apparently not quite a good enough Samaritan to risk life or limb checking on what he'd hit. Chris heard the man's voice very clearly through the cacophony, heard him screaming like a woman giving birth to a breech baby and heard the sound of the car gunning forward over whatever thing he might have run down in the first place.

Apparently the rest of the freak squad didn't much like that. Chris looked back just long enough to see that nothing was following him at the moment, and then he ran again.

Have you ever been desperately lost? Chris Corin thought he'd been lost before, but he was wrong. In the past he'd merely been slightly confused about where he was. He learned that night what lost really meant. Through the darkest streets he'd ever been on in his life, he wandered aimlessly, most of his mind reflecting back on what had happened—or what he thought had happened. Had the people chasing him become monsters? *Well, by God, they sure as hell* looked *like monsters. But that has to be the stress again. Oh, no, wait, who told you it was stress in the first place? Could that be the wonderful police detective who was taking shots at you? The one who just happened to turn into a monster along with the rest of the freak show from the house? Do you think that maybe, just maybe, mind you, he might not be the best source to trust right now?*

Chris was all too aware of the bullet wound in his shoulder, and suspected he might be in shock, but really couldn't bring himself to care all that much. He was far too busy being scared numb. It was the beginning of summer, and from time to time the air got chilly that time of year, but Chris was shaking almost violently. Shaking and sweating. He walked on, stumbling a few times and falling on more than one occasion. He walked past buildings that should have looked familiar but seemed alien, and more than once stopped to stare at structures he could never remember having seen in his entire life that seemed to call to him. There were noises ringing in his head, sounds that should not have been there and sounds that just should not have been. Almost everywhere he went there was a strange odor, like beer that had gone flat and later grown into something gray.

And somehow, he made it home.

He pushed the door open just after two in the morning, his arms trembling with the effort of lifting them to unlock the door and turn the knob. After that Brittany and Katie were at his sides, leading him into the house and making concerned noises that didn't make too much sense. He sat down on the couch.

He closed his eyes.

That was the last he knew for a few hours.

III

Katie let him rest until the sun came up.

When he opened his eyes again, his shirt was gone and he had a patch on his shoulder. He was in his bed, though he had no idea how he'd gotten there, and the sun was spilling through his window and carving lightning strikes across his retinas. Moving his arm up to block the painful light was an experience he could have done without. His arm felt like someone had wrapped barbed wire around each separate muscle and decided to pull roughly in multiple directions. The worst part was, that was his good arm. The other one didn't want to move at all. It took time, but he managed to work both arms until he could move them again without actually screaming. He managed with his legs as well, but it wasn't easy. After a few minutes of stretching—and whimpering—Chris finally got himself out of bed.

He looked at himself in the bathroom mirror and blinked several times before realizing that he was, in fact, looking at himself. His eyes were bloodshot and surrounded by puffy flesh that was several shades darker than it should have been. His face was stubbly, which was unexpected, considering that he normally shaved only three times a week and he'd shaved just the day before. His left shoulder was covered with a heavy layer of gauze, some of which was not rust colored. He pulled the tape and cotton fabric away and looked carefully at the wound. Despite the blood flow that had seemed like it would never end, Chris's bullet wound was actually rather mild. The lead had cut through skin and a little muscle, but it had not left him torn apart as he'd feared. He felt better after seeing that, and he got himself dressed, pleased to whimper only now and then.

He moved down the stairs after that, rolling his shoulders as best he could in an effort to actually make them mobile again. Once he was satisfied that he could at least pretend to be capable of motion, Chris moved downstairs in search of Katie and Brittany and to see if Jerry had made it back yet.

The two girls were in the dining room, and Chris would have found them even if they hadn't been speaking, solely because the smell of breakfast foods cooking was enough to make his stomach knot up with anticipation. He actually caught himself salivating.

Katie was dressed in a pair of Brittany's pajamas, as was Brittany herself. The PJs were loose on his sister, but his friend filled them out almost to the busting point. He smiled his good morning as best he could and sat down at the table and forced himself to focus on the scrambled eggs, bacon and toast that was all but overflowing the small table.

"Good morning." Katie's voice was slightly forced, a little too cheerful, but he didn't sense she'd reached the point where that tone was a sign of pending disaster. Normally she saved that particular tone for Jerry. Her face looked older by almost a decade. Stress did not sit well on her shoulders.

"G'morning." He looked around and smiled at his sister. "Has Jerry shown up yet? We got separated."

Brittany shook her head and gave him a look that clearly stated he was being a moron. "No duh, you got separated. And no, we haven't seen him yet."

Katie brushed a strand of hair away from her face and as much as he didn't want to notice, Chris couldn't help but think about how attractive she was. Her eyes were downcast and she spoke with less cheer than she'd used a moment before. "I've tried Jerry's phone about a zillion times. He isn't answering."

"Shit." Chris ran his hand through his short hair, sighing deeply. That wasn't the news he'd been hoping for. "Maybe his battery died?" She looked at him and he looked back for a few seconds before blinking. "Oh, damn, Katie. I've got his phone." She breathed an almost epic sigh of relief. "I probably turned it off after I called Crawford."

Brittany grabbed a plate and started covering it with food. When she was done she set it down in front of her brother. He nodded gratefully and started eating. He was so damned hungry his stomach actually felt nauseated. He didn't bother speaking for a few minutes, but instead scarfed down the breakfast foods like they were the only possible cure to a hideous disease. He and Katie and, to a smaller extent, Brittany, discussed the night before in detail while he worked on his seconds.

When he was done Katie insisted on checking his shoulder. She hemmed and hawed and made little clucking noises. "You should see a real doctor, Chris. I mean it. It's not bleeding, but that's a nasty hole."

He shook his head and then paused to gulp down the large glass of milk his sister gave him. There was a part of him that was wondering why she was behaving so nicely, but he didn't let it stop him from appreciating the gesture. "Can't do it."

"Why not?" That one came from Brittany.

"Because hospitals have to report gunshot wounds. It was a cop who shot at me. I don't really think the rest of the police department is going to take my side over his."

"Well." Katie looked at him for a few heartbeats and then looked down. "It's not exactly like I've got a medical degree or anything, but you should have it checked."

"You did a lot better than I could have hoped for.

Thanks." Thanks didn't really cover it. He was pretty sure he'd be dead by now if she hadn't stopped the bleeding. He was still having trouble believing that he'd ever managed to get home.

"What if they got him, Chris? What happens if these people got Jerry?"

"You tried him at home? The old number?"

"About a dozen times. His folks are worried sick."

The very thought of Jerry in the hands of Crawford and the rest of the things he was running with was enough to make Chris want to cry. Hell, just the look on Katie's face was enough to break his heart. "I don't think they would hurt him. They want this 'Western Key' too much to risk hurting Jerry. I don't know. Maybe they'll want to trade him for what they want. That's if they even got him, Katie."

"Where else would he be?" Her voice shook, and that too hurt him. It hurt him because she'd been so strong lately and he hated to think of her losing Jerry as much as he hated the idea of himself losing Jerry.

"I don't know. What I do know is that there's a police detective who tried to shoot at us. I think it's time he was reported for that crap, too." Chris stood up from his breakfast and stepped out onto the porch. He couldn't bear to be around Katie just then. Her fears were his fears, and if he saw her crying there was no way in hell he was going to get through the phone call. So he walked out into the warming morning air and used Jerry's cell phone to make the call.

Before it was done he almost wished he hadn't wasted his time and he was worrying about whether or not the battery in the cellular would hold up. He stayed outside, the weather being pleasant and the tension inside not quite as nice, and waded through several switchovers before he finally got through to an officer actually willing to speak to him about the problem.

"This is Detective Callaghan, how can I help you?"

Chris bit his tongue on the "Dirty Harry" comments. "I need to report that one of your detectives took a shot at me yesterday night. He was supposed to be coming to my aid on a breaking-and-entering case where I found the guy who broke into my house, and instead he tried to blow my head off."

"Okay, you're sounding a little edgy, and I can understand why, but why don't you start with the basics. What is the name of the detective you say tried to shoot you?"

"Detective Walter Crawford, with the thirteenth precinct."

The voice on the other end changed a bit, not a really drastic change, but one that put the hairs up on Chris's neck. "I'm sorry, sir, what did you say your name is?"

"I didn't. Not yet."

"I'll need that information, sir." And there it was, that sound in the voice, like the man really, desperately wanted to know his name. It was almost like a straining effort for the man to stay calm or at least to sound calm.

"What I need to know first is whether or not it's common practice for police officers to shoot at unarmed people asking for their help." He realized his voice was rising and made himself calm down. He went from leaning against the porch to pacing, barely even aware that he was moving. "What I want to know, Officer Callaghan, is why one of your detectives was shooting at me and what he might have done with my friend, who was with me at the time and hasn't managed to come home yet. Then maybe I'll discuss my name with you."

There were other people talking in the background behind the cop on the phone, He could hear them whispering urgently. "Sir, can you describe the detective you had dealings with?"

Chris sighed. "Yeah. Average height, receding hairline, brown hair, thick mustache, suit that looked like it came off the rack at Sears, stocky build with a spare tire around the waist and bad teeth."

"Sir, it's imperative that we speak to you immediately." There was that tone. He said it was imperative that they speak, and his voice said they wanted to speak to him immediately but maybe they felt it was best if they played it cool.

"That's what I've been trying to arrange, Detective." Chris frowned. "Listen, what's going on here? Has Crawford been in trouble in the past?"

"Sir, if you saw Detective Walter Crawford, and your description matches his well enough, then you

are one step ahead of us in an ongoing investiga-
tion."

"What do you mean?"

"Walter Crawford has been missing for the last
seven months."

"Excuse me?" Chris was sure he'd heard the man
correctly, but he really didn't like what he'd heard.
His stomach achieved the impossible: It seemed to
freeze solid and simultaneously start rolling on
him, tossing the breakfast he'd consumed like a
ship in a hurricane.

"Walter Crawford signed in for a shift in October
of last year and never came back. He's been missing
for several months, sir. We need to know where
you saw him and what he said. His wife and children haven't seen him and his partner hasn't been
seen since that night either."

Chris clicked the off button on the cell phone.
That feeling was back in his chest, like someone was
slowly squeezing the life out of him. "Fuck . . ." He
walked inside and set the phone carefully on the
coffee table before falling back onto the couch. Both
of the girls looked at him and got those worried
looks again. Their expressions got far worse when
he started hyperventilating.

It took him a few minutes to calm down enough
to explain the situation to them. Brittany was a little
puzzled at first, until he pointed out that a missing
detective was probably just shy of a murdered detective in how many people would be looking for
clues. "I don't want to be their prime suspect on
any of this crap. I don't want them breathing down

my neck and trying to find a motive for me to hurt a policeman. Especially one who tried to kill me last night."

Brittany nodded her understanding. "So what happens now?"

"I don't know. I need to find Jerry if I can. And I need to think." Chris stood up and moved toward the door again.

Katie looked at him and frowned. "Where are you going?"

"I don't know. I don't have any idea. But I have to try to find out something about this 'Western Key' thing. Because if Crawford and the rest DO have Jerry, I need to have a bargaining chip."

"Should we just report Jerry missing in the meantime?" Katie looked at him, her eyes begging for something she could do to make it right.

"I don't know. Maybe." He thought for a minute, wondering what would be the best move. "Try his folks again and see if they've heard from him. If they have, great. If not, maybe it's time to report him missing without knowing anything about where he went."

Katie rolled the notion around in her head and then nodded. "I can do that. Listen, Chris, be careful, okay?"

"Not a problem." He looked at Brittany. "You two take care. I'll be back as soon as I can." Brittany nodded in response. He wasn't thrilled with leaving her alone just then, but he needed time to think and he needed to try his luck with finding out anything at all about the Western Key.

He closed the door on his way out and, as an afterthought, he locked it too.

Chapter Four

I

Chris's arm felt like someone was pushing hot lead through the veins and arteries. Which, when he thought about it, was what Crawford had tried to do with that damned pistol of his. He considered driving and decided against it. The weather was decent, a few clouds coming in, and the humidity was high, but it didn't feel like it would get too hot. The car wasn't in the best shape and he could use the walk to stretch out some of the muscles in his legs and ass that were telling him to go to hell as a result of his unexpected long-distance run.

It was good to get out and just think. Over the last few days he'd been either on the run or brooding inside the house like a caged animal more than he'd been doing anything else. There was a part of him, a greedy and demanding part, that kept whispering to the rest of him and urging him to just keep walking until the whole city was a distant memory. This was supposed to be his vacation. In the world he'd been planning for himself at the start of the summer, he was on his way through Europe right now, not walking down old familiar streets and trying to remember when life had been simple. He didn't even want to think about home. Home was supposed to be the safe place, not the spot where you caught your kid sister getting fondled or the place where monsters tried to rob your dead mother's bedroom. He supposed he was being a bit petulant, but he also figured he'd earned the right.

He made it to the library eventually. He hadn't been there in almost a year, but he still found it comforting. It was quiet in the old brick building, and somehow more solemn than any church he'd ever entered. Churches often had songs and ceremonies. The library just had whispers and cubicles and the rustle of pages being turned. Churches had incense and the perfumes from too many ladies dressed in their Sunday best. Libraries just had the pleasantly musty smell of old paper and newsprint.

He waited almost an hour before he could use one of the computers they had set up for research. It wasn't that hard to operate, and he settled down to start hunting through the Internet files he ran across. He tried a few search engines, typing in the term 'Western Key' and let out a soft moan when he saw that more than a million sites were listed that used the two words together in one way or another. He gave up when he realized most of them dealt with the Florida Keys and any number of hotels. He tried variations on that idea, adding in words like demon, devil, monster and even creatures. None of them netted any results worth the time of searching very far.

After trying the easy way out, he looked through the meager selection of occult books the library offered, with a decided lack of enthusiasm. He found about what he'd expected, which was a long list of books on fairy tales and ghosts. Somehow he didn't think a story or two on a leprechaun or the spirit of someone's dead Aunt Sadie was going to help him much.

He stopped when his stomach gave him a few rumbling warnings that eating would be a nice thing. Looking at the large clock on the wall— which always reminded him of the clocks in virtually every classroom he'd ever sat in; a white circle with black numbers and trim—Chris blinked. Somehow he'd killed over four hours in the library.

It was time to go. He carefully set the last of the books he'd been skimming back on the shelf and then left the sanctuary of the air-conditioned building, stepping into a heat that was much heavier than when he'd entered, and a sky pregnant with darkening clouds.

He couldn't quite bring himself to go home just yet, so he sought comfort in a different way. He walked to the closest florist shop and then walked the few blocks to the cemetery. Chris did what he'd always done when things got a little too strained in his world. He went to see his mother.

II

Brittany and Katie had a long, long talk. It started slowly, with a great deal of reluctance on Brittany's part. She'd known Katie for almost as long as she could remember, and she liked the older girl a lot, but that didn't make it easy to talk to her about private things.

Brittany never liked to talk to anyone about private things. That was why they were private. There were words exchanged, some of them pleasant, most of them not quite kind. Sometimes you had to be cruel to be kind, as the old song said. Katie didn't like having to be an ogre, but when it was necessary she could manage it just fine.

After almost an hour of working at Brittany's defenses, Katie learned the facts of what was making her friend's little sister—and really, a girl who was almost like a sister to her—go a little crazy. Fear. Fear of growing up without a mother. Fear that her brother was only lying to her to keep her quiet. Fear of having her already-broken world ground down into so much bone meal. It was like an anvil sitting on the girl's chest and slowly crushing her down. She was absolutely terrified of being left on her own. With a logic that only made sense to a young woman starting the first serious throes of puberty— an experience that Katie herself was still going through, though she hoped it was past the worst stages—Brittany was doing her best to force her brother's hand. If he really loved her, he'd get angry and yell, but he would never abandon her. If he was lying, she intended to get the worst of the blow over and done with. Oh, to be sure, the words were hardly that clear. Katie had to deduce what she could from what Brit wasn't saying.

But it wasn't difficult, really. Katie had already been there, to a certain extent. She was familiar with the territory, even if she wasn't familiar with the path being taken to explore it.

So they talked. If Chris was expecting a miracle cure for what ailed his sister, he was in for a heaping dose of disappointment. Brittany might be willing to speak of her troubles to Katie, but that didn't mean she was going to suddenly head to the older girl for advice. Even if she did suddenly decide that Katie was wise and knew enough to help her through the problems she was having, it was painfully unlikely that any suggestions given would be taken with more than a grain of salt.

By the time the two had finished their no-holds-barred discussion—which to most people would have seemed perfectly civil and polite, but to the observant (and Chris did not fall into that particular category when it came to women), it would have surely seemed a brutal battle—they were both drained. Catfights were easy when they were out in the open. The quiet ones were always more exhausting, in Katie's experience.

Katie felt a little better when Jerry showed up. He popped through the door without knocking—which was no surprise—and brought lunch with him. He also brought a heavy-duty hug for his honey, which she most definitely needed. "Where the hell were you, Jerry?"

He smiled that little-boy-caught-with-his-hand-in-the-cookie-jar smile of his, the one she could almost never manage to stay angry with, and shrugged his shoulders. "I sort of got lost. It was dark and I got chased a long, long way before I could get my ass to safety."

"Have you spoken to Chris yet? He was fit to be tied when he found out you hadn't made it home."

Jerry chuckled. "No. You're the first person I needed to see. Besides, I thought he was here." He frowned a bit, his hazel eyes looking wet and almost feverish.

"He was. He went out looking for you and for anything he could find out about this key thing Crawford is trying to find."

Jerry put an arm around her shoulders and she leaned in close. He was wearing her favorite cologne, though in a quantity that was almost enough to make her eyes water. "Don't worry. We'll catch up. In the meantime, I brought the very late Chinese food I promised."

Katie was hungrier than she'd thought. She and Jerry and Brittany sat down to eat and she practically inhaled the food set before her. Jerry caught them up on his run from the group in the derelict house and put enough drama in it to keep even Brittany amused. Afterward, he gave Katie a long shoulder rub, working out a lot of the tension that had settled into her muscles over the last day or so.

It was only when they realized that the afternoon

was starting to grow teeth that Jerry left. He was going after Chris, and planned to find him before he could get into any more trouble.

In the end Katie was left with Brittany again. The tension between them had been mellowed a bit by Jerry's presence—and his infinite patience with Brittany. He'd even asked her about a zillion questions without once bringing up the creep she'd been getting touchy-feely with, but with him out of the house they were sort of at a standstill again. Katie started cleaning up the little messes that had built since the last time she'd cleaned up. Brittany didn't offer to help.

That was okay. Katie'd give them a few more days, and then the Corin family would have to take care of their own messes. She had a life of her own to lead.

III

The sod on Eileen's plot was starting to grow in, and the headstone at her grave sat like a silent guardian. Chris gently placed his flowers in the small metallic cup set there for just that reason and sat at the edge of her plot, feeling his depression come back like a fast tide rising to drown him. It'd been long enough now for him to accept that she was dead, but Eileen Corin had left a deep void when she left his life and it had no intention of being filled anytime soon.

His fingers ran over the new grass, the soft blades tickling his palm. A few feet below him, all that remained of his mother was rotting away. That notion didn't bring any comfort to him. He did not speak. He did not ask for her advice. He just sat there for a while, remembering her face and her voice and the looks that some of his friends had gotten on their faces when she walked into a room.

She'd had such a passion for life. Now that passion was gone, and it hurt, damn it all, to think about her. It wasn't supposed to hurt. It was supposed to be good, all of it. When he still counted his years in the single digits, he'd promised to buy his mother a castle. He could still see the look on her face when he'd made his promise, a strange and slightly sad smile that was both wistful and amused. He'd meant it when he made that vow. A few months from now he'd have the money to do it too. Or at least to put one hell of a down payment on any sized house he could desire. Only the need was gone. She'd never live in any place he bought for her. She'd never meet his future girlfriend—assuming he ever found one—and she wouldn't be there if he ever got married.

He'd hoped to find comfort from the simple act of being near his mother, but it wasn't working. He knew that, but still he stayed, fully prepared to spiral down into the worst sort of despair. It didn't matter anymore. Not much did.

"Jesus Christ, Chris. Could you look a little more like a basset hound?" The voice came from behind him and as he started at the sound of it, he saw a shadow growing over him to eclipse the late-afternoon sun.

"Jerry?" He smiled despite himself, looking up at his best friend, who stood behind him with both hands in his pockets, casual as could be. "Good to know you're alive, asshole. Think maybe next time you could call?"

"Think maybe next time you could leave my cellular phone on, so I can?"

"What?"

"I figured you had my phone. I tried calling you like a million times."

Chris groaned. "Well, shit, bro, why didn't you try my house?"

Jerry got that annoying smirk on his face. "Sure. That would go well. Try to call you, get Katie or Brittany and have to explain that I lost you to a bunch of horror movie monsters? Yeah. I can see that."

"Okay, okay, you win." Chris stood up and dusted off his backside, looking at his mother's grave site again.

"She was one of the best, man. But maybe you should give yourself a little more time before you come to visit?"

Chris nodded his agreement, trying not to let the depression get its teeth into him again. "What happened to you?"

"What do you figure? I ran for it and got lost." Jerry looked away, his eyes searching over the headstones in the cemetery. "I couldn't find you, I couldn't find my car. I started walking." He touched Chris's mother's headstone, dusting the top of the monument with his fingers. "You live in

115

a town your whole life, you don't figure you can get lost, but I did it."

"Same here."

"Your arm okay? Where Crawford shot you?"

"Stings like all hell, but I'll live."

"Listen . . . I need to get home. My folks are fit to have cows. I figure I might see you sometime next year, like when I'm old enough for them to actually kick me out of the house." Jerry's eyes wandered over to the distant sidewalk, where a pretty young woman pushed a baby carriage.

"You talk to Katie yet?"

"Yeah, but only long enough to let her know I was alive." He allowed a small smile—a real one as opposed to his normal cynical grimace—to spread over his face. "I figure I'm lucky she loves me. If she didn't, she'd have kicked my ass for keeping her so scared."

"Next time you have monsters chasing down your ass, call the house."

He snorted and looked toward Chris with his usual smile. "Next time, God forbid, I'll keep my own fucking phone."

The two of them headed toward the entrance to the cemetery, nodding a polite hello to the three men who'd started digging at a new plot. People just dying to get into the place . . .

Chris turned left and Jerry to the right. They waved their good-byes and headed in their own directions. Chris was sleepy, and it hit him all at once, like a ton of bricks. Seeing Jerry had wiped a lot of the tension out of him and now he just wanted to rest. He could worry about Crawford and everything else afterward.

He was most of the way home before he realized Jerry had walked in the wrong direction. They should have traveled for almost seven blocks together before separating. For a man who wanted to get home, he didn't seem in too much of a hurry.

The thought was obliterated by the feel of a cold metallic cylinder pressing against his back. He caught a whiff of a musty scent that made him want to gag, and heard Detective Crawford's voice. "Where are you off to? Home?"

"Shit." Chris's eyes cut left and right as he saw movement. Two more men were moving toward him and he felt the barrel of the pistol push hard against his skin.

"Here's the deal. You don't breathe, blink, move or speak unless I tell you to. Break the rules and I'll put a bullet through your spine."

The two men who came up on the sides were smiling and looking around, their eyes moving to cover most of the area. Like the detective, they were dressed in suits and looked respectable. The difference was that their suits were actually tailored and both of them looked like yuppies out for a power lunch, with perfectly groomed hair and pretty-boy faces. Crawford put a companionable arm around Chris's shoulders and slid up next to him, the pistol pressing into his side. "I don't have what you're looking for. Didn't you get that last night?"

The barrel pushed harder against Chris's side, finding a rib to roughly worry against. "What did

I say the rules were?" Chris grunted at the pain but said nothing more. "Good. You're learning. Now walk very nicely with us, and we can get this over with and maybe, if you play nicely, I won't leave you dead."

Crawford led the way and Chris followed obediently. His mind was working overtime, trying to find a way out of this at the same time that it started painting images of what life would be like without the use of anything below his hips. The notion didn't leave him feeling very comfortable.

"Let's get this figured out, Chris." The stocky man was doing his best to sound smooth and placating, but it wasn't working all that well. Mostly, Chris just wanted to break his neck. "I need the Western Key. It's more important to me than I could ever hope to express. I need it bad enough that I sent someone into your house to get it. Sadly, he didn't have any luck finding it. But you already know that." The men walking with them kept up pleasant chatter with each other, speaking loud enough to make it hard for anyone walking past to notice that Crawford was up to something. Chris didn't dare call attention either. There were four or five people on the street and more to come soon, when work let out for a lot of the people in the area, but he couldn't hope to get any help without ending up paralyzed or dead. He ground his teeth together in frustration, wishing Jerry had stayed with him for the walk home. With even one more person, he thought there might have been a chance.

They came to the intersection of Ward Street and

Longfellow, still four blocks or so away from his house, but closer than they had been. Soon enough they would reach his home and Crawford would want him to deliver the key that Chris had never seen.

Crawford's thick fingers dug into his injured shoulder and Chris bit his lip to keep from screaming. "You feel tense, Chris. But honestly, you don't need to be. I just want the key, and when I have it, you'll never see me again." Chris looked at him and shrugged, feeling the end of the pistol graze his skin through the T-shirt. Crawford smiled tightly. Chris noticed for the first time that the man was still wearing the same suit he'd had on a few days before and last night as well, and wondered how the damned thing could still be intact after what he'd seen Crawford changing into. Even the best fabric had to give sooner or later. Of course, the smell coming from Crawford and his clothes showed that the suit was already at least in desperate need of a good dry cleaning. The same moldy stench had come from the burglar in his house.

Crawford looked at him expectantly.

"Did you ask me a question?"

"Yes. I asked if you're certain you don't know where the Western Key is."

"I already said I didn't."

"Well, maybe we'll have better luck with your sister."

"Leave her out of this!"

Crawford pushed the barrel into his ribs again,

hard enough to leave a bruise. "I don't really think you want to yell at me, Chris."

"Look, Brittany doesn't know a damned thing. I know, because I already asked her." Chris looked around and saw still more people. Bryce Darby was leaning against the corner of his mother's house, smoking a cigarette. The sun was bright and almost magnified as it cut through the thickening clouds. The way it ran across Darby's face, he almost looked like a statue with bronzed hair. Darby lived with his father but still came back to the neighborhood from time to time to see his mother. He was wearing jeans and heavy hiking boots, both of which had seen better days. He was also wearing a T-shirt with a picture of Yosemite Sam looking ornery and dangerous in a cartoonish sort of way. Darby and the cartoon gunslinger had a lot in common as far as Chris was concerned. They both had brutal faces, red hair and bad attitudes. The difference was that Bryce Darby was real and fully capable of breaking damned near anyone he saw in half. Bugs Bunny would have been rabbit stew inside of two minutes around the local terror of Chris's early years. Seeing him made Chris want to scowl and then smile as an idea finally came to his mind.

"Look, maybe if you described this key it would help?"

"I don't suppose it could hurt." Crawford shrugged and casually scanned the area. He saw Darby and immediately ignored him. That was better than Chris could have hoped for. "It's a little larger than a quarter, a gold coin with some fine silver filigree and small gems in the center. It's old, too. The original coin is actually a little uneven in shape."

Chris heard the words but paid them little attention. His mind was already working on the Darby angle. He waited until they were even with his old classmate and then looked Bryce directly in the face. Bryce's wide, square face turned as he noticed him, the dark eyes under a broad brow locked with Chris's for a second, and he nodded almost imperceptibly. *Damn, he's in a good mood. Now I have to go and piss him off.* On the best day, with maybe a dozen friends to help him, Chris still didn't like the idea of making the man angry. He wasn't really that much taller than Chris, but he had an unnatural capacity for violence and shoulders that made it almost impossible for him to walk straight through a door. The thought that he might actually get bigger was enough to make most people gape in amazement. If even half the stories he'd heard were true (according to Jerry and a kid they both knew named Tom Murphy, Darby had once curbstomped a grown man's face for threatening to call the police on him—Chris didn't know if he believed it, but he'd never heard Bryce deny it, either) enraging Bryce Darby was probably a better way to get paralyzed than the pistol shoved against his side. It went against his nature to even get Darby's attention. Actually deliberately making him angry? Well, that was almost a guarantee of bodily injuries.

Chris gave Darby the finger. What had been a

nearly pleasant look on Darby's brutish face suddenly became a scowl. One corner of the red-haired boy's mouth lifted in an almost feral way, and suddenly he wasn't leaning against the support post on his mother's stoop any longer. He was standing straight and tall and looking twice as ugly as an IRS audit notice. He lifted one leg and crushed out his cigarette against the worn heel of his boot. His eyes never left Chris's.

Chris made another obscene gesture in his direction and smiled.

Darby started walking his direction with a casual saunter that Chris knew meant nothing but pure trouble.

"Does it sound familiar now, Chris?" Actually, from what little he'd heard, it did sound almost familiar. Chris nodded his head.

"I think I might have seen it, Detective Crawford, but it's gonna be hard to remember where."

"Try very hard. For Brittany's sake." The detective's voice was still roughly pleasant, but Chris caught the threatening undertone without any problem at all.

Chris was about to respond when he felt a hand grab the back of his shirt and yank savagely. He let out a scream of pure shock and so did Crawford.

Bryce hoisted him above his head and threw him into the lawn of the Darby house. Chris hit the nice, soft grass with enough force to dent the ground. Something inside his chest caught fire and he tried to remember how he'd gotten there in the first place. He looked up toward the sky and saw Darby looking down, hands planted on his hips and an ugly expression on his ugly face. "Didn't know you were in the mood to die today, Corin."

"Bryce." He wanted to say more, but the thought of the size-fourteen boot that was getting ready to crush his skull seemed to take away his ability to think rationally. He tried to move, but his body wanted nothing to do with it. In his mind he was already half a block away, but his traitorous nervous system seemed to want to spend a little more time assessing the damage from his rendezvous with the planet.

He could almost feel the bones in his head cracking like eggshells, and in that moment had no doubt whatsoever that Darby was fully capable of beating down an older man and curb-stomping his head into jelly.

Crawford apparently didn't know any better.

He grabbed Darby by the shoulder and tried to spin him around. Bryce's upper body shifted for a moment and then he compensated, nearly knocking the detective off his feet. One of his hands reached over and grabbed the wrist of the offending hand that touched him, and Darby pivoted hard from the waist. Crawford went airborne for a moment and then hit the turf next to Chris.

Chris took that time to get back to his extremely shaky knees. He grabbed the pistol that had rolled away from Crawford's twitching hand and scrambled up to his feet. Bryce—good old predictable Bryce—yanked the pistol from his hand even as he stood.

"I know you weren't gonna use this on me. . . ." The look on Darby's face—something between *Cujo* and the Alien Hive Mother from *Aliens*—made Chris want to wet his pants. The lankier of Crawford's men tried to jump Bryce from behind, and hit him hard enough to make him stagger. On the ground, Crawford made a barking sort of groan and sat up. His eyes looked to the right of Darby and his new rider. Chris looked over just in time to block a swing from the other businessman. The impact of their arms meeting was going to leave a nasty bruise, Chris just knew it. He pushed himself against the man, lowering his body and catching the reject yuppie in his center of gravity. The man folded halfway over his shoulder and Chris lifted. He carried the man's weight easily enough and started running as fast as he could, aiming for the road, with the yuppie letting out a girly scream of indignation all the way. When Chris came to an abrupt stop eight long strides later, the suit and tie kept going. His lean, shocked face changed as he fell, going from a surprised O to a feral snarl that was impossibly wide on his face. He stood up and growled, actually growled like a wounded bear, and started to run toward Chris again, his face warping, splitting open as he moved. Chris saw the skin tear into an X of livid, wounded flesh. Teeth were growing from every part of the opening and Chris jumped back like a panicky rabbit in full reverse, adrenaline kicking him into overdrive again.

He stumbled as he backed up, his hands in front of him, his eyes looking at the strange mouth that kept opening wider and wider, changing the face he saw from a human entity into some nightmarish version of a Venus's-flytrap that drooled heavily as it approached. The man's shoulders and neck seemed to collapse toward each other and the fabric of his suit changed along with his skin, spreading until the entire head and upper torso looked like some serpentine fusion of tweed and skin.

Chris bumped into someone behind him as the thing started charging, the hands changing to look like smaller versions of the face. Darby let out a grunt and then Chris heard, "Fuck off, Corin, I'm busy."

The next second he felt Darby's hand across the small of his back. He'd never realized just how big Bryce's hands were, but he couldn't help noticing now. There was a brief, almost ecstatic second when he thought Darby would throw him again—anything at all that got him farther from Mr. Teeth was a good thing, thanks very much—and then a deep numbing fear when he felt his body pushed forward, toward the snapping drooling freak that was charging.

Chris's feet left the ground from the force of the push, and looking at the thing that managed to convey a grin on its inhuman face, he swung with his right hand as hard as he could. His fist jammed into the head of the demon-yuppie. Not connecting with outer skull, oh, no, that would have been satisfactory. No, his fist went *into* the nasty tooth-filled maw and drove back past the hellish split-lipped, raw opening and slid over the cold tongue and connected with the throat of the creature.

Chris screamed again.

The mouth around his arm—up beyond his elbow—made a stuttering gagging noise and he pushed off from the back of that cold pit as hard as he could, maintaining the scream.

His hand cleared the lips just as the wide open mouth slammed shut with an explosive *clomp*. When he was a kid he used to hit Leary's Pets on Wilmouth and pay a quarter to feed a goldfish to the small sand shark they kept on the premises. The sound it made as it swallowed the goldfish whole was almost exactly the same as the noise of the thing in front of him closing its jaws.

Chris gasped out a breath and took in another as the thing shook the lumpish mass that passed for its head and looked at the bloodred orbs that had once been human-looking eyes as they actually swam over the surface of the face, apparently looking for a better angle to see him from. He let out a wild giggle and pushed both of his hands into the thing's chest.

It staggered back and made a warbling noise deep inside its torso, the mouth opening again like a deadly saw-toothed bloom. Before it could fully recover, he slammed into it again, his own face getting much closer to that mouth than he wanted to think about. One of the opening hand-mouths on the monster touched the bare flesh of his arm and he felt a tooth scraping over his skin like coarse sandpaper. A roar came from the thing—*Oh look, from all three mouths! Ha ha! Isn't that great? Isn't that too fucking neat for words?*—and spilled over him, carrying a rancid cloud of spittle that covered his front and arms.

Chris let out another sound, but this time it was more like a roar of his own. He pushed harder, dropping his shoulder until he caught the hybrid suit-flesh of the thing under the heavy folds of drooping skin that were leaking down from the mouth, and once again found its center of gravity. He gagged under the stench, but managed to push again, this time carrying the beast farther into the road when he finally threw it. He had no plan, no solid method for escaping this nightmare. He just wanted it over. He wanted it dead and gone and wiped from his memory.

He got part of his wish a second later when a van hit the thing as it started to stand again. One second there was a wormy snaky drooling monster scrabbling to rise from the ground and the next there was a honking horn, a screeching sound of tires and a loud boom of flesh on metal, mixed with a shriek of pain that was decidedly not human. Chris looked at the faded blue van with bright yellow legend BEECHER'S FLORAL CREATIONS on the side and looked at the green black smear of fluid coming from under it. He looked up at the window and saw a skinny man with straggly hair looking at him. The man driving the van looked at Chris for half a second, his eyes wide and his face pale and then he gunned the engine and sent the ancient flower-delivery van rocketing down the road. The wheels slipped a bit on something under the van, but it soon caught and took off. Chris couldn't be sure, but he thought he saw something crawling on the undercarriage of the thing. Whatever the case, a thick trail of viscous fluids continued to follow the van.

The sound of Bryce Darby screaming obscenities caught his attention a second later. Crawford was up again and using both hands to fight for the gun. The other yuppie was currently feeling the hospitality of Bryce's boot grinding down hard on his chest.

Neither of them had changed into anything monstrous. He couldn't understand why that was, but they both still looked perfectly human, if more than a little put out at the moment. Chris moved forward quickly, bringing both hands down hard in a double fist, on the back of Crawford's neck. The detective dropped, his hands falling from the pistol. Darby grinned and brought the gun around, aiming it at the face of the man he had pinned to the ground. The man stopped struggling and looked up at him with wide, nervous eyes.

"Now, why don't you get your ass moving before I put a few more holes in it?" Darby lifted his boot and the man scrambled backward away from him. Darby looked over at Chris for the first time since the whole conflict had begun and smiled. "I might have helped if you'd asked, Corin."

"Seriously?" The idea had never even crossed his mind.

"Maybe. Then again, you're a dick, so maybe not."

The two looked at each other for all of three seconds. That was long enough. By the time they remembered Crawford, he'd risen from the ground. His thinning hair was disheveled and his suit looked worse for the wear. His face was swelling on one side, presumably from the gentle ministrations of Darby's fist. His skin looked pasty white and he was sweating. "That's really sweet, boys. But you're both under arrest." He reached into his pants to pull out a small billfold, presumably with his badge inside.

"I already talked to the cops about you, Crawford. They tell me you've been missing for seven months."

Bryce, who'd gotten the look of a caged animal on his face for a second there, relaxed. He aimed the pistol in Crawford's general direction. "Why don't you just leave?" He looked like he was ready to say more, but he never got the chance. The other creature hit him from the side hard enough to knock him completely off his feet. The pistol went flying again, arcing towards the bushes at the side of his house. Bryce Darby didn't go quite as far, hitting the sidewalk in front of his lawn with something fast and gray on top of him. It was moving too fast for Chris to see it clearly. He was grateful for that.

Crawford didn't bother with the pistol this time. He just grabbed Chris by the front of his shirt and pulled him up close for a discussion. "I was trying to be nice about this, boy, but you don't make it easy. I will have the Western Key, with or without your help. And if I have to kill you and your sister and every last person you know to get it, that's okay with me."

Chris hit him in the head. It hurt his fist, but that was okay. It was worth it for the way the man fell back. In fact he liked it so much he did it again. The second blow was off and barely connected. But that was all right. Crawford still staggered when it hit, and Chris felt his own face draw tightly into a grin that he knew would have had most of his friends worrying about his sanity. He was a little worried himself just then, but it had been a rough few days. He reached out and grabbed Crawford's ear along with a handful of hair and pulled savagely, dragging the yelping man halfway around to face him again.

Crawford's yelp changed right along with his face. The entire skull under that face changed too, softening and giving like taffy at his pulling hand. Chris let go, sickened by the changing texture. Crawford's face didn't change completely, but stayed the same, going back to its original shape as soon as Chris released it.

He wanted to attack again, wanted to beat all hell out of Crawford for what he'd already put him through, but his nerves were feeling a bit shot and he couldn't get past the wet texture of the skin he'd just held a second before.

This time it was Crawford who took advantage

of the hesitation. He jabbed a hard fist into the soft flesh of Chris's left shoulder.

Behind him Bryce Darby let out a scream that didn't sound at all pained or angry. He sounded terrified. Chris didn't dare turn to look. He managed to block the next swing Crawford took at him but it wasn't easy. His shoulder felt like it wanted to just fall off and give up. He wasn't far behind agreeing with that idea. Crawford didn't play nicely with others. Chris had never been a fighter. The closest he came was football after school and some boxing training when he was younger. The only reason he'd ever boxed was because his mother wanted to make sure he knew how to defend himself in a fight and paid for lessons at the YMCA.

Whatever else could be said for the detective, he was a fighter. His fists seemed to come from everywhere and Chris was having trouble just defending himself, to hell with actually fighting back.

Darby must have done something nasty if the sound that came from what he was fighting was any indication. The thing did something back that left Darby wailing like a dropped newborn. That is, assuming that the average newborn baby is capable of actually burning the air with his obscenities.

So far it hadn't taken long to fight, but Chris was starting to feel the burn in his muscles. Crawford moved in a half circle around him, his arms ready for more, but his face started to show concern. Not for his fight against Chris, because, frankly, he was kicking Chris's ass. His concern was for something behind Chris, farther away than Darby and whatever he was fighting. Walter Crawford looked past Chris and narrowed his eyes.

"That's it. We'll call this a draw for now."

"What?"

"Too many witnesses for my tastes, boy. Somebody's probably already called the police."

Chris took a swipe at Crawford and connected. The man's head snapped hard to the left and it felt like something in his nose broke. "Fuck you." Not his brightest move, but the idea of anything making Crawford uncomfortable just pleased him to no end. "I say we stay right here and wait for your buddies to show up."

Crawford looked up at him from where he was holding his face. A thick stream of greenish black ichor ran from between his cupped hands. His eyes showed a deep satisfaction that Chris didn't like. The detective shook his head. "No. Not this time. Soon, but not just now." He stepped out of Chris's range and looked around again. "Give my regards to your mother when you see her." The sheer glee on his face when he said those words chilled Chris. Crawford turned on his heel and started running. Chris moved after him and then changed his mind. The man was running away from his house. That was all he could ask for at the moment. Well, okay, the fact that he was exhausted might have had something to do with it. He had doubts he could have made it down the block at a fast clip. As it was, his legs were shaking.

For just one second he allowed himself to think

it was over, then Bryce Darby knocked him to the ground. The man loomed over him, breathing hard, his brown eyes wild and mouth pressed firmly shut until his lips were white. Most of the color had drained from his face and his body looked positively twitchy. Darby had blood running from his hands, from the deep cuts that started at his elbows and ran down to his knuckles.

Chris sat up fast, a flash of guilt going through him when he realized that he'd brought that on Bryce. "Shit, Bryce, I was just trying to get away from them. I never meant for you—"

"Fuck that." Lips swollen from at least one good solid punch parted in a sneer and revealed teeth that were pink with blood. "You owe me. The only reason I'm not taking your head off your shoulders is because I figure you're still in the grace period for your mom dying." He spat a wad of crimson phlegm next to Chris's head. "Next time I see you, you better be moving away from me."

Darby walked past him and into his house, leaving Chris alone on the lawn. What exactly had happened to Darby's sparring partner was anyone's guess. There were several people across the street who were looking at him. He wanted them gone or him gone and figured the latter of the two was the most likely. Like him and like Darby, most of the onlookers were shaken by what they'd seen.

It took a few seconds to actually get to his feet, but after he was standing he managed to walk just fine.

He almost made it home. He was actually passing

the station wagon on his way inside when he thought about Crawford's words again.

Give my regards to your mother when you see her.

It wasn't a threat. The words had the wrong emphasis. They were mocking, not challenging. Crawford had caught up with him only a few blocks away from the cemetery. Jerry had been there, and then he'd just been wondering why Jerry went home the wrong way and then Crawford had been there. Chris dug into his pocket and grabbed the keys, a sinking feeling sliding his stomach all the way down to the ground.

IV

Chris started the car and managed not to hit a tree when he made a three-point turn. He also managed to stop for the traffic signs and behave himself on the road, but it was a close thing.

The front gate to Stovington Memorial Cemetery was open, like it always was, but if it had been closed he'd have run right through it. Chris took the narrow paved paths that led through the various sections of the graveyard at a dangerous speed, almost clipping more than one headstone on the way to his mother's plot.

He stopped ten feet away from where her body lay and knew even as he climbed from the car that something was wrong. The pile of dirt and the shovel were his first clues. Jerry leaning on the granite marker and looking down at someone with a shovel was the second.

His best friend looked his way with an expression that would have been comical if he hadn't been in the process of robbing a grave. Chris didn't find it at all funny. In fact, the sight of Jerry Murphy's expression did nothing but make his blood start boiling. The human body's ability to generate energy was amazing; not more than five minutes earlier Chris would have bet he'd be unconscious by now, and wishing that every muscle in his body would just stop trying to leap away from his skeleton. Now, looking at Jerry and seeing the head of another man in the ground of his mother's desecrated final resting place, he felt no pain whatsoever, just a deep, abiding need to cause permanent injuries to a few people.

"Chris! What are you doing here? I thought you were going home." Jerry tried to put on an innocent expression, but it warred with a deep-seated guilt and something else, an expression Chris had never seen on his friend's face before.

Chris reached down with his right hand and grabbed the shovel resting where Jerry had likely set it to catch a breather. He didn't answer with words. He brought the blade of the shovel in a wide, wild arc and did his best to wrap it around Jerry's head.

Jerry ducked. "JESUS, CHRIS!"

"You better fucking duck, Jerry! I'm gonna kill you!" There was a voice in his head that was trying to remind him that Jerry was his best friend, that Jerry had, in fact, been one of the main reasons he hadn't already gone completely insane after his mother died. The rage he felt at seeing Jerry where he was obliterated that voice of reason.

Jerry backed away with his hands out in front of him and his eyes wide. He still wore that almost laughable look of surprise on his face but Chris still wasn't laughing. Everything he saw seemed to come from behind a deep red lens. Nothing was funny anymore; everything hurt so much that he wanted to scream and keep screaming until there was nothing left of him. Every last shred of kindness or compassion that he had faded for the time being, and he wondered idly if this was what it felt like to be psychotic.

Jerry moved around the headstone and Chris followed. From the hole where his mother's body lay, a hand shot out and grabbed his ankle. He looked down and saw that—*surprise, surprise*—the hand wasn't quite human. It was changing and swelling even as he watched it grip his ankle tighter.

He flipped the shovel in his hands with the sort of precision that would have shamed most Marines doing military drills, and rammed the blade deep into the forearm of the thing holding him. The impact ran from the shovel into his hands and after a brief forward motion, the descent stopped. The hand gripping his leg let go and he heard a scream that sent a pleasant chill running through him. He looked at the arm that was pinned to the edge of the grave, watched it try to pull back from him and lifted his foot. He brought his heel down on the edge of the shovel's blade and stomped as hard as he could. The arm fell away just below the elbow.

Everything from that point to the end of the still-changing hand stayed where it was and spewed out a thick torrent of black, foul-smelling crap that would have had Chris gagging if he weren't so intent on carnage.

What he'd heard a moment before was a scream of pain, pure and simple. What came from the grave now was a roar that shook his bones. It would probably have terrified him to know he was grinning right then. It did terrify Jerry, who had been sneaking up to put a quick stop to the whole mess. This wasn't in the plans.

The figure inside the grave roared again, and Chris looked down to see what was in there. He immediately wished that he hadn't. What was down there looked about twice the size of a mountain gorilla and big enough to swallow him whole. It jumped for him and he brought the shovel up and down in a savage jab that cut into the face of the thing. It screamed again, sounding more human than it had a second ago, and scrambled backward from him in the loose soil, and ruining the top of his mother's casket.

He didn't see much of his mother's remains through the debris, but he saw enough. Her sweet, beautiful face was ruined; savaged first by the car accident, then by decay and finally by the feet of the thing he saw trying to crawl from the other side of the open hole. One thick-toed foot settled directly on her face and he heard something squish and something else crack as her face sank lower.

Chris stared at that foot for a moment, his senses

stretched wide, his nerves seemingly on fire. He breathed in the foul, filthy reek of the thing that was bleeding over his mother's remains, not even noticing the odor on a conscious level. There was just that malformed, graying foot with the claws that actually thickened as he watched. Just that, and the bits of his mother's sunken face that he could see pushed between the toes of the thing like half-dried mud under the foot of some hillbilly.

Chris's world went from dark red to black. He remembered running around to the other side of the open grave, and that was all for several seconds. He came back to himself holding a broken shovel handle in his sweaty hands, and feeling a hot ache moving through both of his arms, focusing far more on the left than on the right. His body was slick with perspiration and just possibly something worse. The thing in the grave was gone, but a trail of ruin lay around him that told him he'd managed somehow to make his point known.

And Jerry was still there, looking at him warily from several feet away. "Chris, calm down, man." He was trying to sound soothing. It wasn't working.

"Goddamn it, Jerry . . . Goddamn YOU." His voice vibrated as he spoke; a high-tension wire caught in a gale force wind.

"I don't have a choice in this, man. They need the Western Key and they need it soon. I had to do this."

"You fucking bury your dad and see if you feel the same way!" Chris was walking toward him before he realized it, one hand still clutching the gore-covered handle. Jerry backed away at a steady pace. "You fucking tell me how it feels when I do it to you!" The world was blurring now, not changing colors. It took him a second to realize he was crying. He'd been through a lot since his mother's death, but this took the cake. This hurt on levels he didn't know existed.

"Come on, bro . . . you know I wouldn't do this if I didn't have to. I loved your mom. Shit, she was like my second mom." Jerry's expression begged for understanding that Chris couldn't find. Part of him wanted to understand, to believe that there could be any reason at all for this atrocity, but it was elusive.

"You need to get away from me, Jerry." It was, he suspected, hard to sound authoritative when your voice was shifting between seriously pissed off and quavering with repressed tears, but he did his best. "You need to get away right now. I can't promise I'm not going to fuck you up."

Jerry backed away, shaking his head. "Chris, man, please. You have to give them the Western Key. They aren't kidding around and I don't want to see you hurt."

"I don't have their fucking key! I don't even know what it is!" Despite the confusion and the grief that were damned near drowning him, Chris started seeing red again. His arms almost let out groans of protest as he started forward again, the makeshift club in his right hand cutting through the

139

air with each step. "If I had the fucking thing they could take it!"

"Chris, your mom had it. She was almost never without it, man. She used it to keep you and Brittany safe." Jerry wasn't backing up anymore, he was standing still, almost inviting Chris to crack his head open. And God, Chris wanted to oblige him.

"I don't even know what it is, Jerry. I never heard of the fucking thing until Crawford and his fucked-up friends tried to steal it from me." He felt the anger dropping. He really didn't want it to. He wanted to be pissed off and filled with hatred, because at least then he had some sort of energy left in him. But it was Jerry. Almost anyone else would have been on the ground and bleeding by now.

The heavy handle dropped from his loose grip, leaving behind a handful of twitching fingers. "They could have it if I knew what it was."

"Chris, you have to know. It was something your mom had with her all the damned time." Jerry's voice was low and soothing and almost desperate to have the knowledge he thought Chris had. "It's supposed to look like a coin of some kind. Gold and silver and rough around the edges." He moved closer, his eyes on Chris and his hands held out placatingly. Chris couldn't think anymore. His head hurt and his body ached and he just wanted to curl up and sleep for a few centuries.

Jerry put out his arms, and despite the anger he felt, Chris wanted to fall into them and cry. Jerry was his friend, had always been his friend, and he needed that bond, that strength Jerry offered.

Jerry's hands grabbed his arms just above the elbows and squeezed hard enough to make him cry out. When exactly did Jerry get so damned strong? "I wish it didn't have to be this way, Chris. I really do." Chris swung with one foot, kicking Jerry in the crotch with all the strength he could muster. The only response he got was an increase in the pressure on his arms, until he felt certain that something would give, be it muscle or bone. Either he was more exhausted than he thought, or his buddy had taken to wearing a cup. "Tell me where the key is or I'll tear you apart." The last words were distorted by strain, and every muscle in Jerry's body seemed to quiver. It was like he was using all of his strength to carry out his threat and the worst part was, Chris was beginning to think he could do it. Jerry breathed out and Chris got a sinking feeling deep inside that had nothing to do with the pain in his arms or the fact that Jerry hadn't even blinked when he racked him in the balls. There was a scent of rancid bread dough carried by the expulsion of air that he knew all too well from Crawford and his friends.

"What did they do to you, Jerry?" His voice was barely above a whisper. Jerry pulled him closer, his face going ugly with rage as Chris's own face was drawn toward him. Chris accommodated his best friend, leaning forward fast to slam his forehead into Jerry's nose. It was rather like head butting a brick wall, and he saw brilliant explosions going off past his closed eyes. But the end result was satisfying. Jerry dropped Chris.

And Chris took full advantage of the situation, backing away as quickly as he could. It was too much. A feeling like he was dropping down the steepest hill on a roller coaster hit his guts and stayed there. It was that damned smell, that yeasty, obnoxious and unclean odor that was screwing with him. The only people he'd ever caught with that stench weren't really human and if they weren't then maybe Jerry wasn't. He could accept the strangers around him becoming monsters— well, he could at least accept the concept even if the reality was painful—but Jerry? He'd known Jerry for as long as he could remember, and there had never been any indication that he was something other than human. Hell, there'd never been any hint that he could do any of the things he was currently involved with, including the desecration of Eileen Corin's grave or attacking Chris himself.

Chris turned tail and ran, moving back to his car as fast as his feet would carry him. He moved solely on instinct and that was probably for the best. Any attempt at rational thought right then would have slowed him down too much or made him overthink the obstacle course of headstones he hurdled and dodged on his way to the station wagon.

He reached for the driver's side door, his heart beating a stuttering tattoo in his chest. The description that he'd gotten from both Crawford and Jerry was finally clicking in his head. The coin was in a necklace he'd seen his mother wear a thousand times. It wasn't something she flaunted and it was never on the outside of her clothing, but he remembered it well enough. He'd seen it on the bathroom counter the morning after she died, cast aside like a piece of cheap costume jewelry after she'd taken her last shower. He'd held the damned thing in his hand for almost ten minutes after he'd heard of her death and then he'd put it back where he found it. Moving it had seemed almost taboo at the time.

Somebody didn't feel the same way about it, and it only took a second to realize who. "Brittany." Her name slipped past his lips without him even thinking about it. He'd seen the chain around her neck just that morning when she'd served him breakfast. It hadn't dawned on him at the time, but it made sense. She wanted Mom's jewelry, had asked him if it was all right to take it, and he'd said yes. What piece could she possibly want more than the one their mother wore almost every single day?

He just had to get the damned thing from her and give it to Crawford and then everything would be all right.

Jerry grabbed him by the shoulder from behind and spun him around to face the fist that came for his face. Chris was too surprised to even think about ducking. Jerry landed a perfect jab on his chin and Chris felt his teeth clack together, narrowly missing the tip of his tongue.

"Thanks, bro. That's exactly what I needed to hear. Brittany's got it? All the better, my man." He shoved Chris against the station wagon hard enough to knock the wind from him. "Just do yourself a favor and stay here. If I get to her first, I'll just take the Western Key and everyone's gonna be fine."

There was a tone in his voice, a little sneer that was almost patronizing. Chris didn't like it, not one bit. More importantly, he didn't trust it. He grabbed the door and yanked it open, sliding into the car as quickly as he could. Jerry made a deep, snarling noise that didn't come from his mouth but from somewhere deep in his throat. Chris started to fumble in his pocket before realizing the keys were still in the ignition. The only reason the car wasn't still running was because he'd forgotten to shift into neutral when he stopped.

Jerry's hand reached in, lunging for Chris. He swatted it hard, though the effort hurt. His body was aching and he was still trying to get a decent breath of air into his lungs. It was all he could manage.

It wasn't enough. Jerry's hand, impossibly strong, caught his shirt and started pulling him out of the car. He grabbed the steering wheel and hauled as hard as he could, trying to keep his grip.

"Chris, dude, I'm not gonna hurt her if she gives me the Western Key. I'm not gonna hurt you unless you try to stop me."

There might have been a chance of him agreeing with Jerry's plan if Jerry hadn't been trying to pull him out of the car and maybe break his neck in the process. Chris leaned his head toward the hand that held him and bit down as hard as he could. There is a difference between sinking your teeth into a good steak and chomping down on your friend's hand. For one thing, a steak doesn't scream and try to pull away. For another, at least in this case, a steak doesn't normally bleed out something foul and green that makes you want to lose your lunch. Chris had tasted his own blood on a few occasions—and several of those went back to his good buddy Bryce Darby—and he'd certainly chowed down on a fair number of rare steaks. What spilled into his mouth from the wound he tore in Jerry's arm had nothing at all to do with the taste of blood. He pulled back and let go of the skin he'd captured, his own body rebelling against the nauseating ichor.

"Have you lost your fucking mind?" Jerry actually had the balls to sound surprised that he'd bitten him. Chris would have laughed if he hadn't been busy gagging. Instead, he took advantage as his best buddy in the whole world pulled his arm out of the car. Chris grabbed the interior door handle and slammed the door shut. What he hadn't counted on was Jerry being slower than he'd guessed. His friend's hand got caught in the closing door. Something inside the hand cracked as Jerry yanked it back, and more of the nasty shit that passed for his blood these days spilled over the edge of the door's interior.

Chris heard the scream, saw Jerry draw back from him and snarl, his face twitching in ways that just weren't right, and then started the car. No time like the present for getting a head start.

He slammed the car into gear and gunned the engine. Jerry was still waving his ruined hand around and howling when Chris hit the main road and started for home. Brittany was all that mattered. He could get sick later, but right now he needed to get to his sister and get the necklace from her before something happened to her.

He never looked in the rearview mirror.

He should have.

Jerry hit the car like a wrecking ball. At least that was what it sounded like. He wasn't stuck yielding right of way to oncoming traffic, didn't have to worry about the low wall around the cemetery and certainly wasn't too worried about things like the laws of nature—laws like: You can't just change shape at will, or get superhuman strength whenever you want it. So Jerry headed him off at the pass while he was actually trying to follow at least a few of the local rules of traffic and physics. Chris only noticed him as he was bringing both hands down on the hood of the car. He might have ignored him completely even then, but the whole station wagon rocked under the impact and the hood buckled like someone had dropped a bowling ball on it from four stories up. Instinct got the better of Chris for a second. Mechanics, his mother and Mr. Hannerty, the driver's education teacher, had taught him to stop when something hit the car. He stopped.

And Jerry looked at him with such venom that he stayed stopped. Jerry, who had spent a hundred nights or so hanging out and sleeping over as they grew up, looked him straight in the eyes and lifted his ruined hand. The fingers were slashed and broken, still more of the black, oily blood spilled from the fingertips that had been caught in the doorjamb. Chris winced just thinking about how much that had to hurt.

Jerry snarled, his lip curling up like Billy Idol doing an impersonation of Elvis Presley, and the ruined hand started changing, growing thicker, with heavy talons almost exploding from his smashed fingertips. Chris looked on from inside the car, remembering the games they'd played as kids. Jerry had always been the good guy when they played superheroes or even just plain old cops and robbers. Jerry had never wanted to be the monster; he'd always wanted to be the knight in shining armor. Now the roles had reversed. Jerry was the thing from the creature feature. And Chris? Well, Chris was at least a squire in a station wagon if not a knight in armor.

And maybe Jerry wasn't really happy with the change in roles. Because he swung that hand and the arm that was changing along with it at the windshield and punched a hole straight through to where Chris sat at the wheel. That nasty-looking claw—reminiscent of the Creature from the Black Lagoon—came through the shattering glass and slapped down across Chris's chest, scraping through his stretched T-shirt and pulling away cotton and skin as easily as Chris might have torn off a sheet of paper towel from a roll. The pain was sharp enough to make him suck in a breath and to get him back on track. Chris stomped on the gas pedal and held on tight as the car jumped forward.

Jerry let out another scream, his arm bending in ways that had nothing to do with his ability to change his shape, and suddenly the monstrous hand was gone from Chris's chest. The pain decided to hang around for a while, but the source of that hot needling sensation vanished as he accelerated down the road.

He saw Jerry in his rearview mirror, stumbling to keep his balance and trying to do something with his arm, which looked to be hanging by a thread. He forced the image from his mind and sped up even more. He had to get home, had to get to Brittany before anything else happened. Just at the moment, he figured damned near any disaster could be waiting for him.

He was right in a way.

Chapter Five

I

Chris got back to his house and pulled the station wagon into the short driveway, his head reeling. The adrenaline that was about the only thing keeping him going anymore was hardly doing the job as well as it had an hour ago. His eyes wanted to cross and he felt like he was going to vomit all over himself if he wasn't careful. The foulness that had spilled into his mouth when he bit Jerry was still the primary flavor and scent in his world and when he caught sight of himself in the rearview mirror, he saw thick stains from the crap all over his lips and chin. His skin as pale as it was and the wild expression he saw on his own face brought to mind any of the "Living Dead" movies, sadly, with him playing the part of one of the zombies. There were little diamonds of safety glass scattered through his dark hair, and a few small scrapes that seemed to be the only color left on his face, excluding the filth running down to his chin.

He cut the motor and staggered from the car, just as the clouds carried out their threat and started spilling rain down toward the earth. The drops felt hot and slightly greasy. He almost made it to the front door before he finally fell to his knees and started vomiting. The nasty taste he would have sworn could never get any worse proved him wrong when it mixed with his stomach acids and the remains of his breakfast. He kept trying to get rid of what he'd eaten long after it was gone, and the pain from the dry heaves only accentuated every other part of his body that protested his day's activities.

Eventually he got his reflexes back under control. By that point his eyes were watering and his knees felt like someone had carefully removed all of the bones from them. Standing up became a new challenge and one that he was barely up to at that. The rain pelting his body did nothing to make him feel cleansed. If anything, it seemed he was somehow dirtier than he had been before the storm broke.

He opened the door to his house, feeling that something was wrong even with that simple action. There was no noise from the television, no sound of a stereo playing anywhere. Chris locked the door and moved into the living room with a strange feeling that he'd done all of this before. He half expected to find Brittany with her top off, being groped by a man older than he was. Instead he found an empty room.

He was too tired for a serious case of panic, but he managed to jog through most of the rooms in the house and discovered that Brittany wasn't home. He also found a note in the kitchen, stuck to the refrigerator door, in Katie's neat, precise handwriting. The note read:

Chris,
    Brittany and I went out for a late lunch and some window shopping. We won't be too long. Dinner's on me when we get back.
    Hugs,
    Katie
    PS Mexican tonight. The real stuff, from Los Reyes.

Chris set the note on the table and moved over to the sink, where he washed his face and arms until they were pink from scrubbing. He flopped back on the couch in the living room and closed his eyes.

When he opened them again, it was to the sound of someone knocking on the door that he could barely see in the darkness. If he'd been in pain when he woke up that morning, then what he was feeling now must have a name that simply didn't exist in the English language. Damn near every part of his body felt swollen and beaten down. He reached over and turned on the light on the end table next to the old sofa and moved toward the door on automatic pilot for about half the distance, his joints practically creaking with every step. Just as he reached the short hallway that led to the front door the dread of what might be waiting there awoke. What if it was Jerry, or Crawford? What if both of them were together and they'd brought a few friends? He stopped walking, his stomach doing its very best to knot itself into some new and daring shape. It wasn't quite panic that was going through him, but it very much wanted to be. He didn't want to move, didn't want to answer the door. His heart was blasting at his ribcage like a caged animal and he couldn't for the life of him draw in a breath.

It would have been embarrassing if he hadn't been on the verge of tears.

He might have actually started crying if he hadn't heard Katie's voice on the other side of the door. Like magic, the attack ended before he could truly be swallowed by it. He went to the door and opened it for her. Katie looked at him, her brown hair wet down to her scalp and her skin glistening from the rain. She'd never looked more perfect to him, despite the strange expression she wore.

"Shit, Chris." She rolled her eyes and scowled at him, the rain dripping from her in an almost-constant stream. "Whatever happened to actually answering the door when someone knocks?" She pushed past him and walked into the house, a trail of water glistening in her wake. He waited at the door, looking for the next person to enter. There wasn't one. "I swear I thought I was going to drown out there."

"Katie, where's—"

"I have the food, so you can finally eat. I'm willing to bet you haven't touched a thing all day with the way you've been acting." Katie reached under her wet blouse and pulled out a greasy paper bag that looked almost as thoroughly soaked. She moved down the hallway toward the kitchen and Chris closed the door to follow her. How was it that she could literally take control of the room just by opening her mouth? Sometimes he wished he had that sort of ability himself. Katie dropped the bag on the table, looking around the kitchen as if she'd forgotten where she'd placed something.

"Katie? Listen, I hate to—"

"I got you a chile relleno and three tacos. There's also extra hot sauce for everything. It's what you had last time and I figured it would be okay this time around."

"Katie, where's Brittany?"

Katie's eyebrows were drawn together and she shook the wet bangs from her forehead. "Where's Brittany?"

"Katie, that's what I just asked you. . . ."

"She was here when I left, Chris. I only went to the bank to get some money from the automatic teller and then straight over to pick up the dinner order. . . ." She looked at him in the light of the kitchen and must not have liked what she saw. "Ohmygod, Chris! What happened?" Her fingers brushed over his left cheek lightly, and he hissed at the sudden stinging pain.

Chris leaned against the wall and let it hold him

in place. His legs were doing that damned boneless thing again and if he tried moving he knew he'd wind up with his ass on the linoleum.

"Oh shit. Oh shit . . . Katie, what if they got her?"

"Who, Chris? Crawford?"

"Crawford . . . or Jerry."

Katie might have looked more surprised if he'd hauled off and slapped her face with all of his might, but he had doubts.

"What do you mean about Jerry?"

"Katie . . ." He hadn't really meant to start that way. He'd wanted to maybe break the news that something was wrong with Jerry a little more gently than that.

"I'm serious, damn it! You tell me what you mean, right now."

"I saw Jerry at the cemetery when I went to see my mom. He was helping one of Crawford's boys dig her out of the ground."

"That's bullshit! How can you say that?!" Chris felt his heart drop down into his stomach and start cooking in his digestive acids. Katie's face went through a dozen changes, but all of them were natural. That didn't make them any easier to watch. She went from shock to anger to full-blown outrage and then into the first creeping doubts in an instant. Then she masked whatever she was feeling with anger again.

"Katie. I'll try to explain it as we go, but I need your help to find Brittany right now."

"Did you check her room?"

"No, but I think she'd have answered if she were

here." He sighed. "We can look around first if you want, as long as we're quick about it."

"You're damned right I want to look around first. And I want to know what you meant about Jerry."

They spent five fruitless minutes looking for Brittany and discovering what Chris already knew. She wasn't in the house.

"Look, I need to find her before Crawford does. She's got the damned key thing they keep going on about."

Katie's eyes flew wide at that. "Do you think he'll hurt her?"

He looked at her with half-lidded eyes, the battering his face had taken speaking for him.

"Okay. Good point. Let's go."

Chris felt the tension growing deep into his neck and shoulders. It felt like someone who was far too strong for anyone's good had clamped massive hands on his shoulders and was pressing down. Much more of it and he figured his arms would just fall off and flop around for a while.

They left the house, stepped into the much lighter rain and headed toward Katie's car, only pausing long enough for Katie to actually look at the damage that had been done to the station wagon. She shook her head, her lips thinned into a slash by whatever thoughts were going through her head. Chris waited at the car until she unlocked the doors and then climbed inside the little lime-green Corolla.

"Where to?" Her words were crisp, precise, businesslike. She was pissed.

"I guess over at the mall is the best bet. She hangs out there a lot."

Katie nodded and started driving. Chris was torn between being nervous about her mood—which was justifiably bleak—and being in too much pain to care. He could deal with one or the other, but the two combined was a bit much, especially in light of the day he was having.

"So tell me what happened." It wasn't a request. It was an order. He complied, pausing from time to time to gather his thoughts. To her credit, she managed to not ask him any questions until he was done.

"It wasn't Jerry."

"Shit, Katie, you don't think I know my best friend by now?"

"Jerry would never do anything like that. He isn't capable. Forget that you said he was changing into something else. Even if he could do that, he would never hurt you. He doesn't have it in him."

Chris laughed softly, rolling his eyes toward the roof of the car and praying silently for strength and patience. "You don't know Jerry as well as you think you do."

Katie turned her head to look at him, her hand guiding the car almost by autopilot as she turned a corner. "I think I know Jerry pretty well by now, Chris."

"I'm not saying you don't, but I can tell you for a fact that he's very capable when it comes to fights." He looked out the window of the car, not wanting to face her when he said the words. "I've seen him fight. He's sort of a bruiser when he wants to be."

"I know he fights, Chris. I know he fights and I know you fight. It happens. But it isn't like he's a boxing contender or something. He just has trouble walking away from a challenge."

"He's calmer than he used to be, Katie. But he likes getting in a good ass kicking."

"Don't. Just don't. Any way you look at it, Jerry wouldn't fight you that way." Her voice was getting a sharper edge. He knew he was sliding into dangerous territory.

"Look. Until this morning I would have agreed with you, but I'm the one he was knocking around."

"Chris . . ."

"No. Katie, hear me out. I didn't wreck my car. I didn't get the window taken out by vandals. Jerry did that. Jerry put his fucking hand through the hood of my car and took out the windshield besides." She started to speak again and he raised his voice to be heard. "I'm the one who was there, Katie. I saw him on my mother's grave, leaning back and relaxing while one of the motherfucking freaks was digging her out of the ground! Are you getting what I'm saying here? I saw him robbing my mother's grave!" It took him a second to realize he was screaming. His vision was going red again just thinking about it. "Listen . . . I don't know what's going on here. All I know is that Jerry is working with the cop who tried to kill us both last night. I don't know why, I don't even care right now. Because what they're working on is taking something from Brittany and I don't really think they give a damn if they have to kill her to get it."

"I'm just saying that Jerry wouldn't do that!"

"I know what you're saying and I'm telling you you're wrong. I don't know if they threatened him or you or his family or whatever, but I know Jerry and the way he talked, the way he acted, except for that weird shit with changing his shape, that was all Jerry. Maybe Crawford did something to him, but that was Jerry who was trying to kill me."

They drove on in silence for several minutes, cruising the streets and looking for any sign of Brittany. Katie glared out the windows, almost daring anyone to cut her off. Chris pitied anyone that foolish.

It was dark out and even though summer proper was here and kids were out of school, there weren't many teenagers on the main strips where they normally hung out. The rain had mostly stopped but there was still enough precipitation falling to discourage the idea of just hanging around on the street corners. There were a few, most of them having a good time and a few looking puzzled by the lack of activity, like they knew there was a party going on and they hadn't been given the right address. Chris looked at every one of them he saw, hoping to find a familiar face. Someone, anyone who could tell him where his sister might be.

He wasn't having any luck at all.

She was out there though and he knew it. It was just a question of who found her first.

II

Chris's stomach growled at him, which was something of a miracle as far as he was concerned. He had trouble believing his body could be hungry after what he'd been through. His mind reeled at the very idea of eating anything after what had been in his mouth earlier and what he'd seen over the last twenty-four hours. Still, there it was, a gnawing little fire deep in his guts. One more discomfort in a sea of them.

Three hours and half a tank of gas had covered almost every spot they could imagine Brittany ever considered hanging out. So far they'd had no luck—excluding the bad variety—and they were barely speaking to each other. Most of what was said came in the form of noncommittal grunts and suggestions about where to look.

Chris let himself think, and that wasn't necessarily a good thing. Thinking led him down paths he truly and desperately wanted to avoid. Thinking made him consider the things he'd seen and they did not agree with his philosophies.

Katie stopped at the intersection of Wieuca and Clegg, near the Club of the Week. It was sort of an ongoing joke in the neighborhood. The place had opened as a nightclub around four years earlier, and had changed its name and style roughly every other month since then. It had been a yuppie bar, a country-western bar, a disco and a pub on various occasions. What it had not been was successful for any of the proprietors until Carl Willis took over the operation. Willis was a no one who'd gone to school at the same dive as Chris and Jerry and the whole lot, graduating a few years earlier. There was every reason to believe that Carl would be as big a failure as everyone else who'd owned the place, but so far he'd beat the averages. When Carl opened his new club on the spot first thing he did was change the name to Club of the Week, which earned a few chuckles among the locals. The second thing he did was open it without a liquor license, which should have been the death of the place. Instead, he opened the doors to teenagers, charging a small entry fee on nights when there was live music and then just charging an arm and a leg for sodas and munchies. The food was average if greasy, and the music was mostly hip-hop and bebop in an odd combination. The place was also a smash success. Most nights during the summer you could count on a few hundred kids coming and going, spending more money than they should have to crowd into the place and dance or play arcade games with their chums. It was rather like an underage meat market and Chris hated the place. Naturally, that meant Brittany loved it.

Katie spoke softly, her voice still bitter. "Should we try here?" He rolled his shoulders and craned his head around, seeking any hint that she was nearby. Several small popping sounds came from his exhausted muscles as he looked the place over. A small army of kids—mostly in their early teens—stood waiting to get inside.

"Yeah. I can't imagine where else she'd be."

"Um . . . Maybe we better wait a few minutes."

"Why?"

"Bryce Darby is coming this way."

"Screw it. He can kick my ass if he wants. Everyone else has." Katie nodded and sighed and parked half a block from the club. They moved in that direction together, through the light rain, and it annoyed Chris to realize that he was limping. He could hardly manage to walk, true enough, but that didn't mean he liked showing it.

They ran across Bryce almost directly in front of the club. The bass from the music was pounding loudly enough to make the blacked-out windows pulse and shake. As neither of them usually bothered with the place, they were a little surprised to realize he was supposed to be there. His usual boots were in place, as were his jeans, but Yosemite Sam had been replaced by another black shirt. This one said: *I'm the bouncer. Don't make me bounce YOU.* The fact that the shirt fit him like a second skin didn't make it less intimidating.

Darby's face was neutral, which for him meant he was almost smiling, until he saw Chris. "You want admission, Corin?"

"Have you seen my sister, Bryce?"

"Don't know. Don't care." He took two dollars each from a handful of girls and opened the door for them. He closed the door after them too, and folded the bills into his pants pocket.

"I'm serious, Bryce. I need to find her."

"You can get to the back of the line and pay for admittance." Darby's eyes were narrowed only a little and in the stark neon of the club's exterior, Chris could see the bruises along his thick neck and arms. He could also see the bandages that covered his wrists. "Other than that, I got nothing to say to you."

Katie stepped up, her eyes almost flashing. "Please, Bryce. Do you remember her going in here?"

Bryce looked her over, even as he held out his hand for the next group of teens who wanted entry. Money talked. Everything else could merrily hit the road. He ignored her until he'd taken money and made change. "I don't know. I see a lot of kids. I might have seen a redhead or two, but who the hell looks at 'em when they're mostly around twelve?"

Chris shook his head, disgusted. He pulled out his wallet and started counting out bills. The line was mostly gone and he waited as patiently as he could until it was his turn. Katie stood next to Darby the entire time. She looked everywhere she could, except at Chris. He kept hoping she would get over her bad attitude—not that he actually blamed her for it—but it didn't look like it was going to happen anytime soon.

Darby took his money. Darby opened the door. Aside from these actions, Darby did nothing at all. Chris supposed he should be grateful for that. Darby still looked like he was in the mood to bust Chris's head in.

The inside of the club was actually a good deal more pleasant than he'd expected. The dance floor was large, but rather than making the entire place into a giant teeming mosh pit, Carl Willis had left it as a genuine bar and grill. There were roughly fifteen tables, most of them already overflowing with kids, and a long bar where still more teenagers sat. The music blaring through the place was something by Mandy Moore, and while he still preferred almost anything to pop music, she was less offensive than a lot of the crap that was being generated for teens. Sadly, the place was also dark enough to make it almost impossible for him to see any of the people clearly enough to recognize them until he was almost standing next to them. Kids he'd seen a hundred times before came and went through his view, most of them doing things that would have gotten them grounded in an instant, but little or none of it illegal. The strongest thing anyone was drinking was a Pepsi as far as he could tell, and the worst they were smoking was tobacco. They were mostly too young for cigarettes, but that was hardly ever a deterrent. Still, he'd kick Brittany's butt if he caught her pulling any of that shit.

Of course, he'd have to find her first. Katie moved next to him, looking around and moving from table to table, asking a few of the people she recognized if they'd seen Brittany anywhere. She had better luck than he. A few of the kids said they'd seen her a little while ago. She'd been here. None of them knew if she was still hanging around.

The Mandy Moore song ended, replaced by 'N Sync. They were singing about a relationship gone bad and the guy splitting. Chris was beginning to wish his life was that easy.

163

He spotted a familiar face, one of Brittany's friends, a flighty little blonde named Kelly. He hadn't seen her in a while and the last few months her body had been playing catch up. She'd become positively chesty. Either that or she was wearing a stuffed bra under her low-cut blouse. She looked at him for a few seconds before the gears in her head clicked and she recognized him. Her smile would have left him desperate to know her better under different circumstances. "Oh, hey! You looking for Brittany?"

"Yeah. I heard she's been around, have you seen her?"

Kelly frowned fetchingly and looked around the room for a minute. "She was over there, in the corner, like, maybe ten minutes ago with her boyfriend."

"Boyfriend?"

"Yeah, Bobby Johanssen? I can't believe she's dating an older guy." Her voice sounded almost envious.

"Tall, sort of thin, with long brown hair?"

She nodded, her whole face lighting up as Chris felt his stomach start falling. "Yeah, he's a looker."

Chris thought he looked like something left over from the worst part of the hippie era, but that wasn't really what any of this was about. What it was about was a creep he'd caught feeling his sister and who was with her again. Another thorn in addition to everything else that was going on. He made a mental note to castrate the guy after he got Brittany to safety.

It took him a second to realize that Kelly had been speaking to him. "I'm sorry, what was that?"

"I said I think they were headed toward the restrooms." She pointed to the back of the establishment, on the other side of the crowded dance floor. "Over there."

"Thanks, Kelly!"

She smiled at him again and waved, going back to her pack of friends. One of them said something that had her nodding her head and the whole group of them giggled. Chris moved away, focused solely on finding Brittany before she got herself into even more trouble.

The people on the dance floor were crowded together into one large, seething mass of undulations. Under different circumstances he might have been either amused or even tempted to join in. Right now he just wanted through. He pushed into the crowd and started bulldozing his way past the bodies pressing against him, ignoring the complaints that came his way. Somehow or another, Katie managed to catch up with him just as he was breaking through the crowd on the other end of the dancers. He pointed toward the restrooms and she nodded, following him.

The hallway that led to the bathrooms also led to the offices and the emergency fire exit. There were almost as many people there as were in the rest of the place, but there was a big difference in the bottleneck facing him. He could see Brittany at the other end of the hallway, struggling with Crawford. Next to her, pinned to the wall by Jerry and at least one other man, was the creep Chris'd seen in the house when he caught his sister with her shirt off.

Chris looked at the bumper-to-bumper bodies between him and his objective and lowered his head. Most of them were facing the other direction, their eyes glued to Brittany, where she fought with the older man, or on Jerry, who was currently holding Bobby Johanssen off the ground by his neck. Katie let in a breath sharp enough for Chris to hear over the din around him and then softly called out Jerry's name. If the man heard, he failed to turn and face her.

Chris charged, his voice bellowing out of him like a drill sergeant screaming in the faces of brand-new recruits. "MOVE IT OR LOSE IT!" Most of the people turned to face him at the sound of his voice. A few of them seemed frozen in place and he helped them on their way, shoving bodies left and right as he headed to where Crawford's hands were touching his little sister. Brittany screamed his name and pushed frantically to get away from Crawford, with no real luck. The man out-massed her by at least a hundred pounds and his hands had a firm grip on her biceps. A boy around fifteen was standing in the way. Chris knocked him to the side and slammed himself into Crawford with all the strength he could muster.

Crawford had a look of complete surprise on his face. Like this was the last place in the world he expected to encounter Chris. Chris wondered for a second how the hell the man could have gotten past Bryce Darby, but it was a fleeting thought that held

Join the Leisure Horror Book Club and
GET 2 FREE BOOKS NOW—
An $11.98 value!

— Yes! I want to subscribe to — the Leisure Horror Book Club.

Please send me my **2 FREE BOOKS**. I have enclosed $2.00 for shipping/handling. Each month I'll receive the two newest Leisure Horror selections to preview for 10 days. If I decide to keep them, I will pay the Special Members Only discounted price of just $4.25 each, a total of $8.50, plus $2.00 shipping/handling. This is a **SAVINGS OF AT LEAST $3.48** off the bookstore price. There is no minimum number of books I must buy and I may cancel the program at any time. In any case, the **2 FREE BOOKS** are mine to keep.

— Not available in Canada. —

NAME: _____

ADDRESS: _____

CITY: _____ **STATE:** _____

COUNTRY: _____ **ZIP:** _____

TELEPHONE: _____

E-MAIL: _____

SIGNATURE: _____

The Best in Horror!
Get Two Books Totally FREE!

**PLEASE RUSH
MY TWO FREE
BOOKS TO ME
RIGHT AWAY!**

Enclose this card with $2.00
in an envelope and send to:

Leisure Horror Book Club
20 Academy Street
Norwalk, CT 06850-4032

no real weight in comparison to his sister's safety. He hit Crawford hard enough to knock the man off his sister, and hard enough to make him wish he'd brought body armor to soak in some of the impact. Chris felt his shoulder scream in protest even as he pushed the renegade cop against the emergency exit door, which promptly blew open on them both.

A loud screaming siren went off, shrill and obnoxious as it cut through the air, and Chris felt the cooler air from outside as he and Crawford exited the Club of the Week and slammed down on the rough asphalt of the alley behind the club. Chris landed on top, his fist already drawing back to hit the man again.

Katie was screaming, Brittany was screaming, the siren was wailing and Crawford hit him in the face before he could bring his fist down toward the man. The world sort of went away right then and there. He reeled back, the impact from the fist damn near knocking him unconscious. The fight might have been over at that point, but Brittany decided it was time to get a little payback against the fat man who'd been pulling at her blouse and brought her foot down on the side of the man's head.

Crawford let out a yell of his own and pushed Chris aside, rising from the ground to face Brittany, who looked like she might have made an error in judgement. Crawford slapped her hard enough to spin her in a semicircle to prove her right. She staggered back and slumped down on the ground, her cheek already swelling where he'd connected.

Crawford grabbed her blouse again, tearing the

top three buttons open and then reaching inside her shirt. He let out a half-laugh of triumph and pulled back roughly. The medallion—the Western Key—hung from a thin silver chain around Brittany's neck. Her whole body lifted forward as he tugged on the chain, then slumped again as the delicate links broke, freeing the prize he'd been so desperately seeking. "Mine, you little bitch! Mine now!" The voice that spilled from his mouth was barely human. It sounded more like the hiss of a radiator on the edge of a meltdown.

Chris stood up and shook his head, trying to get rid of the ringing sound that was moving through his skull. Crawford started past him, barely acknowledging his presence.

The creep who'd been with Brittany played intervention. Just how he'd gotten away from Jerry and company was anyone's guess, but he'd managed it. Thin arms—they looked to Chris like the arms of a man who'd been doing way too much speed in his formative years; long and lean with wiry muscles—grabbed at the necklace in Crawford's hands. Johanssen actually managed to pull the broken chain and the medallion away from the ex-cop, grinning wildly as he did so.

The smile didn't last. Crawford wiped it away when he swung with his left arm in a brutal arc that crossed the man's throat. Crawford snarled as he attacked. "I told you before, you moron, this is my duty, not yours!" His left hand—or where it should have been—was covered in black fluids, and the normal fingers were gone, replaced by three thick talons that grew from his wrist like hooks. Even as Chris watched, the bony weapons melted, becoming a hand again.

Bobby Johanssen let go of the medallion as he brought both hands to his throat. His face pulled down in a grimace of pain and his eyes grew almost impossibly wide. Brittany was screaming as loudly as the alarm for the fire exit, and her hands drew red marks across her face as she dragged them over her cheeks, on the verge of hysteria.

Crawford pushed Bobby out of his way and Jerry was fast on his heels, not pursuing to stop him, but following to join him. The other two were heading in the same direction. Chris stuck his foot out and tripped the last one. It wasn't really a conscious effort, more like an instinctive reaction to wanting the whole lot of them stopped.

The man fell hard, an expression of complete shock marring his plain face. His head pivoted downward and his feet went up in the air. He landed on his skull with an audible cracking noise that made Chris wince in sympathy. It sounded like a board breaking under extreme pressure.

And he stayed there.

Chris looked away as Johanssen fell to his knees, his hands still covering the wound in his throat. Chris moved in his direction, the ringing in his ears finally winding down enough to let him really think clearly. The man was as good as dead. No one could survive a wound like that, not unless they got him to the hospital in a matter of minutes. Brittany was crawling across the ground toward him, her knees landing on the broken glass and debris of the alley and her face set with a look that was almost as devastating for Chris to see as the expression he'd seen on her face when he found out his mother was dead. Katie was there in a flash, her hands pulling at Brittany's shoulders, her face looking both stern and terrified at the same time. Chris wouldn't have thought it possible for her to make that expression with her features if he hadn't seen it with his own eyes. It was like no expression she'd ever worn before.

Brittany struggled against Katie's restraining hands as Chris bent over the man he'd caught in the act of molesting his sister—it didn't matter that she was willing, not in his eyes—fully prepared to see him die before anything could be done for him.

What he wasn't prepared for was having the man knock him into the brick wall with a flick of his wrist. One second he was getting ready to at least comfort the guy who'd just tried to save his sister's life and the next his hands moved away from the throat that had been so badly torn apart and moved to bitch slap him into next week. This was the same guy he'd almost torn apart in his house only a few days earlier?

Chris hit the wall and his head bounced off the bricks. He figured a few more blows like this and he'd probably just call it time to get a skull replacement. The world went gray and fuzzy. He closed his eyes for a few seconds, trying to clear away the fog that had settled into his brain.

Brittany and Katie screamed at the same time,

joined by several of the kids who'd been watching the whole fight. Chris opened his eyes to see the one he'd tripped get back off the ground, his head actually dented in and spilling black blood. Even as he watched, stringy flaps of skin stretched out, joining together over the deep wound, sealing it. Bobby Johanssen was pulling a similar stunt; his ravaged throat was sealing, the foul black syrupy crud that had been pouring from the open wound slowing down to a trickle and then stopping.

Chris tried to stand up again, he did, but he just couldn't. His legs seemed determined to flop around like fish. Chris wondered if he'd suffered any permanent injuries yet. Three fights in one day was a record for him, and not one he was exactly proud to be a part of, thanks very much.

He felt himself drifting, felt that gray wave moving back in on his head, and let it cover him, drown him in the comfort of feeling nothing. God, it was nice not to hurt all over.

Naturally, that meant it couldn't last. Brittany's screams cut through the fog and Chris bit down on the inside of his mouth until he tasted blood. Yep. That did it. His eyes flew open and he shook his head, spitting a stream of coppery fluid from his mouth.

Brittany was screaming because the guy who'd just cleaned his clock for him was moving toward her, his face snarling and his body hopping like a junkie on the worst legs of serious withdrawal. Every muscle seemed to be doing its own thing, and Chris could guess why. He'd seen enough in the last day to let him catch on a little faster than the average.

His sister was still on the ground, her face looking up toward the face of the thing in front of her. Chris heard a wet, ripping sound and saw what looked like a hundred wet tongues start writhing around in the air where Bobby's face should have been. He wanted to imagine he could understand what she was going through. He wanted to believe that somehow he could get even a vague clue as to what Brittany must be thinking. Katie looked disgusted and afraid, her hands still on Brittany's shoulders, but now simply holding on instead of pulling. Katie looked like she was ready to run and maybe puke her guts out. Brittany looked far, far worse. The first time Chris had met Bobby Johanssen, he'd had his hand on Brittany's breast and she'd had her hand inside the man's pants. That was—dear God, please let it be true—the most she had ever experienced by way of carnal knowledge. But somewhere along the way she'd probably kissed him too. She'd likely even done a little frenching. Well, the odds were good that what she'd done the tongue dance with hadn't had quite so many tongues at the time and seeing it as it was now probably made her rethink the passion she'd shared with him. She was still screaming, or at least she was trying to. Her mouth was stretched wide in an effort to scream, but she wasn't breathing in at all, and that was slowing down her ability to get any real volume. That was okay; the alarm behind her was doing enough for both of them.

Chris reached out with both hands and grabbed a double handful of hair on the back of good ol' Bobby's head. He fought off the desire to let go when he realized the hair was moving, writhing against his palms and fingers. Instead he hauled back with his whole body and pivoted on his hips, his legs braced wide apart. He might be a monster, and he was certainly strong enough to put up a fight, but Bobby Johanssen didn't seem to weigh all that much. Chris slammed him into the wall, enjoying the chance to return the favor.

Bobby fell to the ground, leaving a few of his writhing tongue-tentacles behind to decorate the wall. The sounds he made were akin to a bear gargling with antifreeze. Chris grabbed Brittany's hand and yanked her to her feet. Katie was quick to catch on, and in a few seconds they were running down the alley, heading toward the front of the club and the side street where Katie'd parked her car.

Chris practically screamed with impatience while he waited for Katie to unlock the doors. Brittany was making low keening noises from her throat, and her face looked pale and sweaty. Her eyes were looking everywhere at once. "Come on, come on, come on!"

Katie jammed her key into the lock with trembling hands and screamed back at him, her face strained and her neck muscles corded. "I'm trying! I hate this goddamned lock!" She turned the key and slammed her body against the door of the car. Her lower lip trembled and she looked ready to cry, but finally the door opened. In was only a matter of seconds before she had the rest of the doors unlocked, but it felt like a few eternities to Chris.

They were in the Corolla and moving in short order, and Chris looked down the alley as something bigger than a man cast a shadow on the wall. A shadow that moved toward them at high speed. Fortunately for all involved, Katie's little Toyota was faster. He saw just a hint of something gray and scaly before they turned the corner and were out of sight.

"That wasn't Jerry."

"What? Of course that was Jerry." The words came out automatically. They were not what he'd planned to say.

"No, it wasn't!"

"Katie . . . look, I know it's easier to think that way, but that was Jerry."

"That wasn't Jerry, Chris. It looked like Jerry but it wasn't him."

"Fine. If it wasn't Jerry, who was it?"

"Someone who looks like him but isn't him."

"What? You think since I saw him last night they managed to find his perfect lookalike and have him take Jerry's place? Come on, Katie, that's just not possible."

"Get a clue, you asshole!"

"Excuse me?"

"That thing just ripped its own face open and grew tentacles and teeth! You don't think one of those things could make itself look like Jerry?!?"

He blinked. Actually, the thought had never crossed his mind. Now that it was brought up, however, it made a certain kind of sense. "I never thought of that." His voice was low and awed, and his heart felt like it was going to explode. He'd never thought about that at all. Here he was worrying about how Jerry had betrayed him when all that time, it had been one of Crawford's freaks imitating him. It made sense, and more importantly, it absolved Jerry of all sins. "Oh God, I never even thought about that."

"So if they can imitate him, is he still alive?"

And that was another question altogether, wasn't it? That growing euphoric hope in Chris's chest sank again. There were more questions than answers and he had no way of knowing one way or the other where to start looking for the truth.

In the backseat, Brittany started crying, loud braying sobs that hurt him to hear. He ground his teeth together. There had to be answers out there, but he had no idea where to look and his sister's hysterics weren't making it any easier for him to think of a good place to start.

"We have to go back for him!" Brittany's scream was, to be kind, a bit unexpected.

"What?" Katie asked the question at the same instant and in the exact same shocked tone Chris heard in his own voice.

"We have to go back for Bobby!" Brittany actually started fumbling at her door, risking a spill onto the road, which would have certainly shredded her skin. Chris slapped the door's locking mechanism down and reached back to grab her hand before she could pull it back up.

"Knock it off! Have you lost your mind?"

"Bobby got hurt! He was cut!"

Chris looked at his sister, really looked at her, studied her face and her eyes and the nearly frantic expression she wore. She wasn't really all there just at the moment. He wasn't really in the mood to put up with her not being all there. "Get over it! The police were probably already on their way."

It's hard to make your point known when someone else is joining you in talking at the same time. Katie yelled even louder than he did. "Brittany? Are you crazy? His whole head opened up! He had snake-things where his eyes were supposed to be!" Her voice was shrill and she was panting heavily as she hollered, "Jesus Christ, girl! He wasn't even human!"

"That's not true! He had a cut across his throat! You imagined the rest of it!" But Chris could see her fighting to get the words out. Brittany was mostly anchored in reality. She was doing her best to push what she'd seen out of her mind, but she wasn't having an easy time with it. It went against her nature.

"Brittany! Knock it off!" His voice was louder and harsher than he intended, but he was having serious trouble controlling his emotions. Still, he had to at least try to be rational, because, frankly, both of them were looking as freaked as he was feeling. "He was a freak! He got his neck torn out and then he threw me like I was a football! And even if he is just wounded and not really a monster, he's back at the club, where the cops are gonna show up any time. So sit the hell down and shut up and let me think!"

"This is all your fault, Chris!" Brittany glared pure venom in his direction and he looked back at her, wondering exactly what was going through her mind. She obliged him by continuing the accusation. "None of this would have happened if you'd just given them what they wanted! They turned him into some kind of monster just to get at you!"

He looked at Katie. "Do you see what I have to put up with!?"

He stopped his rant when he saw that Katie was on the verge of tears. Her chest was hitching fast, like she couldn't catch her breath to save her life. Her eyes kept pace as she tried to stop the tears from coming and her mouth was drawn down harshly, marring her beauty in a way that was almost as strange as the whole night had been. Katie shook her head from side to side, not even looking at the road as far as he could tell. He reached over and put one hand on her shoulder, the other on the steering wheel, just in case. "Pull over, Katie."

She nodded and pulled to the side of the road, parking in front of a fire hydrant. As soon as the car had stopped she covered her face with her hands and started crying for real, letting the tears out and breathing raggedly as she tried to take in air around her sobs. Brittany joined the all-tear chorus at the same time. Chris looked from one to the other, not at all certain what he should do.

His mom was the one who always offered comfort in the family. She wasn't there to offer anything. She was dead. It hit him again, like a hammer blow to his stomach. His mother was dead. Screw everything else. None of it seemed to matter; his mother was dead, and damn, but it hurt to think about that.

The three of them sat that way for a while. Each alone and grieving. None willing or able to offer the others comfort.

III

It was the sirens that dragged them back into something like rational thought. The sirens, and then the flashing lights. Four police cars came their way down the narrow road and tore past in a hurry, doubtless heading to the Club of the Week. Katie shook herself loose from her crying fit and started the car again, waiting until the police were past before pulling back out onto the road proper.

They drove in silence for a few minutes, no one talking or making any sounds harsher than a deep breath.

It was Brittany who broke the silence. "What are we going to do?"

"We're going to find out what those assholes are up to and we're going to see if Jerry is okay. And if Katie's right about Jerry, maybe we'll even see if Bobby is okay." The last was solely for his sister's benefit. His experiences with the man had been less than pleasant to date and he couldn't imagine that they'd get any better.

"Where are we going to look?"

"I might know where." He scanned the road for a few moments. "Turn left on Heathrow Avenue ... three lights up." He frowned, trying to remember where the house was, the damned street where he needed to go. Jerry had been driving that night, but on the return trip—*ha! Oh yeah, good buddy! One helluva trip and look Ma, no acid!*—he'd been hoofing it. The problem was, he hadn't really been in a good place when he tried to find his way home. He'd even managed to get himself properly lost for a nice long time.

He looked back at his sister, who had decided that a fetal position was pretty darned comfortable. She was sitting up, with her knees all the way to her chin and her arms wrapped around her skinny legs. Only a teenage girl could possibly sit that way and be comfortable, or even breathe for that matter.

"Brittany? What were you and Bobby planning to do tonight?"

Katie coughed into her hand and whispered at him. "I don't think this is the time to get on her case, Chris."

He waved the comment aside and waited for Brittany to speak. "He wanted to take me out to a house he knows. Him and some of his friends, they were going to watch the meteor shower." Her voice sounded so small, weak in comparison to even her calm tones. She still had that strange glassy look in her eyes; it made them look like bright blue marbles. He felt he could sympathize with her for a change of pace.

"Meteor shower?"

"Yeah. It was in all the papers. There's supposed to be a meteor shower tonight and some kind of sea festival or something."

"Sea festival?" He was beginning to feel like a parrot.

"Not sea festival, but it sounded like that."

"Celestial?" Katie asked while he was still trying to figure out what the hell rhymed with sea festival. "A celestial event?"

"Yeah. Seven planets in alignment or something like that." Brittany looked out the window and lowered her head until her scalp pressed against it. "He said the stars would be right."

"For what?"

"Dunno."

Chris thought he could guess. All it took was remembering the look on his sister's face when he saw her with the creep's hand on her bare breast. He made himself focus on the matters at hand, forced the image away before it could make him angry again. "Did he say where the house was?"

"Tillinghast Lane, I think." She pouted at her own reflection, not really looking at it, not really seeing much of anything around them if he had to guess. "Stupid name for a road."

Chris smiled. "Yes, yes it is. I think I know where we need to go."

"Good." Katie sighed as she drove, her eyes narrowed and her hands clutched the wheel tightly. "That's very good, because we're going to need something to have a clue about where we want to be."

"Why?"

"Look outside, Chris. The fog is getting pretty damned heavy."

He looked. She was right. The clouds from earlier had dumped their rain and then decided it was a good time to take a nap. He could just make out the streetlights at the end of the block as hazy haloes, and the glow was actually fading as he watched. The fog wasn't just coming in, it was growing thicker by the second. "Perfect. That should make this sooo much easier."

"Not really clear on how to get there?"

"No. But we have to find it. If Jerry's there and he's been taken by those things, we have to find him and get him away." And then there was his mother's necklace, their damned "Western Key," whatever the hell that meant. It was personal. He didn't want those bastards to have anything of hers, especially something that meant so much to her. Not exactly rational, and he knew that, but then, not much had seemed very rational of late.

"Well, what are we going to do?"

Chris looked out the windshield, his eyes drawn to the thickening cloud that was obscuring everything around him. It was like trying to see through a heavy gauze that moved and swirled slowly in the air. "Take a left on Heathrow. We'll find it. It might take a while, but we'll find that damned house."

Chapter Six

I

They wove down several streets that all looked familiar and alien at the same time. Chris studied each stretch of the different neighborhoods, looking for anything that would strike a memory. He found several different images recurring as they traveled, none of which were really very helpful and most of them haunting. The fog was almost intoxicating. It changed everything outside the car. Even on rainy nights the landmarks all looked the same, if wetter. But the shroud over the city warped his perspectives. Lampposts looked like figures moving through the darkness, and a couple of times he came close to screaming in panic before he realized that what seemed to be—*monsters! The goddamned things are everywhere!*—people or even stranger shapes were little more than bushes or trees.

Brittany was almost completely silent in the back of the car. He'd had to look a couple of times just to make sure she was still there. She was, but she was almost as still as a store mannequin. She blinked from time to time, but otherwise stayed in her almost-fetal position, with her head resting against the glass. The fog when she breathed was almost as heavy as the fog outside the window.

Katie drove in silence, her thoughts, doubtless, on Jerry and what she'd seen. It was bad for Chris, no doubt there, but the idea of what she was going through made him feel like he was getting off lucky. He'd never been intimate with anyone who'd become something other than human. Even thinking along those lines made his balls shrink and try to pull inside his body as surely as if he'd jumped into ice water.

He figured he'd sooner just cut off his manhood and call it a day.

The road sign was hanging low and at an angle, as if someone had hit it with a hammer a few times. He was so lost in thought that he almost missed it. "Stop the car!"

Katie actually let out a little scream when she heard his voice. "Shit! Are you trying to give me a heart attack?"

"Sorry. The sign just sort of popped up." He tried to grin, but shrugged his shoulders apologetically instead. It was a mistake. The shoulder where he'd been shot let out a lightning flash of pain and the other shoulder mimicked it as best it could. It was just the way his week had been going.

Katie pulled the car over to the side of the road. "Is this the house?"

"No. But it's down the road a bit and I'd rather park here. I don't want them to know we're coming. The car might advertise it a bit."

She killed the engine and turned off the headlights. Chris looked back at his sister. "You okay?"

"Yeah." Her eyes moved and she stared at him. The look on her face was far too old for her years. "Let's just find this place and see what we can do. I'm tired."

Chris nodded and climbed out of the car. The two girls followed suit a moment later. The air was almost chilly, especially when compared to the weather earlier in the day. That thought brought a strained sort of grimace to his face and made his stomach dance. It had only been earlier in the day when everything had gone crazy again? It seemed a lot longer than that.

Chris looked around, trying to gain a proper memory of which way to head down the mist-obscured road. He figured it out when he heard the dogs he'd seen before start barking and yowling. Their chains rattled against their leashes off to his right. He gestured and started walking. Katie and Brittany kept up with him.

They moved as quietly as they could, which was almost pointless with the way the dogs were going at it. The two animals could maybe have made more noise if they were actively using bullhorns, but he had his doubts. He stopped for a second and thought about that. Had there been three dogs before? Yes, he was almost certain there had been. He wondered for a moment about the third dog and a shiver ran through his body. *I don't want to know. That's it. I just don't fucking want to know.*

They were most of the way to the yard where the animals were calling out their warnings when the barking abruptly stopped. The sudden silence made his skin crawl. Brittany's little hands were suddenly on his bicep and she pulled in close to her big brother, just like when she was younger and they'd watch a scary movie together. He took comfort from the gesture. He promised himself that she'd get through this in one piece. He hoped desperately that it was a promise he could keep.

From the edge of the next yard he could see the rickety fencing that surrounded the dogs in their home territory. Two silhouettes moved slowly, pacing around the inside of that wooden barrier. He could see them, but heard nothing, save for the now faint rattle of their leashes. Their lack of any sound raised the hairs on the back of his neck.

"What's up with the dogs?" Katie's voice was a very, very soft whisper. Chris shook his head, not quite trusting himself to speak. Katie pulled a Brittany handhold on his free arm. He took comfort from her grip, too, but in a different way and that rather bothered him.

"I don't know. They weren't really what I'd call quiet the last time I was out here." He slowly stepped closer to the house with the gated yard. Through the fog he could see the lights were on in the room that faced him. There was a man in there, sitting in profile. He was large and looked like he should be a trucker. His hair was thinning on top and ran down his back. It looked like he was wearing a muscle shirt and boxers. He shouldn't have been wearing the shirt and his flabby legs needed to be covered up desperately. The man didn't react to the dogs at all. Not to their barking and not to their silence. He was staring at his TV and that was all. Chris watched him for almost half a minute and never saw him blink even once. That too freaked him out a bit.

Brittany let out a little noise that was something between a squeak and a moan, and Chris turned to see that the two silent dogs were now almost to the edge of the fence. The animals were bigger than he'd guessed. He didn't know a damned thing about dogs; his mother would never allow them in the house. But he knew these two looked roughly the right size for eating Cadillacs. They were also looking at Chris and his cohorts like the trio would be good appetizers.

Chris moved past the fenced-in yard as quickly and as quietly as he could. The dogs were creeping him out and he wanted them gone as soon as possible. They slipped to the end of the property, the dogs walking alongside the fence the entire way. And as they moved toward the next house, the abandoned wreck where Crawford had shot Chris, the dogs jumped the fence. The only sound that gave them away was the double *tang* of their chains snapping.

There was no thought in the action. Chris looked,

blinked, and screamed "RUN!" Brittany and Katie did exactly as he said and ran like mad. Right toward the house where they hoped to find Jerry and right past it too.

The dogs were silent and fast, low-slung, high-speed monsters with the meanest grins he'd ever seen on any face, bar none. Both animals chased them hard, and Chris felt himself slipping behind the two girls, not consciously and certainly not deliberately. The last day had been exhausting and whatever reserves he had left were leaving him fast.

The dogs' breath and the sounds of their panting, on the other hand, were almost enough to get him motivated. There was something very motivating about the idea of not becoming a late-night snack. He was almost certain they would take him down like lions after a lame gazelle, but as soon as his feet left the grass and touched the worn asphalt of the road, the animals stopped chasing them. He looked back once he'd crossed the street and stared at the dogs. He could almost see it on their faces, despite the thickening ground fog, that they wanted him desperately. But something near him scared the two beasts far more than the idea of tearing a chunk out of his ass appealed to them. They paced at the edge of the sidewalk, lips curling and peeling back from teeth big enough to make him weak-kneed, but they didn't even touch the ground after the curb.

Chris panted and placed his hands on his knees as he bent over slightly, trying to draw in a serious breath. Katie barely looked winded, but her eyes were wide and wild. Brittany looked scared, but you'd have never guessed she'd just done a hundred-yard dash from a couple of reserve hellhounds.

"Okay . . . why did they stop? I'm not complaining or anything, don't get me wrong, but why did they stop?" Brittany's voice was at the edge of hysterics, but she was doing a great job of faking a calm she obviously didn't feel.

"I think they're scared."

"Of what? Us? 'Cause even I'm not scared of us." She looked around, wrapping her arms around her own narrow ribcage and frowning petulantly. "And right now I'm pretty scared of everything."

"No, not us. I think they're scared of what's in that house." At least she was responding with more than single syllable comments. That was an improvement on her near comatose state earlier in the night.

Brittany looked at him, eyes showing her typical exasperation. "Which house, Chris?" The fog in the air was almost but not quite capable of being called rain and it fell on her hair like a net rather than actually rolling down the individual hairs. She blinked as enough of the condensation gathered to form a proper drop, which promptly fell into her eye. She blinked it back with a frustrated expression on her face. Just at that moment he could see a lot of their mother in her.

"The one right behind you."

The house had looked ramshackle when he saw it the first time. Now it just looked ominous and intimidating as hell. Almost hidden at first by the low shrubs in the front yard and the heavy fog, the building revealed itself only hesitantly. Still, what it revealed was not conducive to happy thoughts. Two stories tall and decrepit, the place looked like it belonged in a horror movie to begin with, but the addition of the heavy, crawling mists and the encroaching darkness made it almost look alive. There was something else about it, something he couldn't quite make out at a distance, and something he wasn't really sure he wanted to know. Still, Jerry was in there somewhere and if Katie was right, Jerry needed his help. Of course, thinking about the last time he'd seen Jerry made him give serious thought to just packing his bags and running for dear life, but he had to hope, to try.

Jerry wasn't just a friend. He was a brother.

Chris looked back at the dogs where they paced at the curbside, and then he looked at the silent house with its boarded windows. There was light creeping from between some of the wooden slats that had been nailed in place. The wind picked up. Instead of clearing the fog away it just moved it around, gave it life and made it seethe around the corners of the house like a thick, crawling funeral shroud. The last place he wanted to be right now was anywhere near that house. The dogs looked less threatening.

He shook his head and stepped toward the dark building. "Let's see what we can do about sneaking in there."

He started to step forward, to break through the

barrier of bushes around the property, but Katie grabbed his arm and stopped him. He looked at her, his eyebrows wrinkled with curiosity and she pointed toward the front of the place. A small gathering of people came out of the darkness, moving to the narrow front porch. They were dressed in casual clothes, but moved with the solemn, measured strides of people already engaged in a ritual of some kind.

Chris heard the dogs across the street as they scurried away, whimpering, their claws scrabbling over broken sidewalk and then into the hard-packed earth of the closest lawn. Their chains rattled almost musically as the dogs bolted for the safety of their yard.

Chris and Katie looked on with Brittany as the small entourage headed through the door of the wretched place. The light from the opening cast their features into familiarity, even through the drifting precipitation. Crawford headed the group, walking in first. Jerry walked with him, chatting softly like an old chum. Even knowing that this probably wasn't really Jerry, seeing him with Crawford was unsettling and unpleasant. It left a bad taste in Chris's mouth.

The group marched through the door in an awkward double file, slightly jostling each other as they entered the house. The creep who had been with Brittany walked into the house with his head firmly attached to his shoulders. Chris knew he'd healed himself, had watched it happen, but that didn't stop him from wanting to bark out laughter when he saw the guy. Not I-saw-something-funny laughter, but the kind that just wants to come bubbling up when the world stops making sense for too long. His sister had a look on her pretty, pale face that said she could go for a few hysterical chuckles herself. And Katie? Well, Katie was munching on her own lower lip in an effort to keep from making any sounds. Her eyes weren't glazed or dazed at all, but seemed too shiny, like wet marbles.

They just kept coming. He counted ten and saw still more coming from the pea-soup atmosphere. They walked carefully, whispering when they spoke. Most of them looked like damn near anyone on the street, just unfortunate enough to be out in hideous weather, but two of them seemed like they might be having trouble with the idea of staying in a human form. Like maybe the weird shit he'd seen a few of these freaks perform was closer to revealing what they really looked like. Like maybe they weren't human at all and never had been. One man walked by close enough for Brittany to touch, and his skin shifted on his left arm, stretching and straining as something just under the epidermis rearranged itself.

They waited for five minutes after the last of the group had gone inside before they dared move. "Are we ready to go?" Chris looked at Brittany and Katie as he spoke.

Katie nodded. Brittany's head jerked up and down a few times, and he figured that was pretty much as close as she was going to get to giving him an actual affirmative.

They moved around the house, treading carefully over the rough lawn of dead grass and a seemingly endless supply of rocks and pitfalls. Through the veil of condensation, Chris walked to the side of the house and rested his hand on the wood. The texture was all wrong. Tiny flakes fell from the surface at his contact and Chris brought his fingers to his nose, testing the scent from the wood. It smelled faintly of mildew and something darker. Something dead or dying, like rotting vegetation in a swamp of stagnant water. He brushed his fingertips across his jeans and wrinkled his nose in disgust.

From inside the building he heard raised voices speaking in unison. The words were metered, spoken carefully; he could tell that though he could not make out what any of the words might have been. Whatever they were doing, they had apparently already started.

It took time, more than he'd expected, especially with Brittany and Katie helping, but eventually they found a possible point of entry. Almost all the way to the backside of the old house there was a rickety set of double doors that led down to what was most likely an old root cellar. The wood was warped by years of neglect, but the padlock wasn't much more than a couple months old at a guess. He ran his fingers over the cold metal, partially disappointed that it was obviously so sturdy, mostly happy that the access would be denied. Not that he would have admitted that even to himself, but there it was.

Then Brittany had to ruin his brief elation by

reaching out and grabbing the lock in his hand. She frowned as she looked at it, and then she yanked down hard, wrenching the metal halfway from its seat in the old wood. "I don't think this should be too hard." She gave the lock another hard wrench, throwing her slight weight into it and was rewarded by a loud snapping noise and a sudden fall on her ass. Brittany let out a small squeak as she fell back, the lock and the latch it had kept closed both in her hand.

Chris looked at the expression on her face and almost managed to stifle a snicker. The laugh wanted to come out, and it wanted to be loud, but he forced it down like a seasick man holding on to his greasy breakfast bacon. If he started laughing he thought there was every possibility that he'd never stop. The situation wasn't funny, but with the way things were going, he desperately wanted to find something amusing.

Brittany shot him a glare that would have melted the metal in her hand and scrambled up to her hands and knees. Katie leaned over and started lifting one of the doors from where it rested. The hinges that held the door fairly screamed in protest, and Chris felt his skin crawl. He helped her with the heavy wooden hatch, and together they set it in an open position.

The stench that crawled out of the entrance was enough to make all three of them back away. It brought to mind mildewed clothing and bread gone moldy, images of fish rotting in the heat of a summer's day and cesspools of stagnant salt water all at the same time. It wasn't merely strong; it was overwhelming, as was the heat that rose with it.

Chris leaned back and sucked in a deep breath of the relatively fresh air away from that entrance and then he lifted the other door as well. He had expected darkness down inside the cellar, and that was exactly what awaited them. But it was not a clean darkness; it was vile with subtle threat and ripe with the promise of danger.

"I really, really don't like this...." Brittany looked down into the pitch-black entrance and whispered softly. Chris was pretty sure she didn't even realize she was speaking.

Katie leaned over next to Brittany and nodded silently. Chris looked at the two of them and thought about what lay down in the depths of the cellar that could produce this sort of foul, wretched odor. The thought didn't make him want to go in there either. But there was Jerry to consider. Jerry, and what his loss would do to all of them.

"If we're going, let's get it done. But I'm going first." He looked at them and shrugged. "What can I say? I'm a chauvinist." Neither of them seemed to mind too much. Equality of the sexes could go to hell when it came to dark and smelly places.

The doors opened about seventeen inches off the ground. Chris eased himself over the wooden lip, his right foot seeking anything at all to settle down on before he swung his full weight over the side. He found a wooden step, one of several, he guessed, narrow and running straight down the interior wall of the room. With a silent prayer to a god he sometimes had trouble believing in, Chris started down the steps, testing each and every one of them to see if they would hold his weight.

He gagged a few times and his stomach did the dry-heave dance again, but nothing came up. As soon as he was in the room and on the floor, he broke a sweat. Not from fear, but from the over-whelming heat of the place. It was summertime, but early in the season as yet. Whatever was down in the cellar apparently needed the sort of warmth that New England only got in August. It was stifling.

And that damned stench was only getting worse. He looked up and called out in a loud whisper, "Stay there. I'll see if I can find a light switch." Both of the silhouetted heads above him nodded. Chris turned and started feeling his way along the wall, trying to be calm and think clearly. He wasn't having much luck with either effort, but still he moved on. The ground was uneven beneath his feet. He could feel the soft texture of a dirt floor that was not well oiled as he stepped, his feet oc-casionally sinking into the earth a little and at other times seemingly moving over bedrock or something equally firm. With little but his sense of feel to go on, he was far more aware than usual of what he stepped on.

His foot kicked against something that moved. It was a small shift, but it didn't feel like it was caused by his weight settling. He stopped for a moment, listening for any sounds that might give him a hint. Whatever his foot had touched was gone, but there was a soft *slssshh*ing sound, and his ears picked up other noises as well; wet, slow movements that did nothing to help him stay calm.

His hand ran along the wall, feeling the uneven brick that built the foundation of the house. There were cracks in the mortar and he guessed that once upon a time the walls had been a good deal more level. Time had broken them down, maybe, or perhaps it was the heat in the cellar. His fingers ran across something stiff and warmer even than the room. He yanked his hand back as if scalded at the same time that a heavy sloshing noise came from directly in front of him. He managed not to scream, but still jumped when he felt the movement directly ahead.

Something heavy was moving in front of him, bumping and making those odd gurgling sounds inside the warmth of whatever it was he'd collided with. He moved around it, doing his best not to think about the sounds. He touched the thing a dozen times—moving in a roughly circular path around an obstruction that was at least four feet wide—before he finally found the simple sanity of the uneven wall. It felt rough and damaged under his hand, but it felt real. It was a small thing, but it helped him continue through the darkness.

How long it took him to find the light was something he would never really know. All that was certain was that it was several lifetimes too long. By the time his trembling fingers found the pull cord dangling form the ceiling he'd been blinking sweat from his eyes for at least several minutes, and he'd run into somewhere in the neighborhood of five of the strange, warm things he'd come to think of as drums. Why drums? Because every time he touched one of them, it made those wet thumping sounds, and it was easier to think of them as big drums than to think of them as hearts, which was rather what they seemed to be shaped like. They didn't pulse quite like a heart should—as evidenced by the noise his own was making in his ears and the way it wanted to kick free of his chest—but they seemed to be the right general shape, and his touches let him feel that they had some sort of thick vinelike streamers running from them, perhaps as anchors or something far worse. Like maybe arteries and veins. Shape alone was enough for him. He didn't really want to think about what they were doing or why they were doing it.

Naturally, the light took care of that soon enough. He pulled the cord that dangled from above him—and again the feeling of simple familiarity, of something he could explain to his imagination, helped him. He had an instant of bright, searing light and then closed his eyes before he could actually see anything. Not so much because he was afraid of what he would see, though he was, but because the light was just too strong after his eyes had adjusted to the nearly-perfect darkness. His eyes watered at the sudden violation of light. He wiped them with a sweaty hand, which really didn't help, and then squinted until he could finally tolerate the glare.

Chris almost wished he hadn't bothered. What he saw just did not fit into the Chris Corin School of

Normalcy. The cellar was as long as the house itself, which, while not what he expected, wasn't all that unusual. The two lights that draped down from the ceiling on thick cables weren't exactly modern, but that was okay; the house was old enough to forgive that. The few implements hanging along the walls were about what you would expect in an abandoned house—pieces of lawn-care equipment that were too old and battered to be of use to anyone at all. Near the ladder he'd scaled to get down into this little slice of Hell was an old workman's bench that had probably last been used sometime before the Korean War took place. There were a dozen glass jars filled with screws and nails on the bench, but the far end was obscured by something thick and black that resembled what he'd imagined in the darkness. It was little more than a silhouette, and at this distance he could tell himself that it was a sleeping bag, or maybe a stack of old blankets that only looked organic. That was all just fine and dandy, thanks. It was the things he saw growing against the walls that kicked his equilibrium to the ground.

There were more of the growths than he would have expected, many of them growing against the walls and a few of them hanging suspended from the bare rafters of the root cellar's ceiling. Each of the things looked roughly like a heart, he'd been right about that, but the shape alone was the closest similarity. They were thick hided and glistened with grayish secretions, the fluids partially obscuring a much darker gray form that was wrapped in green-tinted fibers that held them where they were and pushed into the closest surfaces like the gnarled roots of ancient trees. The heavy binding structures were dull, their glossier interiors like gems held in crude clasps: strong but not at all attractive. They made Chris remember the first concepts he'd ever had of what a cancer must look like growing in the body—foreign and deadly and hungry to suck the life from whatever good, healthy flesh it might encounter. When his mother had tried to explain cancer to him as a child, he'd painted a mental picture that was disturbingly like the tumorous growths infesting the basement.

The one closest to the entrance of the root cellar shifted as he watched, something within it moving and pushing hard enough to make the entire thing shiver in its confining network of roots. Chris moved back in that direction when he saw Brittany's foot touch the rickety ladder leading up to the real world beyond the demented cancer room he was in. He moved around each and every one of the things between him and his sister, careful not to touch any of them.

"I thought I told you to stay outside?"

"Yeah, until you got the lights on. The lights are on now." Her face bore all the patience of any fourteen-year-old girl. That exasperated look faded the instant she took note of the things that sat in the cellar. "Shit, Chris, what are those things?"

Before he could answer she moved down the steps and made room for Katie, who watched her own feet until she was on solid ground. Katie's face had taken on a decidedly green cast as she was forced to continue smelling the warm, rotting odors. As she looked around the cellar, her skin tone moved more into the gray areas. Brittany was right beside her for the transition. They were both pale and sweating by the time they'd taken in the strange fungal lumps that bloomed from the walls and floor.

"What are they, Chris?"

Both of them looked at him like he should have some sort of answers. Naturally enough, he didn't have a clue. He moved to the first one he'd touched, the one that seemed determined to rattle and slosh more than the others, and studied it carefully without daring to touch it. There was something in there, behind the caul of gray, fibrous stuff that made the center of the thing. Something buried inside that he could almost make out as he looked. Katie moved up beside him and dared to touch the thing. Something inside responded to the touch with a violent push. Katie pulled her hand away as if she'd been burned, and she made a mewing sound of panic.

She waved her hand frantically, dropping a thick broken layer of gray from the palm and fingertips. Chris looked from her hand to the gray surface and saw a spot that was almost translucent. He looked back to Katie. "Are you all right?"

"Yeah." She frowned. "I think so. It just felt really weird."

"Weird icky or weird painful?" Brittany had a

201

way with words. He was still trying to figure out how to ask the same question.

"Weird icky. And I think something in there tried to touch me back." Chris looked at the debris around the room and found a small pile of mildewed newspapers. He grabbed a handful and started brushing at the surface of the thing Katie'd touched. The gray coating fell away like little more than a fragile flour coating, revealing a much darker gray surface that held something still darker within it.

Through the twilight of the outer surface, Chris saw that inner darkness move, twisting around until it could reach out.

Chris looked closely as the thing inside pressed itself as close as it could to the surface of the mass. A human face pushed against the thick exterior, shadowy and almost completely obscured by the heavy liquids surrounding it. The skin through the barrier that separated it from Chris looked worn and half starved, but it also looked very much alive. The face was only vaguely familiar to him, but it was familiar just the same. As he looked on, the mouth on that almost-skeletal face opened wide in a silent scream. Brittany moved closer and then shook her head, her eyes wide and frightened.

Chris stepped back, his heart doing the funkiest rhythm in his chest. His mind was playing tricks too, like telling him that what he was seeing was simply not possible. Oh, he knew what he was seeing, couldn't help but acknowledge it, actually, but there was a big old part of his brain that insisted on telling him he wasn't really looking at what amounted to a pickled person who was alive inside the funky plant thing. His brain was pretty much going out to lunch while he looked at the struggling figure, and just to stop that from happening he looked away from it.

And right into Katie's expectant, worried face. "Who's in there, Chris? Who is in there? You tell me. Is it him?" Her voice made a slow spiral in octaves as she spoke, crawling up the scale of tones to the point where she suddenly sounded like a five-year-old version of herself. He stifled a chuckle at the thought that she might suddenly develop a lisp.

"I don't think it's Jerry." His voice sounded good enough to at least pass muster. He didn't actually start laughing and that was a big relief. Oh, my, how he wanted to laugh. Laughter would at the very least keep the screams at bay. "He looked too skinny."

"Try the next one. Oh, God, try the next one."

Chris did as she ordered, not even thinking about whether or not he should look any further. Thinking wasn't really all it was cracked up to be at the present time. He moved and dusted the surface of the next lumpy mass, stepping back when whatever was inside kicked like a fetus inside its mother's womb.

The thick dusty layer spilled to the ground and this time he caught a lungful of the gray stuff. It tasted like mushrooms mixed with something bitter. He coughed hard, his eyes watering while his lungs felt like they were spontaneously combusting. Back when he was in grade school he'd known a kid with horrid allergies. Almost every spring the boy—his name was Ricky Hastings, if Chris remembered properly—would wind up going to the hospital at least once as a result of pollen in the air. Chris had a flash of panic when he thought about poor Ricky. Because he doubted the nice freaks upstairs would be willing to call 911 if things went wrong down in their cellar.

He coughed hard for almost half a minute, until black spots frosted over his vision and four hands rested on his back while he doubled over. Finally the fit subsided, but his throat felt scoured and his head throbbed.

He had to convince the others that he was okay, though he was hardly feeling anywhere near that particular neighborhood. He was feeling more like a long stretch of very unwell, but what could he do? He knew his sister well enough to think she'd want to see this through and he knew as sure as he was stuck in a cellar full of stuff that belonged in a horror movie that Katie wasn't leaving until she had answers about Jerry. That was assuming that he'd have been willing to leave himself, and despite his mind telling him that doing a hotfoot boogie out of the cellar was a neat idea, he wasn't going to listen.

There was Jerry to consider, certainly, and then there was one other task he needed to do. Somebody had to pay for what had been done to his mother. Her death was bad enough, but the desecration would haunt him forever if he didn't see it handled.

So he managed to get back up and move over to look at what was inside the thing he'd just cleaned. This one looked far worse. The figure was easier to see; the fluids surrounding it were clearer, as if they'd lost their potency somehow. There was a woman inside, her body clothed by little more than shreds of a business suit. The fabric had dissolved in the fluids, and so had much of her body along with it. There were tatters of fabric and tatters of flesh floating in the fluids around her. She seemed to stare at him, but only because her eyelids were gone. For that matter, so was one of her eyes. Like the one previously, this tortured figure within the fluids moved and tried to speak through the liquid that not only surrounded it, but apparently also fed it enough oxygen to breathe. Words, on the other hand, were impossible, even if her lips had still been intact. She'd likely been heavy once, but Chris doubted that was much of a comfort at the present time. Parts of her were still overweight while other areas of her body had little left besides bones. Thick lines ran from the walls of the strange womblike cell that held the woman. These streamers of material ran inward and connected to the tortured woman's torso. He might have thought they were only some way to hold her captive if it weren't for how much of her body had been destroyed by her captivity. Through the holes in her flesh and musculature he could see coarse lines of the gray growths running deep into her body, like an added set of veins and arteries. The thin streamers wove in and out of muscles and layers of flesh and cellulite before diving still deeper. Looking at the raw wounds on her face, he thought he could see them driving deep into her skull, pulsing with a faint movement that had nothing to do with her own slow thrashes in the organic prison.

Chris stepped back in complete revulsion, unable to even breathe for the moment. Above him, in the house that should have been condemned—probably was condemned, but certainly not unoccupied—voices joined together in a deep droning chant that made his scalp crawl. He could not make out the words being spoken—the walls and the floor were too thick for that—but he could catch the tones like a barely audible vibration, and even that soft distorted form of the chanting was enough to make him cringe. He looked over and saw that the chanting had a similar effect not only on Brittany and Katie, but on what remained of the woman in her odd fungal prison. Her remaining eye rolled up and her body convulsed, arms and legs twitching of their own accord while she again screamed silently into the fluids surrounding her.

Chris backed away another three steps and likely would have run if the wall of the cellar hadn't stopped him. But the wall was there and he found his eyes drawn back to the woman in her parasitic womb. She put one half-eaten hand against the inner wall of her prison and pushed. As Chris watched, two fingers snapped free from her hand.

That was pretty much all it took. Chris pushed

past the thing, his gag reflex rebelling, and stumbled back to the ladder. He held on tight, his eyes closing and his stomach trying hard to force its contents across the wall. Nothing came up but a thin wash of watery yellow stomach acid that burned hard and left him feeling even more drained than before. He stayed that way for almost a full minute and then spat several times before wiping his mouth.

All the while, the voices continued, filtering down from above, accompanied by strange whistling noises, rather like epileptic tea kettles trying to groove to their own beat. He had a little mental image of cartoon kettles happily tooting out steam and shook it away. God, how he wanted to just let the images take over and let any little invented reality that came along take the place of the world he was in. He couldn't think of anything that would have made him happier.

He might have let it happen then and there but Brittany's scream took the possibility away. Her voice cut out in a wail of denial and he turned his head fast enough to pull something and get a warm hot flash through his neck.

Brit had both hands over her mouth and the scream came through her fingers. He hated to think what it would have sounded like unhampered. She was taking very small steps backward and shaking her head, her eyes as wide as a badly-drawn anime like the Sailor Moon stuff she liked to watch after school—one of her secret hobbies that he just knew was technically uncool these days. He moved toward her, his eyes almost automatically trailing up to the spot where she stared. Her skin was paler still—*like a fucking corpse, buddy-boy! Pale as a corpse, as your mother in her torn-up grave!*—and he started worrying about how she could possibly survive being that sickly and white.

And then he saw the man he'd hated on sight, the one who'd been fondling her when he came into the house. Bobby Johanssen in all his wretched glory. He wasn't as far gone as the woman in the next alien stew pot, but he definitely looked like a refugee from a concentration camp. His ribs were clearly defined under his skin, which looked like he'd spent the night sleeping in a very large patch of poison oak. His eyes were closed, for which Chris was very, very grateful. But he, like the others, was in agony and moved in a slow dance of pain that threatened to tear overly tense muscles from their natural positions. He could see the snaking tendrils that ran into the man's body like eight extra limbs running from his armpits down to his hips, anchoring him in the cloudy waters that should have drowned him but did not.

Chris turned away from the man with a pang of guilt that he chose to ignore. Whoever he was, whatever he was, as far as Chris was concerned, Jerry was the first priority. He ran to the next of the musky-smelling growths and swiped at the fine dusting, scowling as he went. He shoved his face closer to each of the translucent shells, looking desperately to find one that had his best friend inside, if, in fact, one of them might.

He found Jerry on the seventh try. The features were heavily smudged, like a face seen underneath a stocking on a bank robber, but Chris knew them. He knew every detail of that face almost as well as he knew his own. Jerry looked back at him with eyes that were open but did not see. Beside him, Katie let out a sound that was faint, but filled to overflowing with pain.

"Oh shit. What the hell did they do to him?" Chris tried to grab at the surface of the thing, tried to pull it apart with his bare hands, but couldn't get the purchase necessary to make a decent effort. He even hauled back a fist and slammed it forward with everything he had left to give, and damned near broke his wrist in the effort. The shell of the thing was as tough as rawhide but with less give.

Behind him, Brittany and Katie hissed words at each other, fast whispers that made no sense to Chris in his efforts to find a way for Jerry to get free. He looked around the room and saw the old gardening tools leaning against the wall. There was a rake that had long ago lost most of its teeth. He grabbed it up and tried the heft of the long handle. The wood was dry, but it was hard. All he had to do was try to get the rattling remains of the rake off and he might be able to use it.

He slammed the head of the rake against the ground and ducked as it bounced back at his crotch with a vengeance. Then, a little calmer, he propped the rake against the table and stomped hard on the handle, just a few inches above the rake's head. *I spend three fucking days of my life getting beat on, kicked and assaulted by nightmares, and I don't fucking figure out that a weapon would be nice? Need to get a goddamned clue, Corin. Need to get a fucking real life while you're at it.* It took three stomps to actually get the handle away from the ruined head, and he was pretty damned sure he'd broken something in his foot in the process.

So now he had a weapon, if he could manage to keep his hands on it. Right at the moment he felt like his arms would fall off and his muscles were doing funky little trembling dances that, frankly, weren't very much fun to go through. Maybe it was the heat getting to him, but he felt like someone had pulled all of the muscles out of his body and very quickly replaced them with Jell-O.

He moved back toward Jerry's organic prison and aimed the sharpened end of his rake at it like Ahab taking a harpoon to his great white whale. The jagged wooden point pushed deep into the harder exterior shell, flakes and fragments of the handle breaking away as the convex casing became concave. Then, with a sound like a bass drum exploding, the tough skin ruptured and the wooden pole drove deep into the fluids.

A dark gray ichor vomited out of the thing, thick and warm and smelling far, far worse than the atmosphere around him. The stuff spilled from the hole he'd punched and flowed down the sides of the fungal mass like hot sap that had been heavily scented with fish oil and then left to stagnate. There were a few times in his life when Chris Corin had been truly disgusted. Most of them had to do with

Jerry. The worst to date had been the first time they'd ever gotten drunk. At the age of fifteen they'd managed to convince a local kid who'd just turned twenty-one to buy them a bottle of whiskey. Now, it was a valiant effort on their parts, but by the time they'd killed half the bottle they should have known better and stopped. In fact, Chris had known enough to call it quits, but Jerry was never one to admit defeat with any ease. He killed the rest of the bottle himself and paid the price soon thereafter. Never one to like being alone, he took Chris along for the ride. Sometime after the initial giggling fits, and while Chris was trying to get the world around him to just settle the hell down, damn it, Jerry looked over at his best friend, smiled weakly and then bazooka barfed all over Chris's shirt and pants. The stench of alcohol and vomit— along with the feel of it soaking through his clothes and the simple knowledge of what it was—had been enough to set off a chain reaction that left Chris returning the favor. That was the most disgusting thing Chris had ever experienced to date. This one topped it easily. Under other circumstances he probably would have tossed his cookies right then and there, but he'd done that a few minutes earlier and there was already too much on his mind to let a little thing like his gag reflex get in the way.

Still, it was disgusting, so he backed up.

The thing deflated quickly, and Chris reached for the hole he'd made, grabbing the heavy, rubbery substance and pulling as hard as he could. Despite the fact that both of them looked as sick as he felt, the girls joined him, pulling roughly in an effort to make the opening bigger. Katie dug into the small purse she normally carried—a more battered-looking purse might exist, but Chris had never seen it—and started searching frantically as Brittany and Chris tried to tear through the membrane.

The noise from upstairs was increasing, the sound of dozens of voices seemed amplified until it sounded more like the Mormon Tabernacle Choir, at least in volume. It would be a blatant lie to say he understood any of the words being spoken through the obstructing walls and floors, but he had caught the rhythm of the chants from above. Was it his imagination, or did that rhythm falter for just a moment when they finally started punching through the case? Hard to say. He wasn't really at the top of his game right then, what with the violent need to puke out his stomach and a few other internal organs. What stunned him most of all was that he was absolutely certain you were supposed to adjust to this sort of stench after a while. Somebody hadn't told whatever these things were about that particular rule.

Katie reached past Chris, her hand holding something shiny, and stabbed at the heavy material that covered Jerry's body. The wound he'd torn with the rake handle was stretched taut by both his hands and Brittany's. The metal blade in her hands caught the edge of the ragged opening where they pulled it tight and sank in quickly, cutting the stuff with a loud wet tearing sound that was all too reminiscent of a bad gas attack. Chris and Brittany put their weight into it and yanked back hard. The thing gave out and gave up its contents, spilling a thick warm fluid and Jerry onto the cellar floor.

Jerry rolled across the ground, his clothes still mostly intact, but soaked through and torn where the strange connecting tendrils from inside his second womb had held him anchored. The fibrous umbilicals kept him from rolling too far, keeping him connected to the ruins of the deflated heart-shaped thing. Chris reached down and grabbed one of the cords, pulling at it without really thinking. It tore from Jerry's side, coming free with a loud popping noise and then gave added resistance as a rootlike series of finer gray threads slowly slid out of his best friend's body.

"Chris, you're killing him! Stop it!" Katie grabbed his shoulder and pulled him back, making him stumble. He tried to catch his balance and failed, spilling across the ground and tripping over Jerry in the process. The umbilical feed that ran into Jerry was pulled tight as he fell, and continued to slide out of the opening in his chest

Jerry let out a low moan that became more and more lively as Chris pulled the thing from his side. Along with the moan he vomited more of the foul liquid from his mouth and then started coughing and violently gagging as his eyes opened. He hacked and coughed, crawling slowly to his hands and knees, his entire body shaking with the expulsion of the fluids he was now drowning in. Whatever was in that casing was not meant to be breathed, at least not once he was freed from it.

They all did their best to help him, but there wasn't much they could do. What little Chris remembered from CPR classes he'd taken in high school was meant to be used on an unconscious victim or on someone who was choking. Neither was the case here.

The cord in his hand, almost forgotten until that point, writhed and pulled on its own, yanking back and tearing the rest of the way from the small hole that ran between Jerry's ribs. The rootlike structures moved blindly, apparently seeking a new home, and found brief purchase in Chris's flesh. The thin tendrils burned like wasp stings as they started sinking into his forearm. He reached out with his left hand and hooked one of the things, pulling it back. It came loose only reluctantly, seeking another point of entry almost in an instant.

He threw it to the ground in disgust and stomped down hard on the end of the thing that was still seeking to take root again. His heel ground three of the thinner pseudopods into the dirt, tearing them easily. Where they had penetrated his skin he could see welts rising fast and a small drool of blood spilling down his forearm.

Katie and Brittany were still trying to tend to Jerry, who was finally easing up on the coughing fits. Seven more of the serpentine links to his holding pen remained, and Chris had to fight off the urge to yank them from his friend's body. Jerry apparently didn't feel that same need for caution. He grabbed the one lowest on his left side and pulled hard, letting out a long hiss of air as he did so. His flesh, already pale and wet, grew positively white and his eyes tried their best to roll upward, but Jerry persisted, pulling and fighting as the long streamers of seething threads came out of his body with the same audible pop that had happened when Chris had torn one free. Apparently Katie decided that the things weren't actually keeping Jerry alive. She reached out and grabbed one, tugging with all of her weight until it came loose with a snapping sound. She let out a short scream when the tendrils tried to wrap around her arm and threw the thing to the ground, backing away from it.

In the meantime Brittany had gone back to Bobby Johanssen and taken along Chris's makeshift spear. She took a running start and actually left the ground completely as she shoved the pole into the top of the thing, punching through like a needle going into a blister. The much lighter fluids surrounding him were also thinner, and sprayed from the top of the bladder he was held in, spilling over Brittany in a torrent. She coughed and gagged and hooked the end of her spear into the thick hide that covered Bobby, pulling hard and tearing it down the side. Once they were actually broken, the things cut easily enough.

Bobby spilled out of the trap and onto the ground. The liquids that held him might have been thinner, but they were no less rancid-smelling. While Jerry and Katie were pulling the last of the strange root systems from his body, Brittany started tearing the same things from Bobby with violent results. Perhaps they were more deeply imbedded into him, maybe he was simply further gone, but when she pulled he let loose a wet scream, vomiting thick reddish-black fluids from his lungs and throat as he bucked harshly, his eyes going wide. What Brittany pulled from him ended with a much thicker collection of roots that were in turn far more spread out and bloodied as they pulled free. The sound that came from her actions was less like a soft pop and more like the sound of a green tree branch being broken.

Brittany looked at Chris, her eyes wide and terrified, her expression asking him simply what had gone wrong. He didn't have any answers. He moved over to her side and reached for the next of the connections, trying to figure how to pull it free without practically killing the man, when everything went even crazier.

II

If anyone had asked Chris just how things could have gotten worse, he'd have cackled in their direction and very possibly have kept up the broken laughter until he passed out from lack of oxygen.

He'd forgotten all about the chanting crowds upstairs. They'd completely slipped his mind. The unsettling noises just didn't hold a cup to the sight of Jerry pulling the slippery things from his own sides, or the feel of one of them, just one, mind you, trying to dig deep into Chris's body. Next to the bloody mass that Brittany ripped from her boyfriend, even all that Jerry had gone through paled.

Chris remembered the chanting when it faltered and realized that maybe something more was going on around him when he heard the sound of Jerry screaming—not right here in the cellar with him, oh no, that would make sense. No, he heard his best friend's screams coming from upstairs, in the house proper, where the chanting was going on. He looked to his left, away from Brittany and her problems and over to where Katie and—yep, still there, by God—Jerry were finishing up. The tendrils that had been deep inside of Jerry—and Chris gave thought to what was still inside the half-decayed body of what had been an obese woman and realized for the first time exactly what he had pulled from Jerry and shuddered—were already dying, blackening from their previous gray and shriveling away. He looked toward the source of the sound he'd heard, toward the ceiling above him, and heard a new noise. Heavy footsteps moved away from the chanting—and like an Eveready battery, that noise was still going, boys and girls—and down what had to be a staircase. They thundered overhead for a moment and then turned abruptly. Far to the right of where Chris was now, where he had eventually found the dangling chain to the light, he heard a door open with enough force to slam it against the wall.

The footsteps that moved down the stairs came as a complete surprise. In all of his searching Chris had never even bothered to look for a staircase.

He'd been distracted by other things. Now, from the shadows beyond the light switch, he heard footsteps all but stumbling down the wooden stairs that hid there in the shadows.

And from those shadows spilled a frantic-looking Jerry. No, frantic wasn't really the word so much as furious. Chris had known Jerry for as long as he could remember, but he had never seen a look quite like that on his best friend's face. Then again, it wasn't really his best friend who came toward him with teeth bared and head lowered in anger. It just looked like him, acted like him—okay, sometimes acted like him—and knew everything that he knew. That didn't make it any less freaky to watch as he came stomping through the place.

"You stupid fuck!" His voice had a deeply strained sound to it, like he was holding back a bark of pain. "You're ruining everything!" Jerry on the ground looked at Jerry walking toward Chris and did a double take that would have been hilarious under different circumstances. Right at that moment even the hysterical laughter that kept wanting to break out of Chris's body failed to find the situation funny. Walking Jerry made it almost all the way to Chris before Katie tried to interfere. She stood up, her face as pale and stunned as her boyfriend's and opened her mouth to speak. Walking Jerry shoved her back without a second thought, his eyes looking only at Chris. "We tried to make it easy for you, man! We tried to just get it done and let you have your life back. Why did you have to screw it up?"

He must not have wanted an answer to that question. He backhanded Chris across the face, and Chris saw the room turn around. One second he was facing Jerry and the next he was facing the far side of the room and trying to get the black spots out of his vision. Chris was pretty sure his face was actually still attached to his skull, but he couldn't have proved it without a mirror, and it felt like someone had been working at separating muscles from bones. Before he could recover, Jerry was on him. He felt the hands grab his shirt and the seat of his pants and then he was lifted up toward the ceiling. His hand smashed into the wooden floorboards above him with bruising force, and then he was dropping at high velocity.

That rough dirt floor wasn't quite as hard as concrete, but almost. Chris hit the ground and gave serious thought to just staying there. It simply had to hurt less than trying to move. The Jerry who had put him down had different ideas. He grabbed Chris by the hair and pulled him halfway to his feet with a single yank that left Chris screaming hoarsely as his hair seemed to come out by the roots. His legs weren't in much of a mood to support him, so Jerry really had to work for the full-body lift. The new, even angrier Jerry monster seemed more than capable of handling the task. The pain was enough to steal away pretty much every thought he'd been having: like hornets stinging into a field of fire that just happened to rest on his skull.

"Chris, Chris, Chris." Jerry looked at him and Chris looked back through eyes that were finally capable of seeing again, surprised to see that his friend's face was bubbling and blistering. "Now I have to go and kill you, and part of me feels bad about that." He mustn't have been feeling too bad about it though, because he threw Chris again, slamming him into the wall not far from the ladder and the entrance to the root cellar. The wall was not smooth and left several scrapes that made his scalp feel a little better about what it had been through. Chris hit the ground again, his eyes focusing after only a few seconds. Yep. Staying down was sounding better all the time, but he knew it wasn't going to be allowed. He'd brought this on himself, forced the issue further than was good for his health and now he was going to have to deal with the consequences.

He pushed back away from the safe, comfortable ground on watery knees and made himself start looking for a weapon. He figured he was pretty much on his own here.

Naturally enough, he was wrong. He might have expected help from Katie, but Jerry was completely out of the question. The real Jerry, that is, the one who was soaking wet and barely capable of lifting his arm, let alone coming to his aid. What he did not expect was Brittany's help. Not because he didn't think her capable, but because she was actually the one person he could see who seemed to be having a harder time with the whole damned thing than he was.

Brittany timed it beautifully, whether it was deliberate or not. She got a running start while the

standing Jerry was knocking Chris around like a
Golden Gloves contender sparring with a three-
year-old, and she brought a weapon with her. The
trusty rake handle proved its worth again as she
held the dull end in close like a charging football
quarterback and buried the business end in the side
of Jerry's head.

Granted, the Jerry she skewered was not, in fact,
really Jerry. Also granted, he had shown signs—
like the bubbling skin and the superhuman
strength—that he was probably not even human.
But the fact that he simply stood there as the
wooden handle ran into his skull was enough to
shock every conscious human being in the room.
Brittany fell back from the sight, her eyes going so
wide Chris thought her eyeballs might actually fall
right out of their sockets.

Jerry turned in her direction and growled—a
sound that had nothing whatsoever to do with anything human—a trilling, whistling roar that seemed
to come not from his mouth but from his chest. His
skin, which had been blistering and bubbling for a
few seconds now and was releasing a decidedly unpleasant stench, peeled back from the spot where
he was skewered and blossomed into a new shape,
a new form that was unevenly broken into thin
strips of writhing melting goo. The rake handle
launched away from his head like a javelin and
slammed into the ground not two feet away from
Chris. Despite its crooked appearance, despite the
strange flailing shapes that Jerry's skin had taken
on where the weapon had penetrated, Chris could

clearly see that a new mouth had grown where there should have been only a bloody mass.

Jerry glared pure, unadulterated hatred at Brittany and reached out an arm that fairly exploded as it pointed in her direction. Flesh and bone be damned, whatever he was made of wasn't meat and gristle. Maybe he was having trouble controlling his bodily functions now that he had been separated from the real Jerry, but the thing that had looked like Jerry a few seconds earlier was looking less and less like anything even remotely human. The arm that had reached for Brittany stretched out and mutated into what Chris could think of only as tentacles, despite the fact that they obviously weren't part of any sea creature he'd ever seen. They had the right shape, if none of the proper textures he would have expected. The color was almost exactly the same shade of gray as the ropy anchors that held each of the podlike things in place in the cellar. They moved with a furious speed and grew in length until the whole of what had been the pseudo-Jerry's arm was almost as long as his body. The thick streamers of flesh—which held more bulk than the arm they'd grown from—wrapped around Brittany's thin body and contracted, like a small army of boa constrictors targeting Chris's little sister as their latest meal.

Jerry hauled her back toward him and at the same time, his body altered again, swelling and changing from the hips up. His torso just split, his entire ribcage breaking in half and opening into an orifice large enough to pull at least half of Brittany into its depths. Wickedly-pointed hooks and barbs lined the inner opening and they grew larger as she struggled, kicking and screaming to get away from the nest of ropy tentacles around her.

Adrenaline is nature's way of giving you the choice of fighting or fleeing. Chris wanted desperately to flee, but his body seemed to have its own ideas of what to do with the chemical boost provided. Chris moved over the ground and jumped hard, throwing his full weight into the tackle he put on the Jerry-thing. The body had changed, was still changing, almost melting into something entirely different, but it still had mass and most of its bulk was too high up for its own good. He hit it hard and hit it well and both he and the freakish thing went rolling over each other as they hit the ground again, Brittany trailing along like a kite in a hurricane and shrieking bloody murder into the air.

The atmosphere in the room was like a sauna. The thing Chris landed on was more like an oven set to broil. Whatever was happening to the imitation Jerry was sending its temperature skyrocketing. He didn't know if that was the creature's natural state or a side effect of being unplugged from the real McCoy, but either way, it hurt like hell to be in contact. Chris rolled off the thing as quickly as he could, wincing at the reddening of his hands where he'd touched it.

Brittany managed to pull herself loose, her own flesh reddening where she'd been grabbed by the tendrils. She was shaking and jittery as she crawled away, her blue eyes rolling in her head as she, at least for the moment, gave in to complete panic.

Another problem with whatever was happening was that the thing was getting really, really pissed off. The cavernous mouth it had become slammed shut, barely missing taking off Chris's legs clean up to his balls when the teeth slammed together. Thick spittle—or something worse that he did NOT want to think about—sprayed the air where he'd been a few seconds before.

He wasn't in the clear and he knew it. He knew it without even looking over his shoulder. He looked anyway, just in time to help him duck the pillar of gray flesh that tried very hard to pulp his head. It arced through the air like a missile, lifting up and then swinging down in a smooth curve. He dropped under the bludgeon and watched as it pounded a cavity into the hard-packed floor.

He also saw what he hoped would be his salvation on the ground not far from where the tentacle thing landed. Chris was hardly a mechanically-inclined man. Much to his chagrin, he knew next to nothing about cars and still less about the mysteries surrounding home improvement. But he knew a little. And he certainly knew enough to understand the workings of an extension cord. The power outlet was half hidden by the bulbous shape of another of the green pods holding victims of the things singing their special song upstairs. It was what his mother had always called an octopus. There were several extension cords plugged into one another and those in turn led to other cords. Though he had never guessed it—and certainly hadn't taken the time to find it out, thanks very much—all of the light in the room and apparently several other appliances now buried by the fungal wombs in the cellar were connected through exactly and precisely one outlet. And he was looking at it less than five feet away.

Chris scrambled like a madman, his hands reaching for the overloaded collection of cables. His fingers started tugging even as his eyes tried to trace the various connections to their natural endings. He pulled hard at one that looked like what he wanted and was rewarded with a sudden shift in light from above. The cheap lights were merely exposed bulbs in a stainless-steel cone hanging from the ceiling. He had assumed they were properly fastened in place, when instead, as he now realized, they were held in place by clip-on clamps. He reached for the dangling cord where it rose toward the ceiling and grabbed it just in time to be grabbed himself. A thick, wet muscular column snaked around his legs and pulled him to the ground, dragging him rapidly back toward what the Jerry-thing had become. The heat from that elephant's trunk of flesh was overwhelming. Even through his jeans he felt it searing his calves. His hands held on to the light's cord with a death grip. Chris scissored his legs as best he could, trying to break free from the tentacle of hot gray stuff, with no real success.

This time it was Katie to the rescue. She leaned in at a precarious angle and swung her little silver thing again, scraping at the bulky limb that pulled him closer to an ever-changing blob with a mouth

that simply refused to do anything but grow bigger.
Whatever she held was nice and sharp and cut a
deep slash across the flesh. A thick black substance
poured out in a stream and the tentacle eased up a
bit as the cut flesh rippled like Jell-O that had just
been slapped. Chris kicked hard with his left leg
and managed to free one foot. He braced his tennis
shoe against the writhing pseudopod and pushed
as hard as he could. Several hot flashes ran deep
into his right calf and knee, but he felt himself slide
forward and slip free from the thing.

Chris pushed back again and again, propelling
himself across the ground, covering his ass and
jeans with dirt in the process. The creature slithered
forward enough to attack again, the column of flesh
whipping about like an epileptic serpent before it
shot at his chest.

He lifted the conical rim of the reflector around
the light socket and let the bulb inside take the
brunt of the hit. He let go of the rim at the same
time the gray mass shoved through the thin glass
of the bulb and met up with the live wires now free
from their glass prison. The force was enough to
push him against the wall, enough to bruise his
back and crack his head against the uneven stone.
It hurt, and it damn near knocked him into next
week.

But on the brighter side, the thing trying to drive
him through the wall was having a much worse
time of it. It bucked and twitched almost comically,
the entire bloated body shivering and shaking, except for the single tentacle that was busily fusing

itself to the light socket it was jammed into. The whole mass had been sort of bubbling and fizzing along as the fight progressed, but now it actually boiled. Great pustules of seepage erupted from the thing, spitting and hissing as they opened. What looked to be eyes tried to form and then exploded in a dozen spots, and what could only be mouths opened and shrieked as it twitched and fried, sizzled and finally—he hoped—died.

Chris figured maybe it was dead when it stopped moving. He decided he could officially call it among the deceased when it caught fire; streamers of thick choking smoke rose from the mass and were followed moments later by flickering and dancing tongues of flame.

He sat where he was for almost a full minute, trying to regain some semblance of composure. He wasn't alone. The only person moving downstairs was the real Jerry, who was slowly crawling to his feet, his clothing mud-stained and tattered and his face still devoid of most expression.

Jerry looked around and shook his head. "Somebody want to tell me what's happening?" His voice was slurred and his mouth barely seemed capable of movement.

Chris shook his head, unable to make his mouth form words. Too much of his body was aching in a way he did not like at all. Worse, he had a ringing in his head that refused to go away or calm down.

On the ground, almost completely forgotten by Chris, Bobby Johanssen groaned softly, trying to pull himself away from the thick vines that pushed into his ribcage. He was in bad shape, skinnier than he should have been, which meant he was just shy of Auschwitz-level emaciation. Brittany, at a loss for what else to do to help him, ripped the second of the thick, fibrous things from his ribs. The heavy umbilical came out of him slowly, and well before it was over he had passed out from the pain of the thick roots tearing out of his body.

"Chris, please help me!" Her voice had gone all shrill again, and Chris looked over at his sister. The swelling marks on her face from where she'd been hit or where she'd landed roughly made him get up, though it was not an easy thing to do. His sister needed him and he needed to get her and Katie and Jerry out of here.

Katie helped Jerry to his feet and propelled him toward the ladder. The two of them stumbled a few times, but eventually they got there. Chris moved over to where Brittany and Bobby moved on the ground and then he looked past them to the table he'd seen near the ladder. There wasn't much on it that might be useful, but he dropped to the ground beneath it and found what he sought. It was hardly a perfect cutting tool, but the old box cutter was better than trying to use his hands for what he wanted. He crawled under the table despite his body's protests and pushed through the dirt until he could grasp the tool. One check was enough to tell him that the razorblade inside was broken. He almost cried, but then pulled the blade free and saw to his relief that the other half of the razor had not been used at all. He managed not to cut himself as he reversed the rusty razor inside the cutter.

Brittany started tugging at the third of the tentacles growing from Bobby's chest into the remains of the pod he'd been captured in and Chris stopped her with a gesture. He dropped down next to Brittany and showed her his prize before grabbing the coiled growth she'd been tugging on. The razor was nice and sharp, if a bit rusty, and cut through the rough surface of the gray vine with relative ease. He worked fast, making quick brutal slashes that left the ends of the connectors still rooted in Bobby's sides, but without causing him as much potential damage inside. Chris could see the blood on the two sections that Brittany had torn free and could only imagine what the roots had disturbed on their way out. If Bobby was lucky he wouldn't have massive internal injuries from her hasty if well-intentioned removal of the things.

By the time Chris was finished with the impromptu surgery, Katie had come back from the ladder. She and Brittany started dragging Bobby toward the exit, hauling at his dead weight with relative ease. Chris tried to remember what the hell he was doing in the cellar in the first place. Thinking real cognitive thoughts was not something he seemed well equipped to handle at the moment. He looked down at his hands and the small blisters forming there, almost white in the field of seared red his flesh had become. The skin felt tight and he could already see the swelling.

He looked at the other gray things around the room, ignoring the large pile of burning goo for the moment. He didn't really like to think about that. It made him want to start that annoying laughter again. The deep-down laughter that had nothing to do with funny and everything to do with funny farms. There were easily fifteen or twenty of the damned things, and he didn't much like the idea of thinking about what was in them, but there was no way he could just leave the people inside the cocoons either.

Well, some of them could be left. I don't really think some of them would be able to make it out in one piece and I wouldn't wish that sort of existence on anyone.

He thought of the woman he'd looked at who had bones and internal organs showing and decided she was better off dead than suffering through any attempt at recovery.

Chris moved through the room as quickly as he could, batting at the thick layer of gray on each of the growths and doing his best to peer inside to see what was visible in each. Most of them had been stewing in their juices a little too long. He found two others who were in decent shape, the sort of condition where, if it were him, he'd want someone to try to help him out by freeing him as opposed to giving him a merciful death.

He used the box cutter to punch through the outer casing of each of those two and then ran back to the ladder, ready to call out to Brittany and Katie to let them know he needed their help.

He didn't intend to stay in the cellar long enough to finish the job, because he had a suspicion about what was upstairs and what might not stay up there for very long. Jerry's doppelganger had come screaming down the stairs when they unplugged Jerry from his stew pot. He had a feeling 'Bobby might come down too, and he didn't want Brittany to see that. Jerry had been bad enough, but whatever the case, he had never been intimate with Jerry, or even given the notion thought. He didn't think his sister had ever had the chance to actually have sex with Bobby—or worse, the thing that only looked like him and wasn't THAT a lovely notion—but she'd been willing and ready when Chris had broken up the party. She had enough to deal with without that particular hellish thought.

He looked up to the opened double doors and saw Bobby's feet and lower legs as he was finally pulled up by the two girls. "Brittany! Katie!"

"Yeah?" The voice was Katie's and sounded like she'd just run a marathon.

"I've got two more of these things cut open, the razor is right here. Try to help them, okay?"

Her head peered down at him, heavily shadowed. "Why? Where are you going?" "

"Into the house. I'm going upstairs."

Her face went from startled to full-scale outrage and then to a sort of dumbstruck expression. "What? Why?"

"Because they're doing something up there and I don't like it. I'm gonna try and stop them before they finish whatever it is."

"Chris, no! You're crazy! Leave them alone and get your ass up here!"

"Can't do it. There's stuff that has to be taken care of."

"Like what?" She waved her hands around in a wild gesture that only showed how frustrated she was. She looked beautiful, but then she always did, especially when she was angry.

He hissed when he spoke again, a harsh stage whisper that he didn't want his sister to hear. "Like the other Bobby, goddammit!"

She looked at him blankly for a second and then her eyes flashed and she nodded. "Gotcha. I'm coming back down."

"Just be careful and work fast. Don't look at the others. Don't bother with them. They wouldn't . . . they wouldn't want you to." Her only response was to nod her understanding, her lips pressed together in an almost-white slash.

She started down the ladder, her back to him, and he was about to say something to her when a hand covered his mouth and another reached low and grabbed at his crotch. He managed to shift himself enough to keep his private parts uncrushed, but the groping hand didn't seem to want to take no for an answer and continued trying to get better acquainted. Chris was in no mood for it. He hauled his right arm back and drove his elbow into the face of the person behind him. His elbow sank into flesh with a splat, and he cringed. Whatever he'd hit was either not human or very, very badly broken before he touched it.

And judging by the way it threw him into the wall, he guessed the former. Chris caught himself with his palms before his face would have smashed into the uneven stones. Katie let out a scream from up above and started down his way, her eyes wide and her face showing nothing but panic, but apparently not willing to let him go it alone against whatever it was.

Chris kicked his leg back, an awkward and unbalanced move that would have sent him sprawling if he weren't already braced. His foot landed solidly in the midsection of the figure behind him and he felt the most recent source of his troubles stumble backward. Chris turned fast, not wanting to lose whatever edge he might have gained, and found himself facing the other Bobby.

Bobby, beaten and emaciated as he was, looked a world better than his replacement. This one was bigger, for one thing. Much, much bigger. Not so much taller as bulkier. He could have been an extra in a movie filmed at Muscle Beach, but only if the extra didn't mind that his body was sort of out of proportion. His arms were almost as thick as Chris's thighs, but they were practically dwarfed by the width of his torso. Bobby's doppelganger was not melting, not breaking up in the same way that Jerry's had, but he wasn't looking at all himself. The worst was his face, which was swelling like the rest of him, but doing it in weird little waves that rippled from one side of his head to the other in uneven bulges. One half of his jaw was as broad as a lion's but the other side was as narrow as usual.

Bobby stepped forward, his hands held out in front of him, ready to ward off blows that might come his way. One of his eyes looked at Chris. The other was changing, breaking into smaller orbs the color of dark rubies. Chris watched for a second, both puzzled and stunned by the strange transformation taking place in Bobby's left eye socket. As he watched, the smaller orbs spread out, swimming across the surface of Bobby's face, which had lost all other distinguishing features. Chris looked on, staring into the deep red spiderlike eyes forming a circle on that face and felt oddly detached from the moment.

To that point it had all seemed so random, like whatever changes the creatures went through were almost accidental, something they had no control over. Bobby wasn't playing by that rule.

Bobby took another step forward and something clicked—almost audibly—in Chris's head. He didn't think about what was happening to the freak in front of him, didn't even notice the stench coming from him—which, when compared to a lot of the others around at that moment, was hardly worth noticing—he just pumped his fist into that funky face as hard and as often as he could.

Chris was never going to be a heavyweight contender, nor, for that matter, did he have any real desire to be a boxer. But back when he'd taken the boxing courses at the local YMCA, the coach had thought he had potential. Now he proved it all over the Bobbystein Monster's face. He connected with the flesh between those odd eyes, a solid blow that ran all the way through his arm up to his shoulder. The second punch wasn't as good, but only because

his target was in the process of staggering backward. He compensated on the third and fourth
blows. They were deliciously well placed and left
him feeling a slightly warm and fuzzy glow in the
center of his stomach.

Good ol' freaky Bobby fell on his ass to the
ground. Before he could get up, Chris punted, plac-
ing a beautiful shot across the jawline of that now
slightly squishy face. Hitting Bobby was fun, and
not only because he was a monster. It was extra fun
because Chris was finally able to cut loose on the
prick who had been trying to score with his little
sister. It was a cheap reason to feel good, and he'd
actually have flashes of guilt over it later, but for
the moment he ran with it.

It felt a helluva lot finer than the growing panic
he'd been in since he got into the cellar. Oh, his fist
was feeling a little like it had been sanded with
coarse-grade sandpaper, but that was all right too.
Every time he connected with Bobby's head there
was a deep resonant thump, not unlike the sound
a perfectly ripened pumpkin makes when it's
tapped. Even that odd noise was pleasant, like music to his ears. He liked it so much he made it happen about four more times with his feet and his
hands. Bobby kept trying to get up and he just kept
swinging.

He barely pulled back in time when the Bobster
retaliated. One instant he was swinging at the drum
that was Bobby's head, and the next his target—the
now battered and bumpy spot between the red, un-
blinking ring of eyes on Bobby's new face—simply

exploded into a bloom of barbed teeth that surely would have torn his arm off. The sound of those teeth slamming together where his hand should have been was like the sound of a heavy door violently slamming shut. He felt the spittle from that orifice spray across his fisted hand and backpedaled as quickly as he could.

Bobby wasn't willing to play nicely anymore. The thing didn't make any noise aside from scuttling across the floor and gnashing its teeth repeatedly until all Chris could think of was the windup chattery teeth he'd had as a kid. The shape was still mostly human, but the thing that had looked like Bobby was shuffling across the floor in an almost-prone position, head up and body slung low on legs and arms that had too many joints under the clothing. Even the clothing was wrong. What looked like cloth was apparently a part of the creature. The "fabric" around the collar of the shirt on the nightmare blended smoothly into the actual neck, a strange distortion of color that was unsettling at best. Chris backed up again and again as it lunged at him, until he couldn't back up anymore. There was that wall behind him.

Bobby lunged like a rabid pit bull going for the throat and Chris brought his knee up in a purely reflexive response. It was a good reflex. It saved his life. His knee slammed into the thing's jaw and throat and snapped its head backward with an audible crunch. His knee made a new sound too, and sent a shiver of exquisite pain through his leg all the way to his groin. That sharp dagger was followed almost immediately by a deep wave of heat and a boneless feeling that slithered through his entire leg.

Chris fell back against the wall and tried to stop himself from falling over. Bobby practically did a back flip as he fell away from Chris. Katie helped him along the way, her long-fingered hands grabbing a wad of his stringy hair and hauling him backward with all of her strength and weight. Brittany was right there with her, an expression on her face that was almost as alien as the thing she was pulling. Katie let out a low screaming noise, and Brittany was positively growling. Chris had no idea what they were up to, but was absolutely terrified that Bobby's mouth was going to take off one of their arms. He forced himself to stand up and started heading in their direction, his freshly injured leg doing its best to stop him every time he used it.

He never made it to them before it was over. His leg gave out when he tripped on the handle he'd used several times as a weapon. It rolled under his bad leg and that was all she wrote. He fell flat on his back and gasped harshly as the wind was knocked out of him.

And while he was trying to recover his breath in the befouled air of the root cellar, his two companions dragged the struggling, thrashing thing that had been Bobby Johanssen's twin into the burning remains of what had once looked enough like Jerry to throw off even his best friend.

The Bobby thing finally made a noise. It

screeched out a loud, wailing note that damn near shattered Chris's eardrums and slapped both of the girls away from it as the clothlike outer flesh of its body caught ablaze. Brittany was thrown into the table near the ladder, and hit it hard enough to make her brother wince. Katie was knocked into the wall and slid down to the ground with a jarring thud, her face almost comically dazed, but only almost. The blood coming from her swelling lip stopped it from really being worthy of any chuckles.

There was something about the creatures that definitely did not like fire. Maybe it was that they burned at a lower heat than humans, or that the foul-smelling secretions that kept them slick were filled with natural oils that would make a good fuel. Chris had no idea. Whatever the case, the thing's lower half was burning in barely a second, and by the time three heartbeats had passed, it was fully engulfed in tongues of angry fire.

That didn't mean it was dead or done fighting.

The Bobby-thing turned away from Brittany and Katie and bolted toward the stairwell, leaving a trail of burning prints behind it that resembled nothing quite as much as marshmallows that had gone from toasting to flaming confection while sitting over a campfire.

Had he been one hundred percent sane at that moment, or even vaguely rational, Chris would have let him go. But either his body or his mind decided it was time to play mean and slipped past without him being ready. Chris stuck the rake handle out and hooked one of the burning legs just as the thing went past.

The burning figure waved its arms wildly—spitting a few gobbets of smoldering crap through the air in the process—and splatted into the ground. Splatted. Just sort of hit the rough dirt floor and half exploded in a liquid burning lump. Chris looked at it for a second or two and then turned to look at Katie. "Get to the ones I told you about, okay? You two handle them and I'm going to go upstairs and see what the hell is going on."

Brittany looked at him with wide eyes and walked three steps in his direction on legs that didn't seem to want to bend at the knees. "Where the hell are you going?"

"I'm going upstairs, Brit."

"The hell you are! We have to get outta here!"

"No. YOU have to get outta here. Get the ones that can be helped and leave!"

Her face got that look that said she wanted to argue and Chris moved past where she was starting to block his way, almost tumbling when his knee tried to bend in the wrong direction.

"Chris! Quit being an asshole! We have to get out of here now!" Brittany's voice broke as she screamed at him and he looked her way, knowing he shouldn't, not if he really wanted to finish what he had to. She started to cry, her face almost collapsing downward as her mouth pulled into a pout and her eyes started watering. "You can't leave me! You can't fucking leave me, you hear?"

He shook his head and turned away before he

could weaken. He didn't want to leave. He didn't want to go up those stairs, but even with all the noise they'd been making down in the cellar, the chanting had continued upstairs and that just couldn't be a good thing.

Even as he moved toward the burning remains of Bobby Johannssen's imitator, he could hear the sounds coming from the house proper and they chilled him. There was something wrong with those voices, and something much, much worse with the words being called out. He'd seen enough in the last few days, hell, the last few hours, to make him want to curl up and die, but even with all he'd been through, with the thing that was liquefying in front of him, it was the chanting that made the fine hairs on his neck rise.

"Just go, Brittany! I'll meet you outside!" He started to slip past the flaming puddle that was Bobby, and he kept peering over, expecting it to attack at any second. Just because it wasn't moving, just because it wasn't actively attacking him right this instant, that didn't mean it didn't plan to do something. His ability to trust monsters to stay dead was pretty much at an all-time low. The rake handle was in his right hand, and it felt good, already like an old and trusted friend.

It didn't attack him. He kept his eyes on it for the rest of his trip to the stairs. Brittany kept yelling at him but he didn't listen. He didn't dare.

Somewhere up above him in the broken-down house there was a group of—what? Aliens from outer space? Demons? Mutants from under the po-

lar ice caps?—he-didn't-know-whats who were doing something they shouldn't be. He knew they had
to be stopped, but he couldn't have told you why
to save his life.

Chris looked back one last time, his eyes seeking
Brittany and Katie through the rising flames and
smoke. Good ol' Bobby had gone up in flames and
what was left of him seemed determined to spread
into a nasty blaze. Brittany and Katie were on their
knees in front of one of the fake wombs he'd cut
and bled, using the box cutter to carve tendrils from
one of the survivors who still looked fresh enough
to save.

III

Oh, there were so many things Chris would have
rather done than start up those stairs, and not just
because his knee was screaming in protest with
every move he made. The long corridor of narrow
wooden steps was warped and looked ready to collapse, but that wasn't the reason he hesitated either.

It was the voices. They weren't human, had never
been human and he knew that, but to hear them
with one less barrier between him and whatever it
was that made those noises was beyond unsettling.

Still, he'd come this far and he was not done with
what needed doing, even if he wanted to be. One
foot at a time, one stair at a time, he started climbing, listening to the weird chants and hearing—not
surprisingly—the sounds of one of the things up
there howling in pain, screaming out a roar of frus-

tration for what was happening below him in the root cellar, where the person the thing imitated had been cut free from the weird roots meant to trap him. That was reason enough to move up the stairs. Brittany and Katie needed protection from what was about to come down toward him, and he figured he was better than nothing.

Chris looked around as he finally reached the top of the stairwell, his eyes scanning for another weapon, now that he'd given up his box cutter. The closer he got to the chanting, the less reassuring the weight of his rake handle felt. The only thing he saw around him were the walls and the floor, all of which had been in better shape in the past. To his left, through the narrow hallway—did all old houses have such narrow passages?—he could see the living room, still mostly barren, that he'd spotted through the window only two nights earlier. To his right he could see three doorways, two closed and one where the door had been knocked off its hinges, its wood broken in several places. He figured that last one was the door he needed to go through, and as he got closer, he saw that it did indeed lead to the next level of the house.

Chris wised himself up before he could actually enter the darkened stairwell that led to the second story. He stepped to the side, his knee screaming at him all the while, and cocked his wooden handle back like a baseball bat. About ten seconds later the first of the freakazoids from up the stairs came running down, its body already changing into something that had nothing whatsoever to do with human. Chris cocked his arm back a little farther and swung with everything he had, leaning down into the attack on his good knee.

The long wooden handle shattered against the back of the monster's gray, lumpy head. It didn't crack, it didn't break in two, it shattered. The good news was, so did the back of that lumpy head. Where Bobby had been solid and fleshy, and where Jerry had been practically like taffy, this one was hard, with a crablike shell. The wooden stick broke through the back of that exoskeleton and punched a deep hole into the soft gray interior even as it fairly disintegrated in his hands.

The thing turned fast, its head swiveling like a praying mantis's and Chris tried to step backward, only to have the wall get in his way. The thing looked at him with a face right out of his worst nightmares. There were hornlike growths all over the place, pushing through the remains of what looked like human skin. Just as the back of the thing looked like a crab, so too the front. There was a chitinous opening across the lower part of that face, with moving parts that half-resembled a crab viewed from the underbelly. Tiny pincers writhed and clittered over the opening, seeking something warm and meaty to pull inside for devouring. There was a low, protruding brow over that maw, and two perfect rows of glowing spheres burned with an inner light from beneath that spiky shelf on the forehead. Those orbs glared at him; he could actually sense the intensity with which the thing focused on him to the exclusion of everything else.

The sound it made was rather like nails on a chalkboard. One of the arms—it was long and thin and looked, again, like it belonged on a crab—rose from below that face and swatted Chris with a closed lobster claw of a fist. His teeth slammed into the soft inner lining of his mouth and drew blood. As an added bonus, his head slapped back into the plaster covering the rotting walls and cracked the dull, worn finish.

He didn't see black spots this time. He saw constellations. Something warm trickled down the back of his neck, and Chris dropped like a rag doll. He might have died right then and there if it hadn't been for the other thing that came charging down the stairs to his right.

Chris didn't see it clearly and he was glad of it. The damned thing actually scraped the narrow walls as it moved toward the stairwell to the root cellar, apparently not even concerned with whatever might be in the hallway at the moment.

The crab thing met the clawed freight train passing through on its trek and fell victim to the sheer brute strength of whatever it was. Both of them fell over in a tangle of misshapen limbs, caterwauling their outrage as they tumbled. They attacked each other with a savagery that seemed almost impossible. Chris left them alone, pushing himself off the ground and shaking his head in an effort to stop his skull from ringing and his eyes from seeing the universe from a faraway perspective.

He made it to the stairs and started crawling, his stomach doing slow flip-flops as he ascended. The noise in the hallway was bad, but the sounds that ran down from above him were worse. The vibrations from the chanting made his balls want to pull inside his body and hide away. The sound was audible and sub-audible at the same time, multiple layers of cacophony that sent his nerves into a fever dance and made his bones ache more than they already did.

He thought about his mother's body, rotting and falling apart in the opened grave, thought about the thing he'd seen step on what was left of her mortal form, its heavy foot breaking through her flesh and bone, grinding the remains into a rotted paste. That didn't make the pain go away, but it allowed him to ignore it.

Chris stood up and swallowed dryly at the lump in his throat. His fists balled up again and his face grew positively stormy with anger. His feet didn't walk on the stairs, they slammed down, despite his knee's agonized protests. He looked at the top of the stairs as he moved, his eyes focused on whatever might be waiting for him.

IV

Brittany Corin was not having a good day. She hadn't had a good day in a long, long time, but this one was taking the cake. Bad enough some creepy bastard had mugged her—said fat creep was apparently a cop—bad enough that he'd stolen her mother's necklace, but that was only the tip of the shit mountain she was stuck climbing.

She bit her lower lip, trying to stop the thoughts from coming. She didn't want to think about Bobby or the thing that looked like Bobby, or what they'd done or almost done together. She didn't want to think about the sweet words he'd used on her or the fact that the words were just a way to get his hands on the necklace her mom had almost always worn, the one thing she wanted to keep with her forever as a way to remember her mom. She didn't want to think about a long, long list of things, so she just moved instead. The man they were pulling out of his bubble-thingie was thin and wet and stank to high hell, but he was trying to help them as much as he could, his legs pushing and scrambling as they hauled him toward the ladder. Katie was sweating hard, her face practically dripping, and her gorgeous hair matted to her skull by perspiration. She looked at Brittany and managed a very weak smile as they reached the lowest rung on the ladder.

It took both of them to half push the skinny guy up the wooden rungs. Brittany saw Jerry up there, grabbing the man's arms and pulling for all he was worth. Before she could breathe a sigh of relief, Katie was moving back into the rapidly thickening smoke. She followed, breathing in the heavy air and stifling a cough that desperately wanted to escape.

The floor shifted beneath her. Brittany stopped and looked down at the floor, frowning heavily. The floor couldn't shift; it was dirt. Dirt did not, in her experience, shift when you walked on it. Maybe in California, sure, okay, but not in New England.

She looked down and saw that, in fact, the impossible was happening. Not exactly unusual on this particular day, but still not something she wanted to think about.

She might have thought about it some more, but Katie's voice called out for her and she looked over to where her friend was kneeling, next to the last guy they were supposed to pull out. And you could just go ahead and add that to the list of things not to consider: all the people they were leaving behind. Dead or dying already didn't make it feel any better. They were still people and they deserved better. But she'd looked, damn it all, and she understood why Chris had said to leave them. She didn't think any of them would make it out in one piece even if they did try to get them away from the growing fire. Some of them weren't in one piece anymore anyway.

It took an effort, a real effort, but she managed to get her ass in gear again. She looked at the last one they were saving and groaned. He was bigger than she'd thought. He was easily two hundred twenty-five pounds of bigger than she'd thought. He was also decidedly not conscious. Katie used the box cutter Chris had handed her and sawed quickly at the snake things digging into his skin. They cut pretty fast, but the razor wasn't looking as sharp as it had at the start of this whole thing. Katie cut the last one through and the man blinked his eyes. Brittany reached down and slapped his face lightly a few times. He was sort of handsome in a teacher way, but not really her type. Though why she should be thinking about that at the moment was yet another thing she didn't want to consider.

The man groaned deep in his chest and then coughed a quart or so of the black rotten egg crap from his lungs. The root stems left in his side spit out a thick white substance as he coughed. She managed not to puke. Katie's face said she was thinking about heaving a few biscuits too.

The teacher type was weaker than the last one, but he looked around with wild eyes and saw the fire and managed to stand up. Brittany thanked God for that little favor and started leading him in the right direction.

And then the floor bucked underneath them and all three fell down. Brittany closed her eyes on impact and coughed out what little dirt tried to get into her mouth. The ground was still moving but not as violently as before. With her new up-close and intimate view of the ground, she could see something she hadn't seen before. There were long, even slashes growing in the dirt. The oiled soil beneath them was not, as she'd thought all along, actually earth. It was dirt, to be sure, but under that she could see the edges of wooden boards. It wasn't an earthquake and the ground really did move.

Brittany looked back into the root cellar and grimaced. The fire from the fake Bobby and fake Jerry was getting heavier, growing and spreading like a rampant weed colony. And the allegedly solid ground beneath it—the ground that was well-oiled to make it easier to manage—was catching fire too.

"Katie! We gotta move, girl! The fire's spreading and the floor's gonna give out!"

Katie was already busily helping Mr. Teacher back to his feet. She looked over at Brittany and frowned in concentration. "It's a dirt floor, Brittany. It isn't going anywhere."

Before Brittany could answer, one of the big gray cages exploded. It had been sitting closest to the growing fire and had apparently started boiling from the inside. The thick clotted mass that spilled out had once been human, but now it looked more like egg drop soup left out to rot for a few weeks. Worse still, it was alive. It writhed and tried to scream, vomiting more fluids from its lungs instead.

That was about enough for Katie and for Brittany too. They each grabbed an arm and started pulling the man toward the ladder, faces pale and eyes narrowed. Brittany didn't need to be a mind reader to understand that Katie had reached her limits too. This was too much. It was one thing when they were inside their gray cages, but this? No. No more. It was just too much.

The thing on the ground screamed behind them and Brittany heard a wet flopping sound. It was probably trying to follow them, and that thought sent a chill through her that belied the blazing heat of the burning room.

Mr. Teacher started up the ladder and Katie planted her hands on his ass and practically lifted him up the rest of the way. Once again Jerry was there to catch the guy and pull as best he could.

The man fell out of the way and Katie practically flew up the ladder. She moved fast and she stumbled for about seven steps before she fell to her knees and hands.

Brittany looked back once at the deeply sagging area where the fire was worst and the lumpish thing crawling her way, mewling and groping blindly, before she followed Katie's lead.

She'd been breathing the atmosphere in the root cellar for several minutes and had endured the growing heat, the vile smells and the noxious smoke. The air outside was still cloying, thick with fog, and a heavy gout of smoke rose from below into the nighttime mists. She took in a lungful of fresh air and almost cried at the pleasure it brought her.

Behind and below her, she heard the screams start up. They were agonized, filled with fear and pain and what could only be the sounds of the damned. Through the tears burning at the corners of her eyes, she looked back at the root cellar's broken doors and saw a hand reach out, seeking purchase. She guessed it was a hand, but only because the shape was approximately right. What was left of it looked more like a cottage-cheese sculpture that had been left in the sun for too long, and here and there she could see what she guessed was bone sticking out.

The rest of the thing started pulling itself out of the opening and all she could think of was how much it had to hurt to be that ruined and what sort of effort it took to get that far.

She couldn't bring herself to move over and help it though. Not even a gun pointed at her head would have made her move over and touch that thing.

Still whimpering loudly, whining in agony, it crawled up farther until she could see the top of its head and the exposed part of its brain. The only part of the face she could see clearly was the mouth, which hung open in an endless scream.

Her teeth sank into her lower lip and drew blood, and Brittany stared at the approaching figure, horrified beyond words. She was not afraid of what was under that burnt crust of whatever had been in the pod. She was afraid for it. Male or female, young or old, that poor wretch was climbing away from what could have only been a blessing. Even if it lived, how would it ever be whole again?

Brittany pulled her knees in toward her chest and started crying. She couldn't ever imagine that the thing would want her help and still she wanted to go to it anyway, as repulsive as it was. But she could not make herself do it.

And then the option was taken away from her. The figure reared its head up and let out a shriek that she felt as well as heard before it suddenly vanished back into the tongues of smoke licking at the air. The scream was abruptly cut off a half second later.

Something shifted down in the root cellar and a blast of sparks rose from the opening. Brittany could only look on, her eyes spilling tears she did not feel and blurring her vision. That was all right.

She couldn't think of a thing she wanted to see at that moment.

Somewhere in the house she was looking at without really seeing, her brother was heading upstairs toward God knew what. She wanted to get up and help him, wanted to stop him from seeing things that were even worse than what she'd just experienced. But she couldn't make herself move.

On the ground near her, her brother's best friend, the girl his brother would not admit to wanting, two strangers and her almost boyfriend lay in similar shape.

She wanted to help Chris.

She really did.

But there was nothing left. So instead she cried quietly as the fog gathered closer and thicker and mingled with the foul smoke from the root cellar.

V

Chris felt the house move underneath him and heard the chanting falter for a moment. He kept walking. The chanting started again. The stairs creaked under his weight and for an instant he worried that he'd be heard, but he should have known better. The damned voices were just too loud.

He finished climbing and looked into the single room left to see. There had been more than one room once upon a time, he could tell that just by the jagged remains of the walls that someone had torn down to make the space bigger. Different-colored wallpaper adorned various parts of the walls, some with flowery patterns and some in simple pastels. The room was well lit, but not by any modern conveniences. Oil lamps and candles were scattered all around in a sort of chaos that almost made a pattern. The smoke from the lanterns was cloyingly sweet.

Several figures were gathered together in the center of the massive room. They stood facing the very center of their group, where none other than Detective Crawford stood, holding a handful of chains that in turn led to a collection of coinlike medallions. One of those medallions had belonged to his mother. He'd seen her wear it for as long as he could remember, and though she'd never spoken of it, he knew it had meant a lot to her.

He meant to have it back, even if he had to kill every one of the things in the room with him. But that would take a little thought, and while he didn't think he had a lot of time for looking around, he guessed he could spare a minute or so. None of the group hanging with Crawford was paying him the least bit of attention.

Were there weapons to be found? No. No, that would have made it too easy. Couldn't have that. His eyes sought out everything in the room before finally settling on the group. He saw several small things, little bits and pieces of debris left from when this had been someone's home and not just an empty house, but none of the things he saw was of any real use. There were a few broken pieces that had probably once been a vase, and there were three small, stubby wooden legs that might have had potential if any of them had been more than a few inches long. He might be able to throw one, but the thought that they might actually cause damage never really crossed his mind.

He could use the lanterns, maybe, but he really didn't want to think about it too much. The house was already burning down below and the idea of being caught between fires had absolutely no appeal. As it was he was having doubts about how long the oversized tinderbox they were in would hold up. He should have been running and he knew it, but he still had to take care of that feeling of unfinished business. Maybe he'd finally gone over the edge and was merrily losing his mind. He couldn't say, and really, it didn't matter.

The gathering of freaks was stirring now, shifting from foot to foot like a herd of toddlers waiting for the bathroom. It took a second to realize that not all of the movements came from their legs. There were ripples moving under the skin of some of them. It wasn't a comforting thing to notice.

The only good thing he had going for him was that they just couldn't bring themselves to look away from Crawford. The heavyset man was calling out in a deep voice, leading the rest of them in their chant. His face was drawn in concentration, and his body was trembling too, but not in the same way as the rest of them. His body shook with effort, as if holding a handful of necklaces was almost too much strain for him to bear.

As Chris watched, the medallions swung back and forth, the chains and leather ties holding them swinging as if they were caught in a small cyclone. The floorboards below the group creaked dangerously, and light from the lanterns and candles placed around the room glittered off the flashing coins.

He couldn't decide what to do. Part of him wanted to rush Crawford and knock him on his ass. Part of him wanted to reach for the freak nearest him—the very one who had started the whole mess in the house—and just start swinging. The chanting had become a part of the atmosphere, a part that sent almost constant shivers through his body. Part of him responded to those shivers and wanted nothing so much as to run like hell away from the house and trust the fire to finish everything.

And part of him just wanted to get his mother's necklace. There was nothing rational in the desire, but it was very, very real. They didn't deserve it. They didn't have the right to it. And really, in the long and short of it, that was what all of this came down to for Chris. They weren't worthy of touching anything that was important to his mother or his memories of her.

Chris took a step forward, his mind still chaotic, but his emotions giving him a little more focus. Whatever else, he had to get the medallion back. He was going to take their Western Key and he was going to leave.

He'd made his second step before the groaning vibrations from below increased and the floor shifted again. Oh yes, the place was going to come down. He knew that as sure as he knew his knee was almost useless and his shoulder was still burning and twanging from the gunshot. He moved a few more steps toward the group while they faltered in their chanting again.

When they got back into their rhythm, Chris felt the change in the already sullen air. Something happened, something changed, and he felt it like a bubble of cold emanating from the collection of medallions in Crawford's hand. Only it was a bubble of cold that had substance. He felt it pushing against him, like a thin but hard layer of plastic wrap. He leaned into it, pushing against that odd pressure, and felt it finally break around him, only to close behind him as it continued to expand.

The medallions stopped their frantic motions and fell still within the pressure zone. The chanting continued, but it seemed that each syllable stretched and distorted as it drifted lazily through the air in his direction. He was having trouble breathing, and the air was almost blissfully cold. It soothed across his burned hands and lifted his sweat-dampened hair from his scalp.

The medallions glimmered, a flashing light that danced around the edges of the crude coins and seemed to almost glow within the gems that adorned each of them. As he watched, as the gathered group let out a soft, collective sigh that sounded almost like lovers breaking a perfect kiss, the glow that touched the keys so desperately sought by the gathered creatures—for surely they were none of them human—began to grow. It took only a second, he was sure of that, but that single moment in time seemed to stretch itself. The shimmer from the necklaces danced and twinkled and darted between the ornaments, like the universe's smallest lightning bolts arcing through coin-shaped clouds. The dazzling pyrotechnics expanded, moving faster and faster until the separate little flashes became a constant line of blazing light that seemed to draw the necklaces together into one larger piece.

Then the thunder that almost always followed lightning made itself known. The noise was deafening: a cataclysmic explosion of sound that damn near shattered his eardrums. Chris staggered back, his eyes wide, and felt that strange pressure around him change again, growing in intensity as the air seemed to freeze.

He screamed, but the sound was lost in the roar around him. He felt the scream though, and saw it too, as a cloud of warm breath in the suddenly frigid air.

The lightning blasts continued, moving from the collection of small discs in Crawford's hand to the air almost completely across the room. The streaks of energy whipsawed through the distance and spread out like a fan of flame, cutting the atmosphere and freezing the glass in the windows.

Crawford's face stretched wide in a grin that wasn't completely human-looking. His mouth was impossibly large and his teeth, bared as if he were ready to attack, were shaped more like pickets in a fence than like anything that should have been set in his gums. His eyes seemed to have an inner glow that matched perfectly with the chain-lightning thrashing from the necklaces, and Chris wondered if it was merely reflected energies or something that was actually coursing through the detective's body.

All around the leader of the group, the others writhed in what looked like the throes of passion, minus any partners. Each individual bucked and shook, practically doing a jitterbug, for God's sake. That would have been weird enough, but all of them were changing at the same time. Each body was shifting, the limbs growing or thickening or pulling back into the main body or in one case splitting into multiple limbs, but even through the intense glare from Crawford's pyrotechnics, Chris could see that the changes were not voluntary. Despite the outer appearance of wild, frenzied dancing, the creatures in the room seemed more like they were having epileptic fits. Faces stretched and bloated and bodies warped and heaved as the roaring sound grew still louder.

The air seemed to grow murky as he looked at the dancing freak squad, but he realized a few seconds later that it was only in one part of the room: the place where the lightning kept hitting the air and moving in an arc. The lightning seemed to just stop in midair, forming an almost perfect circle of electrical tongues before it cut off. That was a little weird, but not as disturbing for him as most of the shit he'd seen in the last few hours. What bothered him most was that the area inside that circular shape seemed to be the source of the murkiness he'd spotted. There was a dark, almost black mist spilling from the circle, like sand from a broken hourglass and it was slowly building in pressure until it seemed more like steam than a slight fog.

Even as he looked at the thickening gout of mists, trying not to think about the pain in his ears from the noise or the sudden pressure changes in the air, the heavy column of vapor exploded outward with enough force to knock him back against the wall. The strangers in the room were also knocked around, blown through the air like leaves before a hurricane; all save Crawford, who stood in the same position, untouched by the ripping, freezing winds.

Chris started to get to his feet, struggling against the continuing arctic blast that came from whatever was breathing out the now-continuous cloud of frosty air. The arcing electrical storm coming from Crawford's grasp continued, and he was forced to look away from the nearly blinding light.

He'd almost managed his feet when his damned knee told him to fuck off. There was a hot, screaming streak of pain and he dropped down on his good knee and both hands. So far, his mission to stop the bad guys wasn't exactly working out.

On either side of him cultists rose from where they'd been casually tossed, and he grunted to himself as he pushed up on his one good leg, waving his arms frantically to maintain his balance. The massive room was growing darker as the atmosphere that spilled into the room thickened with whatever foul mixture came through the circle hanging in the middle of the air. He wasn't worried about the people around him. They were all too busy looking at the light show. And even as he thought about the fact that he was surrounded by the very beings who'd made his life a personal hell ever since his mother had died, he felt his own eyes drawn back to the circle the lightning cut in the air.

And saw what was moving behind the venting clouds of black frost.

And felt his blood freeze and his heart stutter when he realized it was looking back.

It was only a glimpse, but it was enough. Chris wasn't a scientist by any stretch of the imagination, but he had seen his share of cheesy movies and amusing science-fiction shows, enough to be able to hazard a guess about what was happening. He finally understood what the Western Key and the other medallions opened: a rip in reality. Not a very large one, to be sure, but large enough.

Looking into the center of the flashing corona of raw power spilling from the coins was like looking through a portal cut into the world. Outside that portal was the real world, the safe, sane reality that had just lately been driving him crazy. The air at the center of the hole was glazed, as if a thin but solid layer of some slick translucent, shimmering substance—a membrane—stood to keep the realities from meeting fully. Like a sieve, it allowed gases through into the world, but—he hoped—stopped anything else from passing. Looking into the center of the rip was more like staring into a madman's worst nightmares. And then having those nightmares stare right back.

It was an eye. He was pretty sure of that, though it looked nothing at all like an eye should look. Oh, to be sure, it had shape and color and he could even see what he guessed was an iris, but it still didn't look at all right. There was an eyelid. He could definitely see that, the folds of flesh surrounding the thing he was looking at. Either the image he saw was magnified heavily or he could easily stand in the wrinkles surrounding that orb. What he guessed was the iris of the thing was mottled with dark shades of gray and green, flecked with fragments of a deep red and even finer shreds of silver. And running through this vast expanse of colors were what seemed like hundreds of black spots of varying sizes and shapes. They were what convinced him that the abstract thing before him was an eye. Because the black pools—which seemed to actually be under the iris—changed shapes and sizes easily. They changed when they looked at him, as if tightening their size to better focus on him.

He saw it looking and he felt it too, a strange deep revulsion washing over him from that bloated staring thing. It was disgusted by his appearance, as if he were the monster, not the other way around.

The lightning stopped jumping from the Western Key and what he assumed had to be the Eastern, Northern, Southern and several other points on the compass. Oh, they still flashed with glimmers of their own light, but it no longer arced through the air to where that giant obscenity was looking at

Chris. The circular rip in the air didn't go away with the lightning.

Chris looked over at Detective Crawford, forcing himself to stop, for the love of God, looking at the eye that was looking at him. He felt that wave of *wrongness* coming from the eye and knew it was directed at him. Worse still, he felt the way it wanted to respond, to smash him into the ground like an obscene bug. He had to look away, mostly because that thick bitter emotion was starting to make him see himself the way whatever that eye belonged to was seeing him. He could feel the alien presence actually distorting his mind, intentionally or not, the longer he looked at it.

So he turned his attention to Crawford, and let himself think about everything the man had done to him.

Rage can be a powerful tool. Chris let it take over again, let it devour his fear and the pain in his knee and the thousand other aches in his body that seemed to have settled in for the long haul. He let it shut down the parts of his mind that worried about Brittany and Jerry and Katie and what had happened to his mother, and dwelled instead on Crawford.

Adrenaline kicked into overtaxed muscles and filled them with renewed energy. His hands clenched and relaxed, clenched and relaxed even as his heart rate increased and his vision went decidedly red.

The stocky detective was far too busy concentrating on what he held in his hand to give Chris any real consideration. All around him the things that had looked human when Chris entered were doing their best to make themselves look human again. Some of them were succeeding, but more than a few seemed to be having the same problems that Jerry's doppelganger had run across earlier. Chris wondered if the fire had gotten much worse in the root cellar.

Then he shunted the thoughts off to the side and charged at Crawford, head lowered like a bull on the run, arms reaching for the necklaces held in the man's grip. He was charged up and filled with anger, ready to take on the world.

What a pity his knee didn't feel the same way. Chris made four steps before he felt his leg buckle amid a brilliant lance of pain that stole all of his thunder. His hands lunged for the medallions and he felt his fingers hook into several of the cords and chains they dangled from. Two chains snapped and spilled their prizes across the floor. Four others held and were pulled down in Chris's grasp. A few more stayed in Crawford's hand.

Chris hit the ground like a sack of bricks, his teeth clacking together with his tongue as a buffer. One more pain to add to a growing list of injuries. Detective Walter Crawford's evil twin looked down at him with a stunned expression on his face.

Chris rolled sideways as the man reached for him, pulling the necklaces in his grip along for the ride.

And decided a second later that he might have made a mistake. The circular tear in the world in front of him shifted, stretching and bucking, and the edges of the hole tore wider, allowing him to see more of the thing on the other side. Crawford was screaming something but he couldn't hear it. The sound of thunder he'd heard before was doubled, and the chill in the air became a full-scale attack. The air shrieked as if it were being murdered, and the windows in the room shivered. Chris thought for sure his ears would rupture; even his eyes felt like some invisible monster was pushing them into their sockets with brutal thumbs. The wall facing the street made a loud groaning noise and then collapsed outward in a shower of dust and rotted wood.

And something started reaching through that opening into the cold depths. Something bigger than he'd ever imagined any living thing could be.

VI

Brittany drifted for a while, letting herself fantasize about a nice, safe world where her mother was still alive, where her father—a man she had never even met—was a part of her life, where Bobby Johanssen was not a living skeleton with deep wounds in his side and where monsters were not a part of reality. It was a nice place to visit.

She wished she could stay.

She might have, too, if not for the explosion that blew all the windows out of the top level of the house she was sitting next to. One second she was dreaming about Bobby's lips kissing her own and the next she was blinking herself back to reality as the house let out a roar and glass fell from the windows in a rain of crystalline knives.

Brittany pulled herself into a ball and lowered her head, letting out a mumbled prayer as the fractured windows fell down around her and the other people sitting in the yard. One thing she'd noticed early on about the place was that most of the windows were actually gone, replaced by wooden boards, but there were a few exceptions on the third floor and she'd had the misfortune to sit in just the wrong spot.

The shards rained down around her in a brief hailstorm, most of them bouncing off the grass in the yard. One particularly nasty-looking piece sank into the ground only half a foot from where she was doing her best to play ostrich, burying the first four inches of its length into the earth.

She looked at it with wide, watering eyes and noticed that it fairly steamed as it started to warm up. Even from where she was, she could feel the cold coming off the rime-encrusted fragment.

Katie turned to look at the house, her face pale and her eyes blinking rapidly. Jerry was practically in her arms, looking much worse for wear, and he rolled himself over, with some effort, to better see what was happening.

The windows above were vomiting out a sickly glow, which was partially obscured by the unnaturally dark fog that crept down from them, falling from where a few of the boards had been blown away from the openings. Through the clouds and fog that buried the dilapidated neighborhood and the night sky, she could see the mists spilling from the windows, highlighted by that pale green light.

Looking back at the root cellar she saw the smoke was thicker now, black and greasy looking, with an odor that shamed the stuff she'd caught a whiff of earlier. The groaning sounds coming from below didn't make her feel any better. That floor was probably already a massive cinder, assuming it hadn't collapsed.

She heard her brother's screams coming through ruined windows, falling with the mists that caught the funky light, and felt her heart stutter a few times. That pretty much blew any chance of drifting back into her fantasies straight to hell. Brittany made herself stand up and started for the house again, aiming for the front door this time.

Katie staggered after her, calling her name desperately.

Brittany wanted to ignore her, but couldn't. Katie had done so much for her lately, and the girl sounded like she'd die if Brittany didn't stop. She turned, ready to defend the need to go to Chris, and saw Katie in motion, already leaving the ground like a defensive lineman in the NFL ready to bring down a quarterback.

"Katie? What—?" That was as far as she got before the older girl slammed into her, knocking her backward across the lawn. Brittany hit hard, her butt sliding across the grass and glass, getting stained by one and nicked by the other.

Katie was all over her, her arms and legs spreading out like a blanket, and for half a second her mind flashed to whether or not Jerry's girlfriend had suddenly gone lesbian on her. Katie's face was practically in her tits, for chrissakes!

Then she looked past the girl dog-piling on top of her and saw the wooden slab that would have planted itself in her chest if Katie hadn't sent her sprawling. It wasn't a sudden fit of lesbian touchy-feely, but a need to keep Brittany from being a cocktail weenie stabbed through with the world's largest toothpick that had made Katie go rabid. The thick wooden spear shattered into the lawn, breaking into smaller pieces still big enough to be deadly.

"Shit!" Brittany barely even realized she'd spoken. Her eyes were on the ruined section of wall now spread over a good portion of the lawn. That it wasn't spread over her was something of a miracle, and a fact that could be attributed only to Katie's quick thinking. Brittany's heart did a few erratic beats before it finally just went into overdrive.

She remembered her brother's scream and looked up just in time to see a flash of light that turned the world a stark white. Her pupils contracted down to roughly the size of pinheads, and she let out a scream of her own. When the light vanished the night seemed twice as dark as before, and tinted blue from the retinal echoes left by the brilliance.

Beside her, Katie made noises that told Brittany she'd looked up at the same time. They were both as good as blind.

Maybe that wouldn't have been as much of a

worry if Brittany hadn't heard the sound of the front door being ripped from its hinges. She could see that it was the front door, because she could just make out the rectangular shape of the thing as it was launched through the air, wobbling like a diver pushing for a few extra inches before plunging into the water. The wooden railing on the porch lay like discarded victims of some violent fight, scattered along the lawn. The door's edge clipped a bush and went into a spiral roll, flipping and breaking as it hit the concrete of the sidewalk.

Brittany made a noise, Katie mirrored it, and Jerry moaned softly, barely conscious but aware that something was going wrong. Brittany heard him grunt, maybe even try to stand up, but she couldn't see him well enough to see if he made it.

Then something big moved from where the front door had been, barreling toward her at high speed. Brittany tried to get out of the way, but whatever it was simply moved too fast for her to dodge. She felt things crawling over her arms, pulling her off the ground with ease, and heard a sound like a garbage disposal with a spoon caught in the blades.

Whatever the thing was, it was trying hard to speak to her, but the words—if they were words, if there was a language being spoken—made no sense. Brittany tried to speak, but the monster's grip only tightened. She was terrified, but also puzzled, because the sounds, the pattern of the sounds the thing made, did not seem angry.

Brittany tried to pull back, and the thing roared with enough force to lift her hair from her shoulders. The deep, moldering stench of cheese gone bad mixed with carrion assaulted her sense of smell, and she quailed at the thought of the mouth on that thing closing on her face.

She was pulled closer to the cavernous opening filled with fangs and other things best not considered too closely. She wanted to scream, to run, and to lash out at the nightmare until she woke up, but she was incapable of getting her body to obey her.

Somewhere behind her she heard Katie screaming, but the words didn't make any more sense than what was spilling from the freakishly large maw of the scaly, greasy thing pulling her still closer.

The ropy bindings writhing over her flesh constricted, and she finally let loose with a shriek as the mouth loomed close enough to casually chew her flesh from her skull. And when she felt the chilled, rancid breaths washing over her face, she knew she was as good as dead.

Right up until the time the thing spoke again, this time in English. "Listen to me. . . ." Brittany froze. Her mind acknowledged the words only reluctantly, mainly because she simply hadn't expected the thing to speak to her. She nodded and it spoke and she listened.

VII

The air in front of Chris was distorted as something massive tried to force itself through the shimmering rift between worlds. That thin, glazing membrane strained but held, only marginally giving and venting still more of the midnight-dark mists into the world. Every time he thought he couldn't smell something worse he was proved wrong. His stomach seemed to want to actually leap out of him via his mouth and flee the room. He completely understood. Chris's hand was numb and the feeling drew slowly up his arm, creeping toward his elbow in a steady wave.

Crawford looked at him, the detective's face paler than milk and his eyes fairly bulging in his head. "Have you lost your mind, boy? Give me the Keys!"

Both of them turned to look at the distorted opening into some other place as the pressure in the room changed again. Chris's eyes fairly bulged in his head as the column of darkness pushed harder, with a sound like thick rubber being stretched to the breaking point. All around him the almost constantly changing figures—some still remarkably humanoid in basic shape and others so off-kilter it made his head hurt—prostrated themselves before the thing tearing into the world. The only exception was Crawford, who screamed in a voice that had no chance of matching the sounds coming from the air in front of them.

Crawford lunged to get his medallions back, and Chris rolled out of the way, hooking the bigger man's ankle with his foot and kicking hard. Crawford was not prepared for resistance and promptly fell to the ground, his balding head striking with enough force to actually crack the wood of the floor beneath him. The detective's hands spasmed and he dropped the last of the necklaces on the ground.

Chris lunged, his fingers hooking the hardwood floor and his fingertips catching what seemed like every splinter the entire house had to offer. His fingers caught the two medallions with broken chains and also snagged the last of the ones Crawford had been carrying a moment before.

The rift in the middle of the room shifted, resuming its original circular shape and allowing the pressure buildup to calm a bit. But only for a moment. Then the thing trying to gain access through the hole started pushing again, fighting against an unseen membrane.

Crawford was up and attacking before Chris could celebrate his minor victory. The man's thick fingers hooked into claws and even as they reached for Chris the nails changed, becoming harder and longer and much, much sharper. Those changing talons caught hold of Chris's right arm and sank deep into flesh, punching through skin with ease.

Chris screamed, swinging his left arm around behind him and letting his elbow speak for him. The edge of his elbow smashed against the side of the detective's head, sending exquisite shivers through the nerve ganglions in his arm. He felt his funny bone flare with internal heat and then go into that oddly ticklish pain that earned that nerve cluster its name. Crawford's whole head swiveled with the impact and he grunted again, but his hands never lost their grip. The man's bulk pushed against Chris, shoving him to the ground while claws cut into muscle and drew blood and screams.

Chris kicked again, his foot scraping across the

man's chest, the heel of his tennis shoe doing its best to push through the stocky detective's body. The kick was hardly perfect, but it did the job, sending the rapidly changing older man stumbling backward again.

Chris scrambled on one open hand, one closed fist and his good right knee, trying to get as far from Crawford as he could. The freezing medallions clinked across the floor in his grasp, their cords and chains knocking together and tangling into one uneven lump.

The air in the room shifted in waves, forcing him farther from the rip and the behemoth still straining to break through somehow. The problem was, as far as he was pushed, the wobbling cut managed to keep pace. And the darkness trying to get through was stretching farther and farther through the rent in space, amid a growing roar of changing pressures.

Chris gained a few inches on Crawford, whose hands seemed determined to find just the right shape to make him into shredded wheat. The detective's appendages had fused together, forming scythelike hooks that cut through the distance between them with deadly intent. The flesh above those weapons was changing too, thickening and growing wicked-looking barbs, which were almost certainly as lethal-looking as the cold, black tips of the hooked hands.

After all he'd already been through, the sight of the weapons blossoming into existence was still enough to freak him out. Forget that the wicked blades were meant to cut him into shreds; the fact that the things formed at all was enough to screw with his sense of reality.

Crawford flung his arms wide, as if to embrace Chris, and Chris reacted in the only way he could: he crawled as fast as his knee would allow.

"I wanted to make it peaceful for you! Quick and painless! You've suffered enough. Give me the Keys and you can still have your life back!" Crawford's voice was deeper than normal, and even carried over the shrieking winds blowing through the doorway opened by the Keys. His voice sounded sincere enough, but the angry expression on his face and the strange new formations his arms were taking reduced Chris's ability to trust him.

"Fuck off!" Crawford glowered. "No offense."

Crawford took offense anyway. He spit to the side and rose up to his full height, which was normally substantial, but even worse from Chris's current position. The detective held out his arms before him, almost like a magician showing that he had nothing up his sleeves. The fabric from the long white dress shirt had merged into the deadly-looking scythes where his hands had been, and Chris was pretty sure that, in fact, the detective had nothing up his sleeves. Then the man's arms ripped, from the blade where fingers should have been to the shoulders, a long line that started at the tip of the middle finger and ran smoothly up the center of each arm as if he were being cut by an invisible saw. There was no blood from the sudden wounds. In fact each long half arm instantly started rounding out and growing thicker. Just to make the whole experience a little more uncomfortable, the man's torso, already heavy, grew wider to accommodate the new limbs. And that was exactly what they were, two new arms to match the old ones, thickening with ease.

And when the four arms were all the size of the ones that had been there before—complete with wickedly hooked blades of bone—the Crawford monster swung the four arms back until they almost touched behind his body, and shot them in arcs toward Chris's face.

Chris dropped to the ground, feeling the air above him sliced into bits while he slithered backward, kicking the floor with his good leg and moving away from the four massive claws. The second strike was closer, and left gouges in the aged wood of the floorboards.

The third strike clipped his head a grazing blow, and Chris hissed at the sharp pain that ran from just above his left ear all the way to his temple. He twitched, and one of the medallions fell from his grasp, the narrow links of the chain sliding smoothly away from the rest. The necklace bounced twice as it struck the floor, and rolled to a spot a few feet away. Crawford fairly leaped at the thing, and Chris lifted his right leg high into the air, then brought it down on the coin-and-jewel design with all of his might.

The medallion shattered. The gold filigreed coin cracked as easily as if it were made of porcelain and then broke into smaller pieces with a brilliant silvery flash that sent aching vibrations through Chris's leg up to his knee. Crawford let out a wailing shriek that cut across Chris's ears like a razor, sending needles of pain deep into his skull, and then the detective went into a frenzy, his body fairly exploding out of its almost human formation, expanding and uncoiling like a hundred snakes from a gag can of peanuts. The writhing pseudopods stayed connected to a central mass that looked rather like an oversized brain being devoured by maggots.

All around the room the chaotically shifting things that had been masquerading as humans followed suit. One of them stood up and left behind a thick layer of skin and clothing, like an insect discarding a dried-out exoskeleton, but in this case dark gray, filthy fluids spilled from the carved-out shell. What rose from that wet husk was surely the stuff of nightmares. It resembled nothing so much as a humanoid shape formed from moldy cottage cheese. There were thick splatters of white that fell from it in an almost constant rain, and heavy ropes of some mucuslike substance that drizzled down as well. The thing's torso blossomed open into a cavernous wound that immediately erupted with unfolding insect legs as thick as Chris's forearm. The entire creature fairly launched itself at the roof, and managed to turn the upper part of its body so that the skittering legs could grab on to the ceiling with ease.

Another of the things—he was pretty sure he remembered the human counterpart from the root cellar on this one, which only made matters worse—opened its human mouth wide, the face stretching impossibly until it ripped across the lower half and disgorged what looked like a constant stream of intestines. The white, ropy things fountained away from the torn head, spilling across the floor and coalescing into a small jungle of blind serpent things with mouths that snapped the air around them. Each mouth was filled with spidery fingers that clutched and scraped, seeking only something to shovel into them.

There were more nightmares around him, each and every one of them giving up any pretense of being human and roaring, shrieking or gibbering madly. Each and every one of them looked at the shattered fragments of the medallion on the ground. While he couldn't exactly read the expressions of those that actually had faces, he could pretty much figure they weren't exactly thrilled with him.

Chris stopped looking at the shape-shifting freak show and concentrated on the task of staying alive. His heart was beating too fast by far and his hand where he clutched the remaining medallions felt like it was as brittle as the necklace he'd broken.

He found it easier to ignore them when the thing floating in the air shifted suddenly, the edges warping and wavering, then lighting up with a spray of pyrotechnics that dazzled his eyes. The light show tripled in intensity as something far larger than the rift tried again to push through. Chris hobbled back away from it in fear, but to no avail. The damned thing followed him.

The only way to get rid of the fucking thing is to give up the necklaces, and I ain't gonna do it! That fucker Crawford can kiss my ass!

Crawford seemed to have other ideas, like chopping his ass into hamburger. The thing that had been Crawford came at him again, the multiple writhing limbs whipping through the air and snaking toward Chris's right hand. Chris slapped at the first of the things with his left hand and regretted it almost instantly. The tentacle was as thick as his wrist and powerful enough to stop his swing on contact.

The Crawford thing easily hauled him into the air and pulled him toward it with a deep grinding roar that shook the fillings in Chris's teeth. Several more of the fleshy gray limbs reached for him, grabbing at his legs and his right arm. Chris let out a yelp when one wrapped around his left knee and tightened like a noose.

The medallions flashed in his right hand, swinging wildly in a half circle, and the tear in the universe responded, wavering madly in the air. Then it buckled briefly, a blast of energy ripped across the distance from the medallions to the opening, and Chris felt his arm catch fire as the energy ran through the necklaces and into his body. Every muscle in his body seemed to convulse at the same time. His legs stiffened and his arms went rigid, his back arched as if he were preparing to dive, and the Keys vibrated, danced and shimmered in his clutching hand.

Chris felt the energy moving through him, coursing through muscles and almost freezing the blood in his veins. His eyes went blind from the insane glare and then saw only a deep nauseating green as the wave of power hit his optic nerves.

He felt like he was plugged into a generator and frying in the electrical current, but he also felt like he was being submerged in deep, cold waters at the same time. He forgot all about the crushing force of the tentacles wrapping around his body, forgot all about every inconsequential little pain he was experiencing, because the new agonies made them trivial at best. Chris knew he screamed, but even the raw tearing in his throat felt like nothing in comparison to the supernova exploding inside every cell of his being.

The medallions cast out even more energy, blasting the air around him in an almost constant barrage. The tentacles that held him were instantly incinerated and the Crawford thing wailed in pain, withdrawing and letting him fall to the ground. Chris landed awkwardly, his legs akimbo and his right arm pinned underneath him, but he never knew it. He was too busy being tortured on every imaginable level.

The images came quickly, frozen moments of his life moving through his mind far faster than he could easily sort them out.

Flash: his mother holding him in her arms, her beautiful face the whole of his world, his body small and weak and barely able to move at his direction. There is a man looking down at him, but the man means nothing. It is his mother who holds his attention. The look on her face is pure and simple, undiluted love.

Flash: He's in the living room, the old familiar sofa is newer, less battered than he recalls ever seeing it and there are people in the room with him. His mother, a giantess, is stroking his hair, her belly swollen with the new brother or sister he is supposed to have soon. He doesn't really want a sibling, but it seems important to his mother, so he has decided not to say anything bad about it. The people all seem familiar, but he can barely place them. The man he saw before is back, even taller than the other giants and smiling at him, reaching down with one massive hand to ruffle his hair. He hates having his hair messed up, but it always makes the man smile. The man has a name—Daddy—but he is almost never around. Still, Mommy is happiest when Daddy is there, so he allows the hand to muss his fine baby hair. Mommy must always be happy, not like when she talks on the phone to the woman she says is *her* mommy. And that is a strange concept, mommies having mommies. He looks to his mother's round, full stomach and wonders if what is in there will be a mommy someday.

Flash: He now understands what a little sister is. It's a red-faced thing that screams and makes demands of Mommy's time. Mommy is always so tired these days and Daddy is gone. He hasn't come back for a long time. The thing called Brittany is screaming again, the tiny mouth open and drooling as it wails and calls endlessly for Mommy. Mommy is on the couch, sleeping, or crying again. He doesn't know which, he just wishes that Brittany would—

WHAT?

Flash: Mrs. Darby is watching over him and Brittany. She's a pleasant woman who seems to always need to talk. Her son, Bryce, is a pudgy, dirty kid who always scowls. Yesterday Chris tried to talk to him and Bryce pushed him to the ground. And now, Bryce is looking at him with a mean face and heading his way. What did he do to Bryce to make him so—

WHAT THE?

Flash: Krista Markovich from down the street keeps making weird faces at him and every time she does, he gets a falling feeling in his stomach. Jerry says she likes him and wants to kiss him. But that doesn't make sense. She never talks to him and normally runs away when he tries to be friendly.

Flash: Brittany comes home in tears. Bryce Darby called her a name. Chris doesn't know what a "cunt" is, but if it was Bryce saying it, it can't be good. Just as early as last year, he'd have just told Mrs. Darby and she would have handled it, but these days she isn't very happy. These days she has taken to drinking a lot of her meals—and he doesn't really know what THAT means either, but his mom keeps saying it—and she's been less friendly than she used to be. That means he'll have to handle it himself, because no one picks on Brittany, unless it's him and that's his right as her older brother.

WHAT THE HELL?

Flash: Courtney's house is normally off-limits, but right now her parents are out of town and Mom is working the graveyard shift again and Brittany is staying at her friend Nikki's place. So he and Courtney are on her bed and most of their clothes are on the floor. God! She always smells so good and the way she kisses is definitely making his little soldier stand at attention. He touches her breast through the thin bra she is wearing, marveling at how soft and warm it feels in his hand. Her tongue tastes like cinnamon and she's pushing it softly into his mouth and her hand is going down lower, scratching her nails across his belly and lower still, pushing past the band of his boxer shorts—*thank you GOD for reminding me to wear a good pair*—and her fingers are searching for and finding his—

WHAT THE HELL ARE?

Flash: There's a part of him that aches at the idea of losing Courtney, that looks at her short blond hair and remembers the feel of it in his fingers while she was doing things to him. That part is growing smaller every day. It hurts that she dumped him and it hurts worse that she wants to be friends, but she's tight with Katie and Katie is far beyond merely tight with Jerry and Jerry is his best friend and why the hell did Courtney have to start shopping around on him? Why couldn't she just—

WHAT THE HELL ARE YOU?

Flash: He doesn't love Katie. He tells himself that every day. It isn't love, just a seriously powerful desire to get into her pants. It would be easier to ignore if she wasn't around every day. It would be MUCH easier to ignore if she wasn't so damned hot. When did she become so attractive? Oh, she'd always been nice to look at, but these days when she smiled at him, he wanted that smile to last forever. It's late at night and everyone is asleep. Jerry and Katie left more than an hour ago. He can't help thinking about her as his hand imitates what Courtney's did to him that first time they ever—

WHAT THE HELL ARE YOU DOING?

Flash: Brittany and Mom are fighting again. Sometimes he wishes he could just shake Brittany until she got some damned sense in her head. She could be so sweet sometimes, like when she cleaned the living room last week and it was his turn, and then she could be such a complete raging bitch the next minute.

WHAT THE HELL ARE YOU DOING IN?

Flash: Brittany is having a sleepover, which is decidedly uncool. The last thing he needed is an army of fourteen-year-old girls stampeding through the house. Especially when most of them tend to come on like they were God's gift to men. They might think it's fun flirting with him, but he can do without it. He can do without it even more when most of them are in nighties. Fourteen is too damned young and even thinking about them sexually is wrong, but he hasn't been with anyone in a while and his body doesn't much give a damn about his morals. Just to add to the fun, his mom thinks the whole thing amusing. He can tell by the smirk on her face.

WHAT THE HELL ARE YOU DOING IN MY?

Flash: Two days to his birthday and everything is looking like gold. He doesn't know how far he can get in Europe on seventeen hundred dollars, but he figures if he takes it easy and skips out on everything but youth hostels as places to go, he can get a good way. High school is over and it's almost time to go to college, but he still doesn't have a clue about what he's going to do with his life. Does everyone feel that way? Jerry seems to know what he's doing and almost no one has more common sense than Katie. He looks at his bags—an old Army surplus duffel bag and a carry-on shaving kit that he will probably never use. They'll do the job well enough. One last chance, one last chance to have fun and be a kid before he has to start getting serious about everything. His mom is always fretting about the bills, and maybe he can come back and do something to help out more, even if she keeps saying she can handle it.

WHAT THE HELL ARE YOU DOING IN MY HEAD?

The images kept coming, snapshots from his life that an alien thing was looking over as casually as he'd flip through a magazine. He tried to fight it, to pull back his personal thoughts and feelings and dirty little secrets, but whatever the hell was on the other side of that rift was too damned powerful. He might as well have tried to drink the ocean down in one gulp for all the success he was having.

That massive force peered down at him from where it hid and peeled back layers of his memories, exposing them and sullying them. Chris struggled, snarled and lashed out, wanting nothing more than to be out of this place, away from this desecration. And the more he fought, the more completely he was ensnared. He sought, finally, to look back at what was studying him, to understand what it was that was trying to enter this world.

And that, boys and girls, was a mistake.

The images came in a flood of biblical proportions, a collage of alien thoughts and memories that was far too much for him to absorb.

There was the Void, a vast darkness that dwarfed even the notion of anything else in the universe.

And then there was Light, immense and never before seen, bringing agony to flesh and eyes that had never known anything but Darkness. The Light was a hateful thing: alive and uncaring of the pain it brought.

The thing escaped from the searing pain of the Light and drove deep into the waters and the cool, soothing Darkness the waters offered as solace. Time passed, untold fathoms of time. Eventually the waters vanished, swallowed by lands that had never been there before and while the Light was still there, it was not as painful as before. The light had become tolerable and even pleasant in a vague way.

The thing stayed where it was, unmoving, uncaring until it was buried beneath ages of sediment and a world grew around it. There was life, though none like Chris had ever seen before, and there was change in the very shape of the world. There were dimensions and textures that were almost as alien as the eye he'd seen and the very intelligence he looked into as it in turn looked into him. Mountains of crystal and oceans of thick black bodies that writhed and receded like the tides, clouds that rained down something white and hungry. Something vast and shadowy, too large to clearly be defined, blocked out the sun and the stars. He tried his best to understand the memories he experienced.

A microbe looking up into the face of a scientist and trying to read the thoughts there would have had better luck. The images that assaulted him meant nothing, but sent shivers of terror through his body. In a place and time that meant nothing and whose images made his brain ache, he saw a world of shapes that should not have existed moving in vast droves, moving into the darkness of a shadow cast by something impossibly large. He knew the shadow fell from the form he looked through, and that the miniscule creatures were there to worship and adore the thing and knew just as well that it couldn't have cared less about them. If it was a god, it wasn't a very caring one. Beyond indifference, the thing that cast the shadow toyed with the smaller creatures like a malevolent child with fragile playthings. Thousands were crushed for amusement, and equal numbers had far worse fates. If there was rhyme or reason to the violence, he couldn't begin to fathom it.

From time to time, at what seemed random intervals, the shadow caster shifted its mind away from where it was and sought out other places, other worlds to toy with and despoil. When that grew tiresome, the thing sought out other realities and found them with ease. Still, the places found could not be maintained. It was always drawn away, pulled back to the place where its shadow fell. A growing resentment festered in the thing, blossoming into something darker still.

The sun on the planet grew old, and still the endless tortures and endless attempts to leave continued until there was almost nothing left to amuse the thing. It sought new sources of . . . what? Entertainment? There was more to what the thing did, what it was doing and had been doing for what appeared to be an eternity or two, but he couldn't figure out what. He could see actions but not see the consequences or the reason for those actions.

And while he tried to understand the thing that was tearing through his memories, it continued its own search through his mind. He remembered hearing that there were no nerves, no pain receptors anywhere in the brain, but he felt pretty damned certain that someone had screwed up on that one. Chris's brain felt like it was on fire. The more he fought the more it seemed to burn and sizzle within his skull. He gave up trying to see into the mind of whatever had gripped his own thoughts so completely and struggled instead to stop the invasion from happening any longer.

He fought, yes, and he screamed and railed and

battered against the rape of his memories and destruction of his very self. But in the end it stopped on its own, without any assistance from him. It stopped and left Chris to fall on the ground again, his skin feeling stretched and pulled, his head throbbing with pressure and his eyes almost blinded by the aftermath of what he'd been through.

The air stank, ripe with the rotting mushroom stench of the things that surrounded him and the odor of something far worse blowing in on the draft coming through the rip in space. He felt warmth run from his nose and saw the growing stain of the blood spilling from his face and onto the ancient wooden floors. The room had been cold a moment before—at least he thought it was a moment, but it could have just as easily been a hundred years with what he'd seen—and was now growing warmer. No. Not the room. The floor. The fire in the root cellar must have grown larger. Despite the film that seemed to cover his eyes, he could see the first wisps of smoke sliding into the room, pushing in despite the pressure changes.

He could also see the gathering force of nightmares slithering as quietly as they could toward him, seeking to take what he held in his hand and finish what they had started. They wanted to let that *thing* into the world.

"Oh . . . fuck no, you don't . . ." He barely recognized the voice as his own. It was coarse and dry and strained from his screams, each of which he was now feeling in the back of his throat.

He shouldn't have spoken. He realized that as soon as he did it. Because now they knew he was conscious, where before they only suspected. More importantly, the things knew he was aware of them. They moved forward, a tidal wave of obscenities that intended to drown him and take the prize he held captive.

Chris lifted his right hand above his head, his body poised awkwardly with his weight on his bad knee and his left hand, and then brought his fist down as hard as he could on the age-faded floor. The bones in his hand creaked as he struck and caught several of the medallions between his fist and the hard wood.

And once again, he felt the metallic coins with their glistening precious gems against the floor. Once again he felt hard metal breaking as it struck the ground, shattering like fine ceramic under his fist. Fragments of what looked like gold and silver dug into his closed hand as one of the Keys exploded.

The burst of energy that erupted from the broken medallion was much, much stronger than the first one had been and the effects were far more immediate. The first thing that happened was that several of the things recoiled in fear, backing away with a gusto he hadn't thought they possessed.

The second thing that happened was the actual explosion, which knocked him halfway across the room in an instant. The floorboards where he'd been poised collapsed in a rain of wooden flinders and ancient dust. His body was hurled through the air and slammed into the ground almost at his original entrance. He could barely hear any noise save for a powerful ringing, and his lungs refused, just plain refused, to draw in any air. There was something in his eyes, an irritant that made them water and sting, and Chris wanted to wipe at them but his arms didn't much feel like moving either.

The third thing that happened was the roar from whatever it was on the other side of that gateway to the great beyond. He could barely hear, but he could feel the sound come through in waves of vibration heavy enough to set his teeth rattling. If the destruction of the first Key had been effective in getting the attention of the monsters in the room, the second worked for truly making the thing on the other side of that portal pay attention to him. The glowing membrane between realities flashed and flickered like a string of moving lights powered by a generator that was sputtering out.

It looked weaker. It didn't feel weaker at all. The corona flashed and fizzled and flared to life again as it followed the source of its creation: the necklaces Chris still held. The mass that had been pushing to break through a moment ago was gone, but the eye was back, and this time it was truly seeing him instead of just looking in his direction. The endless array of small black pupils dilated, no two of them looking remotely the same, and Chris felt a deep-seated dread fill him.

The ice he felt growing on his hand—not truly visible, but he felt it there, sinking deeper and deeper into his body—spread itself to his mind and

Chris Corin looked on as the thing began to speak to him without words.

It spoke of endless suffering, torments that would go on for eternity and beyond, and the new and interesting tortures it would find to deal with him if he harmed any more of the Keys. The images it vomited into his very mind in order to communicate were vivid enough to leave Chris staggered far more than the explosion had managed. He'd felt soiled and filthy when the entity had looked over his life's memories, but this . . . this was far deeper. There was nothing, no part of the alien mind that spoke to him, that he could consider remotely human. He tried to look away, to close his eyes, but it was no good. The darkness of those pupils seemed to draw him in deeper, to suck his will away and leave him to drown in a cold void.

Chris felt himself sliding into that emptiness and then he knew nothing at all.

Chapter Seven

I

Jerry Murphy woke back into full consciousness slowly, his thoughts seeming to rise from deep within a murky lake like bubbles from a stagnant air pocket. The first thing he became aware of was pain, deep lancing pain the likes of which he'd never felt before. Not even when he broke his leg in three places back in the second grade and they had to cut him open and reset the bones with metal pins drilled into his skeleton.

Even the pain, fresh and brilliant as it was, took a while to penetrate deep enough into his brain for him to notice it. He reflected on the pain as he started reaching for real thoughts, and gradually realized that it wasn't supposed to be there. His ribs felt like they'd been broken with a pickaxe and his torso in general felt like someone was working hot wires down each and every nerve in his chest. Back when he was far too young for his own good, Jerry had suffered a bout of rheumatic fever. He'd spent ten days in the hospital with a temperature that had his brain ready to boil and an almost constant case of the shivers that made his skin crawl. Under the new pain moving through him, he felt that old familiar discomfort, like a barely audible vibration that insisted on being heard, even over the sound of a Metallica concert right in front of the speakers.

The next thing he became aware of was the fog that hid half the world away as he opened his eyes. The fog smelled of rotted vegetation and smoke, and it made his eyes water. Fog wasn't supposed to do that, but apparently no one had explained that to the thick haze in the air.

The sounds came next. Brittany screaming—he'd known Brittany since she was only four years old; he could have recognized her voice in the dark, and this proved it—her voice strained by fear and maybe pain. That was what really started making him alert again. No one got to pick on his little sister without answering to him, even if his little sister wasn't flesh and blood.

"Brit . . . hang on, honey . . . I'm coming." Jerry made himself stand up, and had to make several steps to his left in order to avoid falling right back down. His legs felt like a demented dentist had loaded them down with novocaine, and so, for that matter, did his arms. It was mostly his chest that wanted to catch fire. By the time he'd managed to regain his footing he'd also managed to lose Brittany in the heavy fog. And did it smell more like wood smoke? Yes, he was pretty certain it did.

A second later he heard another scream. This one came from Katie and that, friends and neighbors, was enough to finally bring Jerry back into full awareness. His head snapped in the direction of Katie's agonized yelp and he moved without thinking, ignoring the pain in his sides as adrenaline kicked him into action.

He didn't have far to go to find Katie. He almost stepped on her as she fell out of the fog and landed in the overgrown lawn. Her face was rapidly swelling on one side and her beautiful eyes were half closed and rolled slightly under her lids. He started to lower down to check on her and make certain that she was all right, but Brittany screamed again, a long, loud wail of despair, and Jerry moved toward the sound as fast as he could manage. Katie was alive; he had to tell himself that. Brittany might not be if he didn't get to her soon.

The fog seemed to thin as he moved away from where he'd been. That, or he was adjusting to it. His sides throbbed with each step he took, but he kept going. Behind him a sudden flare of yellow light made him turn for a second, just long enough to realize the building nearby was on fire. It would wait; he had to get to Brittany first.

And just ahead of him he could see her, her thin body held off the ground by what almost looked like a tree composed of maggots. Thin branchlike stems waved around in the air and several of them were holding Brittany off the ground. Even in the nearly complete darkness, he could see the raw fear on her face, and it sent a deeper desperation into him.

Jerry never had any form of training in any form of fighting. Chris had taken boxing courses for a couple of summers and he knew how to deliver a punch. Jerry didn't have a clue about any of that stuff, but he did have a mean temper. Normally that was enough to make a difference. Right now, with the roaring pain in his sides and the numbness damn near everywhere else, he had his doubts.

He lowered his head and charged like a bull, bracing his body for the impact as best he could. Jerry made one major mistake when he struck. He assumed, reasonably enough, that the creature would be limited in its ability to see what was coming from behind.

He realized his error only when the trunk of the thing erupted in a new batch of streaming limbs, each ending in a barbed hook. Seven bonelike blades rammed into his body, piercing his legs, his arms and his right cheek. The thin barbs punched through muscle and flesh with ease and Jerry howled in pain as he was pinned to the ground like a butterfly on corkboard. It was a bit too much for his already stressed system—the world faded out until the fog seemed to take over everything in sight.

Brittany let out another scream, a sound so filled with despair that he thought she must surely be dying. He grabbed the closest skewer and pulled at it, hissing as it moved a fraction of an inch in his face. The thing that had skewered him helped it along by ripping back with that one spur and taking a bit of flesh with it. Jerry heard another scream, high and shrill, and discovered the voice was his own. He could tell by the wet sound of blood spilling into his mouth and then back out through the hole in his cheek.

There are claims that seeing a loved one in peril can lend a person nearly superhuman strength. That may or may not be true, but it will certainly increase adrenaline levels in the average person. Adrenaline is funny stuff. It can boost your heart rate, give a person enough energy to make him feel capable of almost anything and leave that very same person queasy in the extreme, all at the same time.

Jerry wasn't getting much of an adrenaline kick. Brittany, on the other hand, seemed to have enough to spare. She let out another scream, more like a Valkyrie from Norse legends than her more recent cries of fright, and planted both feet in the trunk of the thing that held her. Both Chris and Jerry could have told the monster that Brittany was very hard to hold when she didn't want to be caught anymore. She wiggled her body at speeds that would have shamed most hummingbirds and launched herself away from the thing that had her trapped. The tentacles that held her slipped and the girl he'd long since thought of as his own sister scrambled like a monkey on a hot plate, kicking her legs and pushing with her arms in a near frenzy until she finally managed to break free. She fell to the ground in a low crouch, still weaving and dodging as more of the snaking, rough tentacles tried to grab her again.

Brittany took off at a hard sprint, her eyes making contact with Jerry's for a brief second before she ran out of sight. The tentacle tree roared as she moved out of its range, and started following as fast as it could, which was faster than the prone Jerry could compensate for. Jerry grabbed at the barbs trailing from his left shoulder and right bicep, wincing at the pain, but was not able to do anything for his legs before he was dragged along for the ride. He tried to scream, but there was nothing left in his lungs after he hissed at the exquisite raw-nerve flash that ran through his entire body. The lawn was unkempt and he felt every blade of saw grass that tried to cut him into shreds: a hundred papercut slashes to add to his pain. He managed to hold on to the umbilical lines that dragged him toward the house, but his legs were off the ground and fishhooked to the demon that chased after Brittany. He managed to stay conscious for almost fifteen seconds, which was beginning to feel like a new record to him, before he felt a rock or something just as hard slide up his back and crack into his skull.

After that, there was only darkness.

II

Brittany ran like mad, barely taking the time to look back. Her mind didn't want to think anymore, didn't want to do anything but slide back into itself and the fantasies it created, but she wouldn't let it. She couldn't, not if she wanted to live.

Her head was ringing, pounding deep inside from whatever it was the thing had said to her. She knew it was important, but she couldn't remember. She hadn't really remembered anything at all, hadn't been able to think at all, until Katie got too close and tried to break her out of the grip she'd been held in. Whatever Katie had done to the thing to distract it had worked pretty well; maybe too well, if the shape she'd seen through the fog was her friend. All she could make out was a feminine form in the mists, unmoving.

Jerry on the other hand she could see well enough whenever she had the guts to turn around and look. He was thrashing like a fish on a line and trying to stop some of the nasty-looking tendrils from tearing out his skin. His face was a blurred patch of white in the darkness, his hair absorbed by the night. She had to do something to save him, but so far nothing was coming to mind.

And then she thought about the house and the fire burning in the lowest levels. From what she knew, these things didn't like fire. The idea of getting anywhere near the flames herself wasn't pleasant, but if it was the only option she'd make do.

The fire was spreading, and fast; flames were starting to lick at the edges of the windows on the first floor, and the boards in those windows were already smoldering. The heat, even from thirty feet away, was enough to draw the moisture from her mouth and dry her eyes. Weird sensation, that: a rapidly warming body to counteract the freezing chill that still held her mind.

The entrance to the root cellar was a greedy tongue of flames, and Brittany ran straight toward it, hoping the thing behind her would follow suit. She heard the slapping sounds of it moving across the lawn and the hiss of Jerry being dragged behind. What she did not hear was Jerry making any noises. Her side was starting to feel like someone had taken a hot poker to it, and every breath was beginning to hurt. Brittany didn't know if it was the smoke from the fire or merely that she'd pushed herself too far. Right at the moment she couldn't bring herself to care one way or the other, either. She could worry about how she felt when she got rid of the boogeyman who refused to stay under her bed.

The creature said something, a harsh demanding term in a language that was nothing but gibberish. The words meant nothing, but the tone used for them was obvious. It wanted her to stop and take whatever it felt like dealing out to her.

Her response was just as obvious, though nonverbal. Her middle finger popped up on her left hand and she gestured with it several times as she ran. The thing took it poorly and roared at her.

Brittany allowed herself a very small grin and ran faster. The thing followed, trailing the silent Jerry along in its wake. The cellar's entrance was nothing but flames and every instinct told her to get away from it, but she moved on anyway, pushing her legs to take her even faster, though they hardly wanted to obey. She felt her bangs begin to crisp in the oven heat up ahead and squinted her eyes almost closed as she got to the edge of the fire.

Brittany Corin came as close to flying as she ever had, leaping for all she was worth over the pyre erupting from the cellar. Her hair caught a few licks and she felt a few stray strands burning as her head went through the flames. The fine hairs on her arms caught too, sending sunburn shivers of fever-chill across her arms and torso. For one brief second she thought she would actually combust as the skin on her lips tightened in response to the heat and then the skin on her stomach did the same. One lace on her generic tennis shoes actually did catch fire, but she never even noticed. The small flame extinguished itself when she hit the open door on the other side, splinters punching through the flesh of her left palm and her right forearm before she was on the grass again.

Before she could let herself think about the stinging wooden shards in her arms and hands, or the skinning she managed to give her knee as she turned around, she made her move. Just on the other side of the blazing greedy flames, she saw the maggoty thing coming at her. It had changed shape again, streamlining itself for better speed, and where there had only been tentacles coming from the trunk before, there were now lean, bony arms with wicked-looking hooks at the ends. They made the barbs cutting into Jerry look like pins next to a sword.

The thing leaped toward the fire, planning to follow the shortest path and risk the flames. Brittany slipped her fingers under the open door of the cellar and felt a nail tear down to the quick. She whimpered as she threw her full body weight into lifting the barrier and watched the thing coming closer and closer through the flames. It was worth it, all the pain and the muscles she would later feel pulling, just to see the look of shock on the creature's writhing face as it saw the door rise. It couldn't stop in time. The wooden door was not in the best shape. It had been near ruin before the fire and now the heat from the blaze had weakened it even more. But it was enough. The monster's weight made the door shudder as it impacted and the force with which it hit sent Brittany backward in a wild stumble. She waved her arms wildly and managed to stay on her feet.

The nightmare dragging Jerry wasn't as lucky. With no forward motion to keep it aloft, even for a few more feet, it fell directly into the column of fire, screeching in a high-pitched frenzy as it was dragged down by gravity. Brittany forced herself to move again, pushing the wooden door closed after fighting it back up from where it was falling to the ground. The wood was done for, had already begun to burn, but she used it as a bridge, jumping over the rest of the uncovered flames. She felt the heat again, felt the pain as her skin was blistered by the rising flames, and then she was over and jumping for all she was worth. Not away, but down, landing on the thick cords that were dragging Jerry toward the flames.

Sometimes the best plans don't quite cover every contingency. The idea was simple enough: Catch the monster and use her weight to stop Jerry from following it into the fire. Sadly, Brittany didn't weigh very much. All she managed to do was lose her balance and fall on top of the bloodied, unconscious Jerry. The two of them moved toward the fire, dragged by the monster's struggles and the force of gravity. The thick cables of whatever passed for flesh on the thing coiled and writhed as it struggled to get back out. Brittany managed to get her right leg properly tangled into the foul-smelling pseudopods long before she could have rolled off. Her hands scrabbled for purchase, but could find nothing but grass that quickly tore from the ground. They would have followed the thing down into the burning hellhole if she hadn't managed to catch the wooden lip of the cellar entry's frame with her feet.

The sudden stop was jarring. Brittany's knees almost gave out. She pushed as hard as she could, feeling the wood beneath her—which was already on fire—sag and start to give, but she'd managed to at least put on the brakes. She could feel the tentacles pulling and moving beneath her, trying to escape from the heat and use Jerry's body as a purchase to drag the burning thing out of the fire. The touch of them moving against her skin was disgusting and she couldn't help letting out a yelp of revulsion.

If she didn't get Jerry freed soon, they would still end up in the fire, or worse, with that monster coming back really pissed off about the whole roasted-alive thing. Brittany pushed off against the frame again and felt the wood under her left foot crack. She slid her foot forward into the grass and dug deep with her toes before pushing off again. She felt like she was dragging a car behind her. Only most cars didn't scream and wiggle. The fucking monster was still trying to climb out of the fire, still pulling at all the hook thingies in Jerry and using her own fight to avoid burning as a method of trying to get free.

It might have made it too, but the anchoring lengths of monster flesh holding it to Jerry started burning and when they caught fire, they caught fire fast. One moment Brittany was fighting with all of her strength just to stay where she was and the next she felt the writhing snakes under her stop struggling one after the other. Half a second later her frantic push to escape was sliding her and Jerry away from the flames. She practically used him as a surfboard for a minute, her feet pushing and his body skidding under her. She stopped only when she was certain the thing wasn't coming up after them. She was only certain when she no longer heard its screams.

Muscles she'd taken for granted shuddered in protest of the abuse she'd delivered, and her body ached damned near everywhere. Jerry's heart was beating. She learned that when she rested her head against his chest for a moment to catch her breath. He was still unconscious, and she guessed that was sort of a blessing. With quick, decisive gestures, she started pulling the hooks from his flesh, doing her best to get the barbs out with minimal damage to his flesh.

Behind her, the second floor of the house started burning. Brittany heard it and saw it, but knew there was nothing she could do to get to Chris. She did what she could for Jerry instead. And if she was crying, no one saw the tears. They evaporated in the heat of the building behind her.

III

It was looking into him again and through him, almost as if it knew he hid secrets deep in the recesses of his self. Chris fought to keep from it everything the entity might want to know, but had no luck. The presence sifting through his brain was like a battering ram slamming through rice-paper walls. All his struggles meant nothing at all to the thing. It was just too powerful.

He could not sense its thoughts, but he could feel its disgust for what it was doing. As vile and alien as the thing was, it felt the same way about him. In a vague way he was still aware of the world outside his mind, but only as a distant thing, a faded echo.

At least until he felt the slippery, cold touch of something as repulsive as the mind-raping thing in his head. The chains in his hand were being pried loose and he couldn't allow that to happen, no matter what. Chris bit the inside of his own mouth, felt his teeth punch through the soft interior flesh, and then felt the sudden flash of pain the bite brought.

The thing in his head felt it too, and recoiled from the sensation. He felt confusion and maybe even a little fear emanating from whatever possessed the eye that held him at bay. Was pain a new sensation? Was it somehow more connected than it meant to be to his psyche? He had no idea and he didn't care as long as he could stop it from doing anything more to his head.

He bit down again and felt the mental assault weaken a second time, if only for an instant. Chris moved his hand then, twitched it, and felt the chains there slide a little. He pulled his arm away from where it had rested and heard the medallions clack against each other. That was better. He forced his eyes to shift, averting them from the thing that floated in the air in front of him. The contact was broken and he could feel that hellish empathy fading, but not before he also felt the fury of the thing as it was thwarted again.

He liked the feeling.

Chris rolled to his side, pulling hard at his arm and feeling something sliding away as he tucked himself into a nearly fetal position. All around him the monsters moved, trying to find a way to get at their precious necklaces without making Chris mad enough to break any more of them.

They were being as careful as they could and he could sense their frustration with his sudden awakening. Chris wrapped the cords and chains more tightly around his fist, felt the cold metal links cut into his flesh and the circulation slow down in his fingers.

The voice was almost like Crawford's, but it came out of a nearly shapeless thing, a seething pit of snakes that kept changing even as he looked at it. "The master can give you power. The master can give you everything you've ever desired. Just . . . don't hurt the Keys." All of the threats were gone now, reduced to nothing but a desperate need to see their rituals finished and the dark force they worshipped, the vile thing that had been tearing through his head, released into the world.

"Yeah. That's gonna happen."

Chris hauled his fist into the air and brought it down as hard as he could into the floor. This time it wasn't only one coin that shattered. He felt the frozen coins clash together and break like delicate ice sculptures in the confines of his hand and against the floor. It wasn't all of them, but it was definitely the majority.

A small part of him wondered why, exactly, he felt the need to commit suicide in stupid ways. Most of him was too busy screaming to answer the question or even give it any thought. The pain that lanced through his arm was a living, vicious thing with teeth and an attitude. He had about half a second to think about it before the fireworks began.

The shards vibrated in his hand, pieces of frozen power that cut deep into his flesh like electric carving knives for elves. It was the first time in his life he could ever remember a pain being so intense that he physically could not scream.

The air around him crackled with energy, and a dark green luminescence grew around his hand and rapidly slid up his arm. Wherever the glow touched his skin he felt like his flesh was broiling and freezing simultaneously. Chris looked at his hand, saw the deep cuts, the blood flowing from them and the way the energies spilling from the broken fragments seemed to take the place of the blood that ran out of him, as if trying to fill a void.

The pieces seemed to be trying to work their way deeper into his system, trying to force themselves into his body as if they wanted to take root. That didn't seem like a good idea. Chris scrambled fast, his left hand pulling at the slivers of frozen fire in his right hand, cutting his fingers even more as he pulled desperately.

All that, of course, while the gate into whatever realm the freaks had opened began to falter. The circular rift cast thrashing bolts of lightning into the air, charges that flared but failed to touch anything at all. One of the things—the one that resembled a human carved from cottage cheese and mold—dropped from the ceiling, trying to physically stabilize the rift with its own arms. As soon as the funky curdled flesh touched the opening, the thing shivered and thrashed, arms smoking and boiling instantly. It couldn't have screwed up more if it had decided to mate with a generator. It let out a sound like metal scraping against a grinding stone and burst into flames, falling in a heap in front of the dwindling opening. Small fires ran across the body and mingled with arcs of the same dark green lightning that was running up Chris's arm. In damned near every spot that wasn't burning, the spasming form started to grow, shapes trying to force themselves out of the ruined form, trying, perhaps, to flee before they were consumed. What looked like a head forced through a long tube spilled from the torso, straining an impossibly long neck, trying desperately to be born. The flames ran over the thing before it could come to full size, rapidly blackening the outer surface.

The other things in the room backed away hastily, avoiding the overly greedy fires that devoured what was left with a nearly rabid fury. That made Chris smile absently, because they had apparently not noticed what he'd already realized.

The floor beneath him was much, much hotter than it should have been. The smoke he'd seen earlier, pushing at the edge of the door, was thicker now, and darker in color. The house was on fire, and every last one of the damned things was likely going to burn.

There was a lot of comfort in that thought, even if it meant he had to burn with them. Fair to say Chris Corin wasn't at his sanest just then.

All of that while the room was beginning to truly catch fire. The walls began to blacken a little, just at the edges nearest the door and around the few remaining windows. The hole in the wall where the corner of the structure had given way was not yet ablaze, and Chris had a notion of trying to jump for it. It was only two stories, if he could make it that far before the things around him decided to rip him apart. He had doubts. They were panicky right now, but he figured in a few seconds they'd graduate to righteously angry and looking for his blood. He'd pretty much fucked up whatever it was they were planning, and that suited him just fine.

Of course, the thing on the other side of the portal didn't seem to agree with him. He'd even have said it was truly infuriated. But he figured the worst of what the thing could do was over, because the opening was still dwindling, getting weaker and weaker, fading away, even as the fragments of the Keys tried to tear into his skin and nest somewhere in his body.

The broken pieces then did what their counterparts before them had done: They exploded. None of them was large, but size didn't seem to matter very much. Each and every shard gave off a blinding flare of energies that went from the dark green they started at to a silvery white that left Chris blinded for a moment. Every spot where one of the slivers had pierced his flesh grew numb and that had to be a blessing, because the force of the release was enough to throw him again. His right arm wrenched violently and his body sort of went along for the ride. Even after all of that, the last medallions were caught in his fingers, pulsing and glowing.

The pain caught up with him a second later as he lay cast across the smoldering floor like debris in a junkyard. The impact faded enough to let his nerve endings recover from the sudden shock and where there had been silence, there was suddenly a cacophony of sensations. Heat overlaid cold, which devoured the harsh reality of the holes in his arm, which in turn felt the searing crawling shattering wave of pure agony that rippled through him like a shark's fin cutting through water.

Chris screamed long and loud, not certain if he'd ever be able to stop screaming.

IV

Katie looked at the burning house, looked at Brittany sprawled in a daze on top of Jerry—and was that jealousy she felt for half a second? Surely not! Brittany was just a little girl—and then moaned as the pain came back into her face.

One second she'd been trying to get the tree monster from Hell off Brittany and the next it had attacked her, one of the numerous maggot-encrusted limbs sliding her way. She'd tried to block it, held her hands up and braced herself for the impact, but it had pulled a fast one. While her hands caught the limb, the writhing wormlike bark had blossomed, shooting out a thick streamer of filaments no thicker than hairs, which then swatted at her face, sending a thousand stinging pains into her cheek.

The pain was excruciating but mercifully short. Whatever stung her knocked her unconscious in seconds. She flopped to the ground after letting out a startled squeal and then she knew nothing for a few minutes. It took a little time for her to regain consciousness—how long, she couldn't have told you but it couldn't have been too long because the house was still there even if it was burning brighter than before. And now she was finally able to move

again, to feel her body and all the dozens of aches
that were embracing her nerve endings.

She stood up, walking with the exaggerated care
of the seriously hungover, and moved toward Jerry
and Brittany. Brittany's hands were covered in
blood. Most of it was Jerry's, if the wounds on his
body were any indication. The house beside them
was fully engulfed by the fire and she could hear
the sounds of things shifting as they burned, probably ready to collapse from the rapid weakening of
important structural supports. Maybe it had been a
great old house once, but just of late it had looked
like shit, from what she could see and it hadn't
looked exactly like the sort of place she could call
secure. Now the flames had been chewing away at
everything that held the place together.

Somewhere above her, on the third floor, she
heard a loud explosion, then saw the few remaining
windows blow out. Katie covered Brittany and
Jerry with her own body as best she could, wishing
that either of them was in good enough shape to
help her. Brittany seemed to be almost conscious—
she was moaning and her eyes fluttered under soot-
coated lids—but she wasn't able to do anything but
twitch in an exhausted sleep. Several of the fine
hairs that had bitch-slapped Katie herself into a stu-
por looked like they were anchored in the younger
girl's thin leg, and a long stream of welts ran from
them all the way down to Brittany's ankle.

Drugged, just like Katie had been. She didn't
have to look closely at Jerry to guess he was having
the same troubles.

She grabbed Brittany, throwing her weight into it, and hauled her backward, away from the house and the moderately compromising position she'd been in on top of Jerry. Any possible cause for jealousy was nullified by the fact that both of them were clothed and paralyzed, at the very least.

It took her about a minute to drag Brittany away from the house to what she felt was a safe distance. Then she went back after Jerry, pulling on one leg until he started to slide. He made a faint wet rattling noise when he tried to moan, and that scared the hell out of her. There was also a thin trail of blood on the grass where he had been and that wasn't helping her get comfortable with the way the night was going.

Back at the house she heard Chris screaming, and then that sound was drowned out by something crashing in the root cellar. For a second she thought it was the floor giving way, and then she had reason to doubt that. The crashing kept happening and the sound seemed to be rising up the inside the house rather as if a massive part of the ground was rising into the house proper rather than the wood and nails falling to meet the earth like they should have.

Something big and loud and wet made a noise in that house and the boards at the base of the burning structure exploded outward, sending a hail of flaming debris sideways through the air. There were flames rising from the glassless windows, tongues of greedy heat that fairly boiled into the fog enshrouded night. For a moment the flames spilled out faster and then the window closest to her went black. She wasn't sure, her eyes were feeling the effects of looking into that glaring inferno, but she thought something was in there and moving up, slithering at a slow, deliberate speed.

Something higher made a noise that sent shivers of gooseflesh waltzing from her neck down to her ass and then Chris matched her scream. The window above the blackened one—on the second level—went black as well, and Katie whimpered, barely noticing that she made any sound at all, barely aware of anything in the world beyond the wounded, terrified sound of Chris Corin wailing far above.

Katie covered her mouth with sooty hands, her eyes growing wider in her pale face, as she heard another roar—this time definitely the sound of wood collapsing in a fiery rain. Chris screamed again and she started praying for all she was worth.

It was all she could do. Whatever happened now, Chris was on his own.

V

Chris didn't dare look at his arm, his mind refusing to consider what might be left after what had just happened to him. The only thing he knew was that his arm must surely be gone to cause that much pain. Oh, he knew the arm was still there, but the pain made him want to believe otherwise. If it was gone there was the possibility of reprieve from the endless nauseating agony. It was so intense that he didn't even feel it when the beast that was Detective Crawford grabbed his hand in several fine tentacles and began unthreading the remaining necklaces in his grasp.

Crawford almost got away with the medallions. He had Chris's hand open and the fingers peeled back before Chris became aware of him. Even then he might have gotten the remaining Keys freed before Chris had overcome his near blackout and stopped the theft.

But the thing on the other side got impatient.

The barrier—and to Chris's mind it still seemed rather like a living membrane, a tissue that had substance and possibly even felt when it was touched—had held against the prodding of the monstrous entity on the other side. He had watched it fluctuate repeatedly as the shape pushed against its surface, shimmering and distorting the thing on the other side of its skin and likely that distortion was a mercy, because Chris didn't want to think about what it might look like undiluted.

When he'd broken so many of the Keys, Chris took for granted that the thing on the other side was going to have to abandon whatever plans it had for coming through and causing damage to this reality, a universe where it obviously didn't belong.

He was wrong.

The membrane didn't tear so much as it shattered. The massive form on the other side pushed hard and that distorting barrier collapsed like a plate-glass window hit by a freight train. What came through after the odd torn skin between worlds was dark gray and massive, larger than he could easily comprehend. It could have been called a hand if someone wanted to stretch the definition to the breaking point, but only in that it had smaller limbs attached to a larger limb. There were several fingers, more than there were supposed to be on a human hand at least, and thick webs of scabrous flesh between those fingers that fluttered in the breeze caused by the rift. Long, wickedly barbed claws sprouted from the end of each finger, one of them burned at the end, doubtless a side effect of touching, however briefly, the ring of burning colors that linked the worlds. The failing aura that marked the rip in the universe let out a sound, a deep wailing howl of noise as the column of flesh shoved farther into this world amid still more flashes of lightning and sparks. The sound was what bothered him the most. It was a noise that made Chris imagine what a universe might sound like as it was being raped.

The rift was closing. That was all there was to it. The circle of lightning was cutting into the wet-looking flesh of the thing trying to push through, but that massive writhing hand still pushed into the room, despite what had to be a serious level of pain. Where the limb was extending into this reality the skin of the thing looked seared black. In a few spots there was a dark gray, foul-smelling substance—all too reminiscent of the nightmarish cellar—falling to the floorboards. Even as the substance hit it started to smoke; the heat from below was getting to the point where Chris thought fire was only seconds from blooming in the room. Despite the searing heat, the goo that struck the ground grew, solidifying and spreading, a virulent fungal mass that seemed to carpet the entire room through the heat. The smell of searing demon-flesh was sickening and the overwhelming scent of mold and yeast was enough to make Chris's eyes water fiercely. Damned near every part of his body was affected, even his lungs, which had almost recovered from his earlier allergic reaction to the unnatural dust, were itching again.

The air vibrated, distorted around the thick arm pushing and straining into the world. The far side of the large room was almost filled with black mists, but the shape of the clouding substance on that side wavered and rippled, mimicking a reflection on water as the thing kept forcing itself deeper and farther into Chris's world.

He was terrified. Whalelike, the thing ripped into the world and stretched toward him, seeking him through the gap that should have been closing but was kept open by the violating mass. Chris pushed himself backward across the floor, while the thing that had once looked like Detective Crawford prostrated itself in front of the approaching titan.

The monstrous alien form on the ground was brushed aside, thrown across the room and lost in the murky depths of the growing darkness as the gigantic hand stretched out, seeking where Chris had been a moment ago. The force was immense and the effort to exert it barely substantial. The Crawford-monster hit the wall on the far side of the room hard enough for Chris to feel the vibration in his feet. The warbling shriek it let out as it flew ended a second before that tremor ran up his legs. And while the idea that Crawford might be dead was pleasing, it was easily eclipsed by the thought that what had done the monster in was actively seeking him.

Chris tried to push himself across the floor, away from the black mold that was growing in a wave and almost ready to overtake him. Already the first fine hairs of fungus were crawling over his pants and shoes. Even whatever passed for blood in the thing seemed to want him.

He never really had a chance. With the air behind him bucking against the violation it received and the room in front of him almost completely blacked out, he barely made it ten feet before the hand grabbed him. Chris screamed, his voice breaking like a kid in the worst throes of puberty as he was lifted from the ground and hauled into the air.

Everything he'd felt in his mind before, he felt again as he was touched by the cold, rough shark hide of the thing that had looked into him and basically torn his memories into bite-sized chunks. The skin of the thing cut at his flesh like sandpaper, wrapping around him with unholy strength and dragging him back toward the erupting firestorm that marked the hole in the universe.

Chris had seen enough in his unexpected tour of the leviathan's mind to know he wanted nothing to do with what was on the other side. He pushed as hard as he could, trying to break the grip around his body, but with no luck. The last of the medallions in his right hand started sparking and humming as he was drawn closer and closer to the rolling lightning border around the gate.

The eye that had so thoroughly enthralled him was hidden away, blocked by the appendage that held the gate open. The corona of sparks and fire that danced around the opening seared the alien flesh again as it passed through, back into its own reality. He could tell the thing felt it too, by the way it kept crushing him in its grip whenever the energies around it flared brighter.

The grip around his chest tightened convulsively and Chris woofed out his breath, felt his vision blacken as it kept pushing and squeezing, stopping him from getting a decent lungful of air. His eyes bulged in his skull and felt like they wanted to pop completely out. He closed them and swung the necklaces in his hand in a semicircle. The arm holding him twitched with every arc of the necklaces and Chris experimented. It took a few seconds of squinting his eyes open enough to see what was happening, but as Chris watched he began to understand a bit. The damned opening was still connected to the jewelry he held. Each time the coin-shaped medallions arced closer to the rip in space, the energies around the edge flashed more brilliantly. As they moved away, the light show dimmed, however marginally.

Simple math. Lose the Keys, lose the portal. Chris tried to get his hand up enough to crush the coins against the flesh that held him, that was slowly crushing him to death. No luck. The best he could manage was to push them into its flesh, and that wasn't helping him at all. Hell, if anything, it seemed to revitalize the thing that was drawing him into the pyrotechnics.

He clenched his hand around the small cluster of coins and squeezed, but found he had the same problem. He couldn't get enough of a decent grip to make a difference. He was also fast running out of options.

Then Chris caught his one and only lucky break, though most people would hardly call it that. The floor beneath him gave up the fight to resist the encroaching flames. The floorboards were first illuminated from below, with thin light spreading between the slats and growing brighter and then sending up small tongues of fire amid a rising hail of sparks.

The effect on the growing black fungus was immediate. The foul-smelling stuff burned away damned fast, leaving behind a fine white ash that rose into the air and spread even more miasma into the atmosphere of the room. The fire spread as quickly as the wash of mold itself and burned so brightly that Chris felt the heat even in the air. Several of the things in the room let out panicked squeals and Chris could only imagine—whether he wanted to or not—the sight of them as they caught fire.

The fire flared briefly and then died, but several more flames had caught in that flash paper wave, and the grip of the thing wrapped around him seemed to falter for a moment. He didn't have the time or strength to break free, but he managed to pull his right arm—which had not, in fact, blown from his body but merely felt like it had been—from where it had been pinned against his chest. He pushed the necklaces closer to the crackling circle that braceletted the thick inhuman arm he was trapped against and watched as, again, the energies flared brighter. And the remains of the portal slid back as they had before, always maintaining the same distance from his body.

And that brilliant fiery light burned up the length of the creature's arm. He heard the unholy sound it emitted as it screamed, and more importantly he felt that scream in both his body and his mind. It was one part pain and at least two parts pure hatred. The webbed, thick-fingered hand wrapped around Chris's torso flexed as it tried to pull back. He heard a few loud, wet cracks come from the region of his chest as pain suddenly lanced through him. He made a noise that couldn't really be called a scream. The air was forced from his lungs and his eyes bulged. His blood pressure soared high enough to make him fear his head would simply explode.

The floor underneath him collapsed, opening up into a raging firestorm as the flames ate away the ancient supports. The thing wrapped around his chest suddenly let go, the roar of pain coming through the rip in the cosmos reverberating through his body, even as he finally managed to draw in another breath.

It took a second for him to realize there was no floor anymore. By that time he'd started falling into the fires below. Chris now returned the favor the monster had done for him. He grabbed hold of the thing's rough flesh and held on for all he was worth. His sides felt like they'd already been caught in the fire, and his hands felt like cheese in a grater, but he managed to hold on, eyes looking at the flames rising under him.

The circle of energies around the arm was sputtering, growing weaker perhaps, or only being obscured by the foul environment and the smoke. Chris pulled himself up the thick arm, feeling more skin cut away from his hands in the process. He had absolutely no intention of staying on the thing, and that was probably for the best as it was pulling back, trying to escape the flames and the circle of agony wrapped around its limb. The contracting noose of lightning looked like it was actually cutting deeply into the flesh. More of that thick, foul soup that seemed to be the blood of the thing was spilled out and fell into the fires below, catching ablaze and dropping like falling stars into the flames. Chris felt his hair crinkling in the heat and felt his feet trying to slip from the rough, uneven surface he stood on.

"Fuck . . . what the hell do I do now?" He could barely hear himself over the cacophony in the burning room. That was okay; he didn't really need to hear himself, he just needed to know he could still speak.

The arm that had become his bridge over the fires

suddenly moved, pulling away from the heat, trying to withdraw back into its own world. A minute earlier Chris would have been ecstatic; now he just did his best not to fall off the limb and into the burning pit below.

Flesh seared and spit and burned all the brighter as the thing tried to pull away. Chris stumbled and fell, hitting the floorboards just at the edge of the fire, sure he was going to die.

He felt the wood under him sag dangerously, groaning as it started to collapse, and pushed off for all he was worth, trying to catch the flesh that was rapidly withdrawing even as it lost several inches of its outer layers in the tightening ring of pyrotechnics. That mental roar continued, and with it came images of pain and suffering like few Chris had ever seen before. Not images of the thing that was trying to get away. Oh, no, that would have been a blessing. No, these were images of Chris and Brittany and his mother and his best friends. Flash fire shots of every imaginable type of torture inflicted on him and his. It wasn't a random thing and he knew it. That entity, be it god, demon or other, was making him a promise.

Then, as if to prove his guess, it actually spoke in his mind, using words for the very first time. "You are marked, Christopher Corin. You have made an enemy this day." The voice was like a hundred bee stings in his mind and he staggered, slipping backward as he heard it.

Backward, to where the ground wasn't. He waved his arms, he danced with his feet and he shook his whole body in an effort to stay upright. The flames licked eagerly at his heels and the backs of his legs, all the way up to his buttocks. The jeans held, for which he was grateful, but the heat was enough to evoke another yelp from already strained vocal cords.

He should have plummeted into the depths of the fire. Instead he felt a massive weight rushing up from below. Chris looked back over his shoulder, fully expecting to see his death in the form of a fireball as the pressure changed and he was lifted back from the edge of the fire pit the floor had become.

He might have preferred the fire.

What he saw instead was all mouth, a deep, cavernous throat surrounded by what looked like thousands of teeth descending in wet cold rows. There were long streamers of gray flesh, almost like catfish whiskers, trailing below the thing. Several of them ended in what looked like bulbous hearts, but most were ruined, deflated shells that had once held human beings within them.

Chris felt the air change again as the massive thing came to a stop, the gigantic maw glistening in the light of the fire. He could see very little aside from the mouth and he was grateful for the lack of knowledge. He didn't want to know what the rest of the monster looked like. What he saw already was more than his mind wanted to accept and he felt laughter start coming out of his mouth.

SHIT! Out of the fucking frying pan and into the fire, baby! That sonuvabitch is gonna swallow me like a worm! Oh, that got him giggling even more. He had a vivid image of himself at the bottom of a tequila bottle, swimming around while a group of wormy-looking things with lots of thick whiskers sat around playing poker and taking shots. *HA! The worm eats YOU, buddy! Isn't that a scream!*

Chris saw the arc of lightning finally dwindle, saw the massive hand that had clutched him seared and marked as it withdrew. He turned and looked at the worm that wanted to sample his flesh and looked back at the lightning ball that shimmered in the blackened depths of the room he had almost vacated via the ruined floor.

There was no logic to it. There was only a small, petty need to make a final statement about how little he liked the way his world was ending. Chris threw the remaining medallions at the glowing ball of lightning—and did he see that monstrous eye again, looking at him as the wound in the universe started at last to seal itself? Yes, he just possibly did. Did he see the pupil on that watery eye grow wider as the medallions arced through the air like glittering gold comets? Very possibly so.

Mostly what he knew he saw was the Keys hitting the last of the energies they had brought forth. The coins breaking and catching—suspending themselves in the frying electrical field, glowing brighter and brighter, their odd green glow somehow dwarfed by the crackling electrical discharge. There was a second of satisfaction, a gloating pleasure in knowing that that fucking doorway would never open again.

And then self-preservation set in and Chris ran as hard as he could, feeling his knee screaming in protest, feeling his agonized arm throwing bolts of pain through to his shoulder, feeling the wooden floor below him buckle upward in a slow-moving wave of wood and fire as the thing coming up from below humped and forced its way into the blasted room from below.

It roared, that gigantic mouth, and a cold spray of wet, foul-smelling fluids sprayed from its jaws amid the sound waves that actually pushed at Chris's clothes hard enough to make them ripple.

Chris was on the third floor of a burning building that was already crumbling around him. He couldn't have cared less. There was a giant worm with teeth as big as his body snarling after him and tearing all hell out of the floor and that too was not a serious consideration. Something big enough to eat tractor-trailers and pick him up like he was the smallest of flies had just promised him eternal torments and that too was inconsequential.

All Chris could think about was what was going to happen when that brightening ball of lightning that held worlds joined together got caught in the explosion from the broken Keys.

He pushed himself harder, pumping his legs for all he was worth, his face drawn down in a wide howl of fear. His knee was on fire, the battered joint shrieking out pain signs like he maybe hadn't caught on that it was hurt badly.

He did not look back to see the almost comical look of panic on the gigantic face below him. He wouldn't have been able to read the expression anyway. The giant column that held the maw in place tried to back away and failed.

The world behind Chris went stark white, and the walls around him blew out like the footage he'd seen of houses at old nuclear testing grounds. Chris felt himself cast through the air and tried to scream, but with no luck. There was nothing left in his lungs to expel. The second wave of force knocked him unconscious, which was truly a blessing. He didn't feel anything at all when he hit the ground almost a hundred yards later.

Chapter Eight

I

Chris dreamed.

He was floating in a darkness that was not at all comfortable. It was terrifying, because he knew he was not alone in that darkness.

There were things out there, and they wanted him dead. He didn't know what they were and he didn't want to know. He just wanted them gone away forever. He could not see them, but he could hear them, whispering to each other, hissing in that perfect darkness. And he could feel them from time to time, touching his flesh and maybe thinking about where to bite down first.

There was a part of him that had touched them, that understood certain things, much as he wanted to forget them. There was something in the ground, something that had been waiting a very long time, and it had finally been within minutes of achieving its goal. It had made people, you see, made them in the image of real people, and it had worked slowly and carefully, planning out how to use its spawn to its best advantage.

There were others, not really like it, but close enough to be considered family. Each of those others was resting in a faraway place and wanted to be here instead. They had been here before, and been taken away though he couldn't have told you how.

They wanted to be over here and they were hungry.

They were not here, and so they starved.

They were not supposed to be here, and that bothered them a great deal.

It bothered them so much that they would do anything to get over here again.

That was his dream.

And in his dream they kept trying to get closer. Trying to get to him and to his family and to everything he held dear, so they could make those things their own.

In his dream there were people in the world who wanted to help them, wanted for whatever sick reasons they might have to make this world another toy, another possession of the ancient things that lingered in forgotten places.

The Outsiders wanted back in.

The Outsiders wanted to do things. Dark things that would leave the world completely changed and would surely drive every living thing in the world completely mad, if anything even survived their coming.

The Outsiders slept and dreamt of not only the world, but the whole of reality. As they had for untold centuries, they slept.

The Outsiders were sleeping, dreaming of playing with their shining toy as they had in the past. Dreaming as they had for countless centuries.

The Outsiders had needs. They were starving where they were.

The Outsiders needed to escape from the places where they slept and waited, needed to find their way back to the universe, before they wasted away.

The Outsiders wanted to change the world, the whole of the universe to suit their needs, and someday they would have that power again.

But maybe now the Outsiders were beginning to awaken.

It was that thought that finally made Chris Corin wake up himself.

II

He came out of his sleep with ease. He just opened his eyes, stifling the scream that wanted to creep past his clenched lips. It almost escaped, managing to become a moan instead of a shriek.

He heard the voices dimly, but they were good voices, familiar voices. He felt hands touching his face, and made his eyes open. Brittany was standing over him, looking far too tall to be his little sister. She could not possibly be his little sister, in fact, because she was smiling too broadly, looked way too happy to see him and that was just plain unnatural.

"Wut choo milngat?" He'd meant to say, "What are you smiling at?" but his lips were dry and sticky.

Brittany answered by hugging her skinny body to his and damn near cutting off his air supply. He was stunned when he realized the warm, wet drops falling from her face were tears.

The next face he saw made his own eyes sting. "Yo, twerp, you're cutting of his air." Jerry's broad friendly face looked at him, leaning down like Brittany's had done, but from farther away and with just a touch more cynicism.

"Wha hopned?" He winced, his throat making him aware of a discomfort that was apparently waking up as he awoke. Somebody had rudely shoved a burning coal down his neck while he was sleeping; at least that's what it felt like.

"You tell us, bro. We were just waiting for you."

A nurse who looked like she could take on full battalions of Marines with her bare hands reached past Jerry and lifted Chris with one arm. Her head was pressed to a cell phone that rested on her shoulder and her spare arm was fluffing the pillows Chris had been resting against.

Jerry backed away from the woman with both arms held up in a sign of surrender. Chris knew there was a story behind the move, but couldn't begin to guess what that story was.

Apparently Brittany was not as intimidated by

the nurse, and reached past her to give Chris the sweetest gift he had ever received. A Styrofoam cup full of water and ice chips. No one had to tell him to drink slowly. It was all he could manage, but after a few sips he felt the raging flames in his throat ease up, extinguishing.

The smile he gave his sister was pure love.

She smiled back, and he looked over her skinny frame, noticing the bandages on her arms for the first time. "What happened?" That was better. His voice was no longer a croak.

Between doctors paying quick visits to make sure he was alive and to tend to several batches of stitches and patches of burn ointment on his body, she told him and Jerry spoke as well. For Jerry the whole thing was pretty much a wash. He'd been running with Chris, trying to escape the freak show that followed them and he hadn't made it. He thought for sure he was a dead man, but instead he wound up plugged into whatever it was that used his brain and his memories. Did he know what was happening at the time? Not really. For him it was more like a dream than anything else; he knew what was happening, but only in the vague, disassociated way a dreamer can recall details of a fading nightmare.

Chris listened attentively, and Brittany pretended to, but it was obvious she'd heard the story before and just as obvious that she wanted to forget the entire thing happened.

Naturally, it wasn't meant to be that easy. Long before Chris could have figured out the words for his own version of what had occurred, the police came by. Detective Martin Callaghan was short and wide and looked like hefting the occasional freight train was his idea of good clean fun. Where Crawford had been portly, Callaghan was pure muscle of the sort you can only get when you spend too damned much time at the gym. What little hair he had was dark brown and kept cropped so close to his head that Chris could see his scalp with ease. Brittany looked at him and practically melted.

By that point Chris was hurting too much to really notice. All of the aches and pains he hadn't been feeling were letting him know that they felt overlooked. The doctors were impressed that he was intact, actually. His right hand had stitches he'd chosen not to think about and his left knee was a mass of swollen soft tissues that, in his estimation, went well beyond the sprain they were calling it. His skin was both frostbitten and burned in a dozen places; fortunately, none of the injuries would be permanent. The worst of it was what he'd done to his back when he took a little ride through the stratosphere on his way to a rough landing all the way across the street.

Detective Callaghan couldn't have given a flying fuck about his injuries. He just wanted answers. The look on Jerry's face and the look on his sister's face told him he had to tread carefully. Fortunately for Chris, the nurse who'd been fluffing his pillows between assaults on the armed forces was right there and shooed the officer outside for a few minutes, explaining that if he'd waited that long he could wait a few more minutes before he spoke to Chris. She ushered out Jerry and Brittany as well and set to changing a few bandages that had been changed already.

Chris looked at her, wondering what exactly was going through her head.

She answered his question while he was still trying to figure out how to ask it.

"Your sister, the little redhead? She likes to talk a bit. She's been here every day and we've gotten to know each other a mite more than some would think." Her voice was softer and more pleasant than the craggy face she wore. Her attitude in front of others, and that included Chris but apparently not his little sister, was pure New England: brusque and efficient. "She told me about what happened to the lot of you as best she could. Normally I would have trouble believing a story like that."

She took the wrappings off his right hand and examined the stitches there with the hawk eye of a jeweler checking out a flat of freshly cut diamonds. Her eyes remained off his face while she worked, but it was obvious she was looking at him. "Normally, I would. There are always exceptions to prove the rules." She sighed and moved to his knee, looking at the ugly swelling and smiling with satisfaction. It was a tight, small smile that had nothing whatsoever to do with kindness, but with approval for the way the injury was healing. "The fact of the matter is my sister's body was among those found in the remains of that house." He started to express his condolences automatically and she waved them away. "We were never that close, but we were family. I'll miss her a mite, I suspect. She was always into the strange things, the paranormal, if you prefer. And I know for a fact that she was into activities that were questionable at best."

She finally looked him in the face, her dark brown eyes visible under eyebrows the color of a stormy sky. "I understand you ended her suffering a bit earlier than it might have ended." He looked at her and saw through the stoic exterior to the pain she felt. He also saw in her face and build similarities to the large woman he'd seen half-devoured in the center of one of those chambers and nodded silently.

"That was good of you. And I suspect it was for the best. So I'm giving you a little help to repay a kindness. Your friends and your sister kept it easy. They mentioned the necklace, and the kidnapping of that fella Jerry. They mentioned the grave robbery and that is all, young man. They did not try to explain what happened. They just mentioned those things. No monsters, no goblins and no reasons given for the explosion. Do you understand me?"

Chris nodded silently as she finished with his knee and gave a perfunctory look at the burns on his calves. When she was finished she reached around and fluffed his pillows again. "Make sure that you do. I've known enough detectives in my life to know that some of them are like terriers. They don't like to let go of their chew toys. Don't become a chew toy for this one. I think he could be dangerous."

She left the room without another word, nodding curtly to the detective.

Callaghan did not reintroduce himself. He got straight to business. "You called me a few days back using Jerry Murphy's cell phone. You didn't leave a name and you said you had seen Detective Walter Crawford."

Chris just nodded.

"Why wouldn't you leave your name?"

"I had a policeman shooting at me for no good reason. I didn't much feel like having two policemen shooting at me."

Callaghan's gray eyes studied him from a face that looked carved from stone. "Fair enough. Why didn't you report the desecration at your mother's grave site when it happened?"

"I was busy trying to avoid having Crawford kill me."

The man nodded. "The incident involving Detective Crawford and one Bryce Darby?"

"And two other men. Don't forget them. Same problem. Crawford wanted a necklace he called the Western Key. I had no clue what he was talking about and he was using a gun to ask me again. Darby was there and helped me." And there was the stickler. Bryce could easily tell a different story, probably would, in fact, and there was nothing Chris could do about it.

Callaghan nodded his head. "That pretty much matches up with what Darby said."

Chris blinked, but otherwise left his poker face in place. That was unexpected.

"What happened at the house?"

"Which house?"

"Tillinghast Lane. The one that blew up."

"I don't remember much. I remember the fire and trying to get some people out of the place."

Callaghan looked at him with those cold gray eyes for a long, long time. It was a war of wills and Chris had to force himself to keep looking at the detective long after he wanted to curl up and hide. The detective was a scary man and it had nothing to do with his muscles. His eyes were dead, or at least very good at giving the impression that there was nothing warm or kind about him. He was about as unreadable as anyone Chris had ever met.

"Fair enough." The man slapped down a business card on the little rolling desk that seemed to come standard with every single hospital bed on the planet. "If you think of anything else, please give me a call, Mr. Corin."

"I will, sir."

The man stood up, his shoulders rolling under a suit that looked like it cost too much for a police officer to afford. "I don't know what happened out there, Mr. Corin, but I understand you saved a few lives, you and your friends." He turned without so much as a smile creasing his thin lips. "You should be proud of yourself."

Before he could respond the detective was gone. The room was empty for a moment and Chris sighed. Proud? No, not proud. Just glad to be alive.

He moved the Styrofoam cup off his little rolling desk and opened the top of it. Toothpaste, a comb, a couple of Brittany's teeny-bop magazines. Not really a shocker that she'd claimed the thing for her own. There was also a mirror that flipped up and he used it. His reflected face was a bit of a shock to him. It looked like he hadn't shaved in at least a week or two, though to that point he had no idea how long he'd actually been in the hospital. The hair on his chin and under his nose was thick and wild, curling in what seemed to be a hundred random directions. He doubted he'd ever be able to grow a real beard or even a mustache that didn't look like crap. There were a few fading bruises on his face, and his skin had a spot or two that were too shiny, as if the skin had just healed.

He barely looked like himself. He looked too old, too thin and too desperate.

But what really slapped him around were his eyes. He'd had his eyes for as long as he could remember, had stared into their reflection on a few million occasions, and seen them every time he did anything, even stuff as woefully mundane as brushing his teeth. Courtney had once told him that he had the most amazing blue eyes she'd ever seen and he'd responded that they were a hereditary trait. His mother and his sister had the exact same color. He'd told her that through a blush, as they had just started dating back then and he had been very, very flustered by her compliment and by what she'd been doing with her hand just then.

But the eyes looking back at him were green. Not

hazel, not blue green or jade or any of a dozen different possible combinations of colors that could look like green. Oh no. They were green, damn it, as green as beer on St. Patrick's Day and as green as the lawn he knew he had to get to mowing soon. He looked at them and away again several times, convinced that they would magically change back if he did it enough times.

He only stopped when Katie came in carrying food, followed by Jerry and Brittany. Courtney was along for the ride too, and that was an added distraction. The food was DeLucci's. There was a second when he was afraid he wouldn't be able to eat it. For one single moment all he could see was his mother's face, lovely in life and ruined in death. The last time he'd had DeLucci's was on his birthday. God, that seemed a long time ago. Then the scent of the food hit his stomach and he felt no nausea or fear or even melancholy. Instead he felt a tight rumble grow and reverberate deep inside of him.

He was hungry. And the food tasted no poorer for any associations with his mother's death. It was still the best damned Italian food in town, as far as he was concerned.

That was enough. He would worry about the color of his eyes later. He would let himself fret over the dark dreams and the lost time, when he was asleep for what had to be days on end, sometime after eating. For now he had his sister and his friends and it was enough.

Chris ate, and before the meal was over he managed to smile and to laugh and to almost convince himself that he could easily fall for Courtney before he reminded himself that she was not always as sweet as she was being right then.

It was enough to be alive.

It was a start at least.

James A. Moore
FIREWORKS

It begins on a happy day. The small town of Collier gathers on the Fourth of July to watch the fireworks. But in the middle of the celebration, the shocked spectators witness something almost beyond comprehension, something too horrifying to believe. The lucky ones are killed immediately. They escape the true terror that is yet to come, terror that will come from an even more surprising source. . . .

It's quiet now in Collier. The townspeople are waiting, resting, gathering their strength. They know the quiet will soon be shattered. They know the screaming will soon begin. But they don't know what will be left when the screaming stops.

DEEP IN THE DARKNESS
MICHAEL LAIMO

Dr. Michael Cayle wants the best for his wife and young daughter. That's why he moves the family from Manhattan to accept a private practice in the small New England town of Ashborough. Everything there seems so quaint and peaceful—at first. But Ashborough is a town with secrets. Unimaginable secrets.

Many of the townspeople are strangely nervous, and some speak quietly of legends that no sane person could believe. But what Michael discovers in the woods, drenched in blood, makes him wonder. Soon he will be forced to believe, when he learns the terrifying identity of the golden eyes that peer at him balefully from deep in the darkness.
